Game of Justice

Brad Madison Legal Thriller Book 3

J.J. Miller

Innkeeper Publishing

Books by J.J. Miller

THE BRAD MADISON SERIES

Force of Justice

Divine Justice

Game of Justice

Blood and Justice

Veil of Justice

THE CADENCE ELLIOTT SERIES

I Swear To Tell

The Lawyer's Truth

Stay in touch with J.J.

Sign up for J.J.'s newsletter

Email: jj@jjmillerbooks.com

Facebook: @jjmillerbooks

Website: jjmillerbooks.com

Contents

CHAPTER 1

As the two men hauled the woman toward the cliff, the storm's first drops of rain doused her face and blended with her blood. The drug they'd given her had turned her body rag-doll limp and rendered her all but speechless but it didn't dull the horror she felt at the sound of the pounding waves coming closer. It was as though the sea was ravenous for her, somehow knowing that the men were set to toss her into its jaws.

Just moments earlier, in the parked car, the woman realized they were going to kill her. Whatever they had put into her drink had taken effect.

They must have drugged her at the younger man's apartment, she thought. That's where the mood had gotten weird; just after she made that stupid joke about what she thought the two of them were up to.

The joke was meant to feel them out, to pave the way for her to ask them some more serious questions. But it didn't just fall flat, it crashed with a chilling thud. The younger man was visibly jolted. The older man, whom she hardly knew, gave her a wry grin. But she didn't have to be psychic to see that his amusement was forced.

She then decided to try and extract candor from the uneasy mood and pushed forward with a bold accusation about the men. She tried to sound like she knew exactly what their game was and that there was no point in them denying it.

Their stone-cold silence unnerved her even more.

She then quickly tried to backpedal, saying her friend Erin dared her to raise the subject with them.

She waited for the men to respond, thinking they still might confess to an unwelcome truth. But they offered no affirmation whatsoever. They just stared at her. She thought she saw hatred in the older man's eyes.

She felt compelled to speak next.

"Don't worry. It's not like I've pitched it to my editor. You're not going to be front-page news." She was flailing, trying desperately to dispel the tension, but only making things worse.

Abruptly, the men sought to make light of it.

"You are so wide of the mark, it's not funny," the younger man said. "It's complete and utter nonsense."

"Who's this friend of yours Erin?" asked the older man, looking at her like she'd lost her mind. "And where the hell does she get this kind of crap from? I never thought reporters would be so desperate for a story."

"Forget it," she said with a laugh and excused herself to go to the bathroom.

She thought she heard them arguing in hushed tones.

When she returned, the older man apologized for reacting so awkwardly.

"Look, you really caught us off-guard with that stuff. I didn't think you could be serious. But, hey, listen—it's cool. Everything's cool. No offense taken, okay?"

She nodded, somewhat relieved.

"You've sure got some balls on you, though," the older man said, shaking his head and smiling. "For a second there, I thought I was sitting with Barbara frickin' Walters."

She warmed at the compliment. They hugged and laughed. The good mood was reinstated but not fully—an undertone of tension remained. Where did she stand with these two? Should she ask more of what she wanted to know? Or should she just drop it?

Then the older man seemed to read her mind.

"Listen, you want a story? I'll tell you a story. And, I swear, it'll make your toes curl. Might set you on the path to breaking something big."

She asked him, practically begged him, to elaborate.

"Later," he said. "But I promise I'll fill you in tonight, okay. Now are we here to party or what?"

He then pulled out a small Ziploc bag of cocaine and racked up two lines each. He told her it was the best gear in LA and that he had a bottomless supply. He said anytime she wanted some to just give him a call.

With the coke and a few more drinks, her disquiet gave way to excitement. She was wired.

What was the older man going to share with her?

Could it be the story that would make everyone in the *LA Times* newsroom take her seriously as a journalist?

She was stuck in the Lifestyle section, churning out breezy articles on anything from Lady Gaga's cosmetics line to the top ten vegan dips. She could write that kind of piffle in her sleep but had long ago lost the buzz of seeing her byline attached to it.

No one else in the newsroom saw her as being stuck. To them she was perfectly positioned. What more could that quiet, pretty blonde girl from Tennessee aspire to?

Plenty, but her confidence was so underdone she could barely tell her closest friends that she wanted to be an investigative reporter, and even that took some convincing.

Could the older man's information be the game changer? She was twenty-six now. It was time, once and for all, to forge a new career path, one that she felt was her true calling. She couldn't wait to hear what he had to say.

After more lines, the older man pulled another small bag out of his pocket and slid it across the coffee table to her.

"Here. Take this. I've got more than I know what to do with," he said. Her eyes lit up. That quiet, pretty blonde girl from Tennessee did love her cocaine.

The older man went to the kitchen to fix some margaritas.

She stepped out to the balcony with the younger man. The night sky over the Pacific was lit up now and then by distant lightning.

"Let's go watch the storm," said the older man, joining them on the balcony with the drinks. "The lightning show over the ocean will be incredible."

She said she didn't want to, that she was happy to stay put, do more lines and drink more margaritas. She walked back inside with her phone in hand to change the music on Spotify.

She didn't see what was coming.

The older man stepped up behind her, swung her around by the shoulder and punched her in the face with all his force, his right fist cracking into her cheek. She fell backward and brought her hands up to her face. When she took them away, she saw they were covered in blood. She started screaming at him, but he leaned in and punched her again. And again.

She collapsed onto the tiles then tried to get to her feet but couldn't.

"Come on," said the older man. "Let's get her into the car."

"What about the blood?" said the younger man.

"Get some paper from the john. Wipe her down. Make sure there's none on the floor."

From that point on, it was like she was just a spectator of her ordeal.

The older man drove. The younger man sat in the back with her, occasionally wiping her face with Kleenex.

It was a huge effort for her to speak.

"What's going on?" she moaned. "Where are we going?"

The younger man spoke to her softly.

"Don't worry. Just keep quiet. I'll take care of you."

And, for some reason, she believed him. But why did he stand by and say nothing of the attack?

What have I done to deserve this?! What?!

She had no answer. All she knew was that she was now in grave danger and that she was utterly powerless to save herself.

After thirty minutes the car pulled over and the older man got out from behind the wheel.

"Where are we?" she asked hazily, hoping her worst fears were only that.

Her door flung open and she was yanked out roughly into the night. She tried to scream, but it only came out as a whimper.

They grabbed her painfully on each side and escorted her toward the sea.

A flash of lightning exposed the location to her.

It was a place she recognized.

A year ago, she'd come here in despair, when she thought her world had collapsed beyond hope and she'd wanted to end it all, to end her pain with one final act of resolve. But she'd called him to say goodbye and he'd come and taken her home and gotten her help.

Now, though, she did not welcome death; she desperately wanted to live. She summoned every ounce of strength to fight, but her limbs could not rise to her will. In contrast to her limp body, her mind was as turbulent as the sea, cresting in bursts of panic, fear, disbelief and desperation.

What have they given me?

Why do they want to kill me?

How could he do this to me?

"Car!" the older man hissed and the three of them fell forward. She hit the ground face first. The older man fell on top of her.

"Keep your mouth shut!"

When she opened her mouth to breathe, it filled with dirt and grass.

They lifted her up. She started coughing after inhaling dirt down her throat.

Then she felt the rain on her face and the shudder of the crashing surf through her feet.

They hauled her over a wall and kept marching.

When they reached the edge of the bluff, they stopped.

Maybe they're having second thoughts.

Maybe this is just a warning after all.

"Grab her legs," said the older man.

She looked out over the ocean as they swung her over the brink and back.

Now came the horrible certainty that this was it.

As though reaching out for help where there was none, she thought of her mother and father, who both loved her dearly. And she wanted to hug them so tightly and never let go until she'd woken from this nightmare.

But this was not the work of imagination.

Suddenly, her insides were swept hollow by the rushing descent. The terror of falling was all-consuming; her muted scream lost amid the clamor of the wild surf.

CHAPTER 2

I shouldn't hate on Jim Rafferty but I will. Take it as me cashing in some frequent flier miles on a friendship spanning twenty-odd years.

I don't know what was worse: the way he pointed his little finger as he popped an aioli-laden french fry into his mouth or the smug rapture that came over that fairway-tanned, entitled face of his as he chewed. Leaning back and taking in the view of Los Angeles from the patio of the prestigious California Club, Jim looked like a man so comfortable in his element you might as well have called it a birthright.

And maybe he was always destined to be here, despite this being the very thing our younger selves swore we'd never become: a fully franked member of the Establishment, someone who perpetuated rather than addressed inequality, someone who devoted his whole working life to serving the rich and in return getting the gold-plated version of the American dream: the mansion, the prestige cars, the private schools, the uber-exclusive club memberships.

That was how we saw it back then when we were cramming for exams at Stanford with Audrey Hollander—without doubt the smartest of us three—and listing the countries we wanted to help via the Peace Corps and then later with USAID or even the UN. We knew graduates not much older than us who were advising government ministers in Africa and Central Asia. They were building new legal justice systems for broken countries on the mend. How's that for serving the world, making an impact?

But that was a long time ago, a time when our idealism ran down to the marrow. Look at fat cat Rafferty now. He has it all and I'm sure he'd tell you he deserves it. You know, all those fourteen-hour days he puts in. Like no one else works fourteen-hour days and for a fraction of what he banks. Like no one has earned it more than him.

I'm no socialist, but this whole swanky lunch scenario was putting a bad taste in my mouth that the grilled sea bass and unoaked chardonnay couldn't wash off. But then I'd arrived with a bad taste in my mouth. The truth was that I, too, was the subject of my own contempt. This little get-together was actually my idea.

I'd come not to bury Jim but to butter him up. A couple of lean years, a new landlord who'd almost doubled my office rent in eighteen months and a belly full of nefarious clients had me looking out for other options. And so Jim came to mind.

On the face of it, I came armed with a couple of ideas on how we might collaborate. But that's the spin: the truth is I wanted to hitch my wagon to the corporate gravy train while I still could. I'd come prepared to offer myself to Jim's firm—Cooper, Densmore and Krieger—a collection of uber-rich lawyers who advised the people who owned Los Angeles, and I hated myself for it.

"How's the fish?" Jim asked as he leaned forward to cut into his filet mignon.

"Very good," I said distractedly. It was time to ask what I'd come to ask. "Jim, remember a year ago you approached me about a job at CDK?"

"Yup, and you should have taken it. I wish you'd listened to me. We've got some real interesting stuff coming on deck that we could have been working on together."

"Well, that's what I wanted to talk about."

"I can't tell you shit. Only that we are going all-out on what's going to be a massive case. You'll be reading about it, that's for sure."

I took a slug of wine.

"No, I understand you can't divulge details of your case. What I meant was I've been thinking and I've reconsidered."

Jim stopped chewing momentarily before dabbing his mouth with his napkin and reaching for his glass.

"Reconsidered what?"

"The job offer. I've decided I want in. That is if the offer's still open."

Jim leaned back in his chair.

"You're talking about the offer you threw back in my face a year ago, right?"

"Well, now—"

"You mean the offer that I put to you on behalf of our managing partner who was so keen to hire you it was like he thought you were the fucking Don Draper of the law?"

"Jim," I said. But Jim wasn't going to be interrupted.

"You mean that day when you had the gall to crap all over my career choices, my firm, and told me there was no way in hell you were going to sell out like I did?"

"I'm not sure I put it like that."

"Believe me, you put it like that. I had to drag my ass back to the office and tell Harold Krieger that, basically, I was full of shit. He had his sights set on you like Captain Ahab and I assured him that I could get him his fucking white whale. Sliced and diced. Served up to him like sashimi. I was stupid enough to tell him that I was sure my old Stanford buddy could be persuaded into becoming a senior partner at CDK. With your high-profile cases and connections, there was even a suggestion that that tight-ass bastard would even waive the half-mill joining fee. And I was stupid enough to believe you were a chance. You'd proven yourself as a crack trial lawyer, you'd made the papers with some brilliant wins. Every firm in the city would have given their left nut to have you, but I'd promised Krieger that if anyone could haul you in it was me."

"Jim, I'm sorry."

"You're sorry? That's the first I've heard it. Exactly when did you start to feel sorry about what went down?"

"Jim, I felt bad about—"

"You didn't feel bad about anything, you arrogant son of a bitch. I never heard from you until a few weeks ago. You know you almost cost me *my* senior partnership?"

Jim's face was burning with resentment. I'd hurt him more than I could have imagined, and I'd never cared to ask.

"No. I wasn't aware that my decision had any impact on you at all. I'm sorry, Jim. What can I say? I was caught up in my own world. I didn't feel I needed anyone."

"That's right. You were about to sign Tremaine Drake, one of the biggest drug dealers in California."

I may have grown somewhat tired of defending crooks, but I never tired of reminding people we're all entitled to a fair trial.

It's chiseled into the Constitution. Worse was hearing other lawyers trying to make themselves sound virtuous by maligning defense attorneys. I tried to keep it nice.

"Everybody's got a right to a sturdy defense, Jim. You know, the Sixth Amendment and all?"

"Keep telling yourself that, like it's the noblest of truths."

"Well, it just about is as far as the law's concerned: making sure innocent people don't get punished for crimes they didn't commit."

"Right. You get Tremaine Drake off conspiracy to distribute twenty keys of heroin, among other charges; he hands you a check, walks away and next thing three of his lieutenants are executed on the mere suspicion of betrayal. Case closed. Society can't thank you enough, Brad."

I didn't want this to become an argument. I had to bring it back to the personal. Him and me.

"I'm not trying to tell you things have changed, buddy. I've changed."

"What do you mean?"

"I've had a change of heart."

"About what exactly?"

"If Harold is still out to land his white whale, well, you can deliver it to him."

"You want in?"

"I want in."

"Really?"

"Really."

Jim picked up his napkin and wiped his mouth.

"Well, that's too bad, Brad."

"Too bad? If this is about the half-million buy-in—"

"Five hundred grand won't get you an equity partnership at CDK now, Brad. Nothing will."

"What are you talking about? Last year—"

"Last year was last year. This year, Harold Krieger has a dartboard with your fucking face on it. At least he did for a while. But I can tell you he's not interested in you whatsoever. You know why?"

"No. Why?"

"First is your love-in with Tremaine Drake."

"A love-in?" I could accept Jim unloading on me for letting him down last year but only up to a point. But I bit my tongue.

"Yeah, a love-in. Like it or not, Brad, your brand changes with every high-profile client you choose. And you chose the lowest of the fucking low. What, you were thinking you could dangle the billings from a drug lord as a carrot for us to let you in?"

I had to admit I was kind of thinking that.

"Well, you're out of your mind," Jim continued. "You want to sleep well at night being the courtroom Zorro for that scumbag, go right ahead. But don't expect Krieger to be impressed. You tainted yourself with the Drake case, and you know it."

"It's called justice, Jim. It's not my fault the state of California failed to meet the burden of proof."

"Cast yourself as the white knight any way you choose, Brad. A blind man can see through that bullshit."

"You're claiming the moral high ground? Really?" I could hold my tongue no longer; job scrounging be damned. "Are you seriously saying there's a moral chasm between who I defend and who you protect? The fucking corporate vampires of this world who defraud investors, who screw dying policyholders, who use public funds to fuel their political ambitions. What was that case you closed a month or so ago? Oh, that's right. Paul Spears, CEO of Calbright Properties. Paid off City Hall to get a zoning exemption for a fifty-million-dollar development in West Hollywood, and you pulled the legal strings that allowed him to get away with it."

"That's different. It was—"

"I bet you wrote that revised land-use ordinance. Didn't you?"

"Look—"

"For Paul Spears, no less. One of the most corrupt developers in the city. And he's so much better than Tremaine Drake? How?"

Jim held up his hands for a truce. For a moment, I wondered if there was a scrap of honor in anything either of us did. Both of us took a few deep breaths then we ate in silence for a minute or so.

"We're a long way from Stanford, Brad."

That reminded me of the other proposal I had for him.

"It doesn't have to be like that, Jim."

"What do you mean?"

"We can still deliver on that promise we made to each other all those years ago."

He scoffed, took a sip. "Yeah? How exactly?"

"Start our own firm." Jim's face went blank. I pressed on. "One that takes on class-action cases. I'm sure we could convince Audrey to come on board. Last time I checked she was lecturing at Stanford. We could—"

"I'm going to stop you there," Jim said, putting both elbows on the table and leaning in. "Jesus, Brad. Listen to yourself. Do you actually believe this three-amigo bullshit? Let me be clear:

I'm fine with where I'm at. You may not like it that I'm happy at CDK, but I don't care. Harold Krieger has got a few more years and I'm gunning for his managing partner spot. And after a few years there, I'll be running for office." Jim's future was a series of Tetris blocks that he would spin to fit exactly where he wanted them to go. "So, you understand that I'm perfectly okay where I am. But clearly you're not? What's going on?"

What's going on? Good question. And the truth mostly came down to money. The new landlord that had taken over my floor eighteen months ago had raised the rent twice already. Last week he was at it again. I couldn't keep justifying staying there. And that train of thought had me wondering if I could justify other things I was doing with my life, making money defending the likes of Tremaine Drake for one. But I had big financial commitments. There was no alimony for my ex-wife—Claire was doing very well for herself as a designer—but I'd insisted on covering our daughter Bella's education, which was currently at thirty grand a year for fifth grade at the Crossroads School. I also had a mortgage and my escape-LA-once-and-for-all plan to fund. Then there was Megan, my brilliant secretary who I could never do without, whose engagement to her high school beau had fallen through and who now, single and unsure about her future, feared every financial hurdle that came my way spelled the end of her job.

But it was about more than money. I guess I was in the midst of a mid-life crisis without actually realizing it.

"Nothing," I said to Jim. "Just think I need a change."

"Well, if it's just a case of you looking for where the grass is greener, then I don't think you've scoped our firm properly. And that tells me you don't really have your heart set on joining us.

So I wouldn't be recommending you even if that offer was still on the table, which it isn't."

"You said there were a couple of reasons it no longer stands. The first was Drake. What was the other?"

Jim sat back.

"We're all hands on deck with this big new case and there's a freeze on hires. It's a closed shop until further notice."

"What's the case?"

"You know I can't say."

"Yeah, yeah. But what can you say?"

Jim leaned in.

"A massive property development down in Costa Rica has failed. There's going to be some heavy damage to investors here and our client needs to circle the wagons."

Costa Rica… Property development… There was a bell ringing in my head, and I didn't like the sound of it.

"Your client. Who is it?" I was sitting up straight now.

"Brad, you know I can't tell you that."

I leaned forward.

"Jim, I need you to tell me. Okay, not the client. Just the name of the development. That's all."

Jim paused a moment or two before answering in a low voice, almost just mouthing the words.

"Playa Dorada."

My stomach dropped.

I shot straight to my feet.

"I've gotta go," I said.

Alarmed by my reaction, Jim grabbed my arm as I passed and held me.

"Brad, you can't say anything to anyone! I swear, if you do…"

I pulled my arm away.
"Thanks for lunch."

CHAPTER 3

A cold sweat was coming over me as I made for the elevator. I pressed the button. I couldn't wait and took the stairs. Out on the street, I tapped a speed dial.

"Bradley," my mother answered. "How nice to hear from you." Her voice was happy and warm and buoyant as usual.

"Mom, that investment you bought into in Costa Rica."

There was a slight pause before she answered.

"Yes?"

"What's it called again?"

She brightened as though my question was a pleasant surprise compared to what she'd expected.

"Playa Dorada. It's Spanish for Golden Sands."

My shoulders sank as I exhaled deeply.

"Have you heard anything about it recently?" I asked.

Another pause. Then her voice resumed with apprehension. "How did you know?"

"Know what, Mom?"

Her voice began quivering.

"It's gone. It's all gone."

My worst fear was realized.

"How much did you lose?"

"A lot, dear. Almost a million. I have to sit down. I can't bear thinking about it."

"Mom, does Dad know about this?"

"No, dear. Of course not."

It was a stupid question but I'd asked it on reflex. I still wasn't used to Dad being ignored about anything when it came to my parents' lives. But the Alzheimer's had come on quickly. So much so that you'd no more seek his opinion on an investment than you would a toddler's. Mom had good reason to go it alone on what she did with their money. But I was sure she hadn't gone it alone. There was no way she'd drop a million on something so risky all by herself.

My blood was boiling.

My parents had just lost a huge chunk of their retirement savings. And that put me in a hole: there was no way I was going to stand by and watch them be reduced to food stamps. I'd beg, borrow or steal whatever it took to keep them living in the comfort they'd always wanted for themselves.

So much for thinking I had five hundred grand to buy my way into a firm.

All of a sudden, I realized that I was going to struggle just to keep my own practice running.

I felt sick.

From out of nowhere, I was in the middle of a financial catastrophe I never saw coming.

Mom wasn't keen to feed me any details about how this debacle came about, but she didn't have to. I knew exactly who was to blame: a smooth-talking, self-absorbed weasel who, in pursuit of easy money, was ever happy to run his morality gauge down to zero.

My brother.

CHAPTER 4

I knew he wouldn't answer my calls, so I didn't bother trying. That didn't matter—I knew where to find him. At two o'clock on a race-day Thursday, there was only one place he'd be: the track. Santa Anita Park, to be exact.

I cursed his name a thousand times on the twenty-minute drive out to Arcadia, and my fury hadn't abated as I entered the famous racetrack. I made my way up the escalators to the top bar where the balconies overlooked the finish line. I knew this was where he would be—he'd taken to calling it his "lucky spot" years ago. And when I crossed the bar and caught sight of him, that's exactly where he was headed.

There he was in a figure-hugging long-sleeved shirt, jeans, new Vans sneakers and one of those idiotic trilby hats on his head. He clutched a Corona in one hand and the form guide in the other; one of those fools who thinks throwing good money after doped-up animals is what you call "sport."

It had been six years since I'd last seen him and a couple years since we'd last talked, but he was still up to his old crap and hurting the one person who couldn't help but love him. Our mother.

The air hummed with the drone of the caller's voice. A race was in progress and Mitch and two pals necked beers as the field rounded the bend and hit the straight. I stepped out onto the balcony and stood at Mitch's shoulder.

"Got money to burn, have you?" I said. Mitch's head swung around quickly. Although the shock of seeing me was evident, he played it cool.

"What are you doing here? If you want to see me, call. Don't come here."

I grabbed him by the shirt with both hands and slammed him up against the glass window.

"You and I are going to talk right now or I'll take all your fucking tickets and flush them down the john."

Mitch's two buddies stepped closer. One of them raised a hand to touch me. I released my grip on my brother and smacked the guy's hand away, stepping forward.

"You better think very carefully and real quick about your next move. I've got some business to take care of with my brother. And if you don't like that, then you and I can sort things out first." The guy, shocked by my intensity, raised his hands.

"Is this true, Mitch? Is he your brother?"

Mitch nodded.

"Yeah. Drop it, Josh. It's cool. Actually, can you guys give us a minute?"

The other two obliged and slid past us on their way to the bar.

"What's with the hostility, Bro?" said Mitch. "What the hell are you doing here?"

That lying face of his hadn't aged much these past six years. That was always one of his gifts. And how the chicks dug that tanned skin, generous smile, and easy wit of his, not to mention the long, light brown hair he liked to pull back into a ponytail. Nowadays the hair was shorter, but it was slicked back and tied beneath that stupid hat of his. He was a charming piece of work, my younger brother, I'll give him that. He had everything going for him. Even money. What he lacked was the sense to keep it.

While I was at college, he got into real estate. He made plenty of money but knew of only two things to do with it: spend and gamble. The only thing he knew how to do better was to spend and gamble with other people's money. And on the subject of marriage, Mitch only had two problems: gambling and monogamy. Two women had loved him enough to walk down the aisle with him and both ended up walking out to the same divorce lawyer's office.

"I told you to keep Mom out of your schemes. I remember the conversation clearly because I was happy for it to be the last thing I ever said to you. You called me up out of the blue and pitched me some dodgy property investment."

"Brad, that's not right. I didn't pitch you anything dodgy."

"I told you to shove that deal because I was done with your conniving schemes."

"You think I'm going to stand here and take shit from you?"

"I told you not to get Mom involved!" I shouted.

A Hispanic man in a white tie and dark waistcoat appeared at the doorway.

"Is everything okay, Mitch?"

"It's alright, Carlos. My brother's a little upset is all."

Carlos backed away inside.

"I told you to keep that shit away from Mom and what did you do?"

"I don't know, Brad. What did I do?"

Mitch didn't know what I knew, so he wasn't keen to admit to anything.

"You talked her into that Costa Rican development that's gone belly up. Playa Dorada."

His face dropped.

"Brad, I didn't push it on Mom at all. If you think that's what happened, you're wrong!"

"Her money's gone. Mom and Dad are practically broke. Don't try to make out like you didn't persuade her. What did you talk her into?"

"Brad, it was a sure thing. Never been surer of anything in my life. I still don't know what went wrong, or how. I know you don't believe that, but I've been in the property game a long time and I did my due diligence and it all checked out. That's why I felt confident about approaching Mom. I thought I was doing her a favor. And look, the dust hasn't settled on this thing. She may well get her money back."

"That's not what I've heard."

From my conversation with Jim, I knew the money was shot.

"What have you heard?"

"It doesn't matter."

"Look, Mom made it clear she could afford half a mill for one of those properties."

"Half a mill? What are you talking about?"

Mitch realized his mistake immediately.

"She told me she'd lost a mill. So that means she lent you money to buy one for you."

I was struggling not to hit him. He raised his palms.

"Brad. Brad! Look, I can make this right."

"No, you can't. You've just screwed up Mom and Dad's life. And I'm going to have to bail them out. So, you haven't just screwed up their lives, you've screwed up mine too. And I swore to God that would never happen again. That's why I've wanted nothing to do with you."

"I'm going to make this good, Brad. I swear."

"How are you going to do that? Have you got a million tucked away that you can hand over? Because that's the only thing that will fix this mess. Have you got that money?"

Mitch looked ashamed, which surprised me because I always thought that feeling had somehow been surgically removed from him.

"No, not exactly."

"You mean 'no.'"

"No."

For a second I was lost for words. Mitch sensed this moment was an opportunity to deliver his pitch.

"Brad, I work for the guy who put together the whole Playa Dorada deal. What's happened is not right. No one saw it coming, but if there's any way to salvage this mess, he'll find it."

"You really expect me to believe that? Who is this guy anyway?"

"His name's Rubin Ashby. Real smart guy. Like genius smart. If we've been burnt badly by this deal, he has too. I know he put a lot of his own money into this thing. The Costa Ricans must have screwed him over."

"You sound like a naive little girl. You want to help? Then get Mom's money out of this Ashby guy's pocket. Can you do that, Mitch? Can you?"

Mitch shook his head.

"Didn't think so. Whose money are you gambling with today?"

"Mine."

"Show me."

He pulled out a thick bankroll. I snatched it out of his hand.

"Hey? What the fuck, Brad?"

"Consider it a down-payment on your debt to Mom."

I counted the money. It was almost three grand.

"Only nine hundred and ninety-seven thousand to go," I said as I pocketed the cash.

"Jesus, Brad. That's my winnings. How am I supposed to—?"

"Ask someone who cares."

I left him there and walked back into the bar area.

I was ten minutes from the office when my phone rang. It was Megan, my secretary.

"Where are you?" she asked. "I've been calling you for an hour."

"I left my phone in the car. I'm on my way back to the office now. What's up?"

"There's someone here to see you."

"But I don't have any appointments."

"No, I know. He didn't make one. He just arrived."

A walk-in. Is it too much to ask people to pick up the phone and make an appointment?

Megan's voice lowered. I could hear her walk away from her desk and into my office for privacy.

"I told him I didn't know when you'd be back and he said he'd wait as long as it took."

I didn't like the sound of this. It's happened too many times. I know the kind of guy who strolls into a defense attorney's office unannounced and on a mission—unstable, hyped-up, drug-fucked, twitchy and paranoid. I wasn't far away, but I didn't like Megan being alone with a potential lunatic.

"Did he now? Who is he? Is he behaving himself?"

"Yes, he's fine. I'm fine, Mr. Madison, I assure you."

"Did he give you a name?"

"Yes. He said his name was Rubin Ashby."

CHAPTER 5

Rubin Ashby watched me approach from the elevator door. He was in his early sixties and dressed immaculately in a fine navy suit.

When I came up and stood before him, neither of us said a word for a moment. I was taller, but with his chin jutted out it was as though he was looking down on me. His arms were folded with each hand gripping its opposite elbow tightly. His expression was almost blank but with a tinge of displeasure—at first glance I figured he was upset with me, as if I had the gall to keep him waiting even though he'd arrived unannounced.

The reason for my initial silence was that he was one of the most unusual-looking men I'd ever seen. The skin of his face was shiny and smooth, giving literal meaning to the term "plastic surgery." It was a face that had deviated far from its original form, and I wondered how on earth this could be the desired outcome. It had been cut and tucked and stretched into something that looked like the death mask of a younger man. The youthful effect was contradicted by deep creases under his chin and eyes. The wrinkled skin of his throat gave away his age, yet his thick quaff of slicked-back hair showed not a trace of gray. His black eyebrows and eyelashes looked like they'd been glued on.

Suddenly, his face softened into a smile. His arms dropped and his hand came out for mine. Somehow, I felt like he was welcoming me to his office. For someone of average height and average build, he had presence, that's for sure. He had the bearing of a man who gets whatever he wants.

"Mr. Madison," he said. "I apologize for just dropping in on you like this. I understand this is not the way you conduct business. But I'm here with my colleague Otto Benson on an extremely important and rather urgent matter."

Ashby spoke quietly but firmly, with courtesy and an inclusive tone, like he was bringing me into his utmost confidence. His companion—a lean thirty-something with patent leather wingtips, cropped black hair and designer stubble—bowed slightly at the mention of his name.

"It's funny, Mr. Ashby. You're just the person I wanted to see."

"Is that right?"

His eyebrows seemed to want to help convey his surprise but couldn't move.

"Yes, it is." I bent down, placed my briefcase next to Megan's desk and gave her a nod by way of greeting. I then straightened and stood directly in front of Ashby. "You have taken my mother for a million dollars and I'm going to see that you pay every cent of it back."

A polite confusion came over Ashby's face. "I'm not sure what you mean. If there is something I have done to you, or your mother, Mr. Madison, I assure you I am completely unaware of what that might be."

"She bought two of your dodgy properties in Costa Rica. Playa Dorada. And because of you she's pretty much blown the life savings she and my father worked so damned hard for. You took that money. And you are going to give it back."

His eyes were defiant, but he remained utterly calm. He bowed his head for a moment before speaking.

"Mr. Madison, for starters, I have not taken your mother for anything." His voice was low and dry and even. "Yes, I am the head of the group behind that development, but I put a lot of my own money into it. More than anybody else, I can assure you of that. More than I can afford to lose, I'll have you know. So, I am extremely unhappy about the problems that we have been having with the Costa Rican government, but I can assure you I will be doing everything in my power to rectify the matter. Now, if you give me a minute, I can explain to you where things stand and why I'm here."

I hadn't had time to check any coverage of Playa Dorada in the media, but I figured that must be what Jim's firm was preparing for: to protect Ashby and co. from having to pay out smaller investors.

I had to play my cards close to my chest on my source. Not just lawyer confidentiality; I didn't want Ashby to know I had a friend at CDK.

"I'll give you one minute," I said. "And then you and your—"

"Mr. Madison, I understand your anger." Ashby lifted his hands to cut me short. "I'm not happy about this whole situation either. Now, I must be one hundred percent honest with you. I can offer you some reassurance about your mother's money but, unfortunately, no guarantees."

"So, you're not going to help her?"

"Please, Mr. Madison. I'll get to that in due course, but, as I just mentioned, there is another matter of grave importance I wish to discuss with you and it really is quite urgent."

He flipped his hands in the direction of my office door and tried lifting his eyebrows, which only half obeyed.

I reached for the door handle.

"Megan, would you mind…"

"Certainly, Mr. Madison." She hardly needed me to tell her to hold my calls.

I pushed the door open for Ashby. As he stepped forward, he saw me eying his companion warily. He snapped to attention.

"Mr. Benson here is my head of acquisitions," he said. "A most brilliant financier who is across every aspect of my business, so I'd like him to join us."

"I see," I said, looking at Benson. "The brains behind the Costa Rican cluster fuck, I assume?"

Benson's jaw tightened.

Once both men were in my office, Megan rolled her eyes and spoke low.

"You sure you want those two rattlesnakes in your cage, Mr. Madison?"

"I can handle them, Megan."

By the time I took a seat behind my desk, Ashby and Benson were already settled in my two leather client chairs.

"Before I hear you out, Mr. Ashby, I want you to know that I meant what I said upfront. One way or another, you are going to return my mother's money and not a cent less than she paid."

Ashby crossed his legs and regarded me with his lips pressed into a thoughtful pout.

"Mr. Madison, I don't appreciate being spoken to in such a tone. It is uncalled for. But I'll forgive you, given your emotions are running high."

I thought better of snapping back.

Ashby crossed his legs and interlaced his fingers over his knee. "Now, I'm going to tell you what will happen here today. You and I are going to part ways with a clear understanding that we both can help one another out. You don't have to like me nor do I have to like you, but you and I will be working together whether you like it or not."

"That sounds an awful lot like a threat," I said.

Ashby brushed at the air with his hands but held an unblinking gaze on me.

"Maybe I just have a clearer view of the future than you do. But take it whichever way you want. I'm merely stating the truth. Do you want to know why it's true, Mr. Madison?"

"I'm fascinated," I said sarcastically. "Your minute's almost up."

"I have a friend in need. A dear friend." Ashby lifted his left wrist to look at his watch, a gold Rolex Datejust. "As of three hours ago, about half of which I have spent waiting for you, my friend and employee Mr. Walter Powell was taken in by the LAPD for questioning about a murder. I fear the police are possessed of the absurd notion that Walter threw his former girlfriend off a cliff. And I would like you to go and extricate him immediately."

"Is that right?"

"Yes. I propose to hire you not only to get Walter out of there but to see to it that this ridiculous suspicion is dispelled at the earliest opportunity. The police have already demonstrated that they are not prepared to listen to reason. Walter has a solid alibi, yet I fear they are determined to blame an innocent man for this murder."

"Are you done? Right. That's your minute. Now get the hell out of my office." I stood, went to the door and opened it. "The next time you and I talk it's going to be about one thing and one thing only: the exact date my mother can expect her money back. If I don't get a clear answer from you in seven days, I'll be coming after you. And, one way or another, we are going to settle the ledger on that score. Now get out."

Neither Ashby nor Benson moved an inch.

"I'm not going anywhere," said Ashby, sweeping dust off his knee brusquely. He continued in a low voice, clear, steady and slow. "This may be your office but don't delude yourself that you're the one calling the shots here, Mr. Madison. I'm not going to explain to you where things stand as far as our property deal goes, but I will say this: you are powerless to get one cent from me that I am not prepared to give you. You want to threaten me? You want to try to intimidate me? Okay, I'll walk out of here and you and I will never speak another word. You will not get within shouting distance of me. And if you try you will deeply regret it. That's not a threat, just a statement of fact. So, I can only urge you not to be foolish."

"You can take your advice and—"

"The choice, Mr. Madison," he said, talking over me, all the while remaining seated and looking ahead, "the choice is yours. Get Walter out of this mess and I guarantee that your mother gets her money back and that you will be paid handsomely for your efforts. Or you get nothing, neither for yourself nor for your dear mother, who, like any investor, went into that deal with her eyes wide open. The only person in this room who sees any injustice in her fate is you, let me assure you of that. But make no mistake, I do not care about your mother. I do not care about you. I care about my friend and I was told you were the best person to handle his predicament."

I was recommended to Ashby? By whom?

Then the penny dropped. I resumed my place behind my desk but remained standing. "Did that stupid brother of mine send you?"

A look of slight puzzlement came over Ashby's face.

"Hmmm," he said pensively. "Honestly, I forgot that your brother works for me. But no, it wasn't him."

"Then who was it?"

"Well, I believe you know Harold Krieger? He spoke very highly of you. And then there's our mutual friend, Tremaine Drake. Although I shouldn't really describe Mr. Drake as a friend. We've just got some common interests. But I do remember him once singing your praises and I committed the name to memory. What did he say exactly? Ah yes. 'Brad Madison is the best little lawyer boy in town,' or something to that effect. Was that it, Otto?"

"Word for word, Mr. Ashby. Best little lawyer boy in town."

"You son of a bitch," I seethed.

Ashby rose from his seat calmly and slowly. Benson took his cue and did the same.

"At this point, I'd normally shake your hand, but I can see you wouldn't be amenable to that," Ashby said.

"You don't have my answer."

"I don't need an answer. In a few minutes' time you will realize you don't have a choice." Ashby picked out a business card from his wallet, took a pen from my desk and wrote something. He straightened and tapped the desk. "They have Walter down at headquarters. I've told him to say nothing until you get there. You have one hour, Mr. Madison. If you haven't gotten Walter released by four o'clock, I will assume you have found another way to compensate for your mother's loss."

"You will be the one paying."

"Mr. Madison, of course. That is what I am offering. But, and I hate repeating myself, there is only one way that that's going to happen. I would really appreciate it if you go and help Walter."

As much as Ashby was an affront to me, I was confounded by his insistence. I stopped him at the door. We stood face to face.

"Why me?" I asked. "There are a thousand lawyers out there, ones that will even pretend to like you for the money?"

"I need you, Mr. Madison," said Ashby softly with his chin raised at me. "As for why, I think that will become abundantly clear in time."

Satisfied that his response was adequate, Ashby tilted his head slightly before stepping out of my office.

I followed and stood beside Megan. Once they were in the elevator and gone, I spun around and stormed back into my office, slamming the door behind me. I picked up whatever I could get my hands on, which turned out to be my desk phone, ripped it from its leads and threw it across the room and into my bookcase. My fury was not sated enough, so I stepped toward the bookcase and drove my fist into a volume set of Witkin's guides: two-inch-thick treatises on various topics of California law. Luckily, the books gave way a little, allowing my knuckles to stay intact even as the skin broke and bled.

"Fuck! Fuck! Fuck!"

Megan rushed in, but I waved her off. After she'd left me alone again, I regained my breath slowly. Never before had I hated my job so profoundly.

What kind of a man would I be if I obeyed him?

But what choice did I have?

Ashby was right.

A minute later, I knew exactly what I had to do.

CHAPTER 6

First impressions count for a lot with me, and I didn't care much for Walter Powell. He was a big, broad-shouldered, good-looking kid in his mid-twenties, but he reeked of superiority. When I entered the interview room, he was sitting there with a rod-straight back regarding the two cops standing over him with disdain, as though spending time in their presence was an unsavory imposition he should never have to endure.

"Are you my lawyer?" he said to me. "Thank God. What took you so long?"

I was in two minds as to whether to clip his ear or reply. I erred on the side of civility.

"I wasn't aware you'd called 911, son," I said. "This is the process. This is how long it takes. My name is Brad Madison. And you're coming with me. Unless you want to stay."

I wasn't familiar with Powell's interrogators—Detectives Brian Cousins and Harrison Daylesford—but I'd heard plenty. They made an odd couple.

By all accounts, Detective Brian Cousins—mid-fifties, five-six and wiry—was a pretty straight arrow. He wasn't the type to bring someone in for questioning without believing there was something to it. And that's the way he came across, with his by-the-book haircut and suit and his earnest manner. He was the kind of officer you wouldn't doubt was simply trying to get at the truth.

Detective Harrison Daylesford was of a similar age to Cousins but that's where the physical similarities ended. Daylesford was six feet tall and bore the waistline of a man who sat and ate too much, and the physique of someone who'd never owned a gym card. He sported a thick brown mustache straight out of *Kojak*-era casting in the middle of a big, double-chinned, flabby-jowled face. The word I had on Daylesford was that he was as nasty as he was bent. Not that this was common knowledge or, in fact, substantiated. It was just that, among other things I heard, two clients of mine who now occupy prison cells told me they had friends who'd been framed by Daylesford. No one had any proof of this, of course. It could have been no more than the scuttlebutt of a sewing circle of cons.

Neither cop was happy to see me.

"Detective," I said to Cousins, "how is my client of use to you?"

Cousins told me that Powell's ex—Nicola Beauchamp—had been found at the bottom of a cliff in San Pedro four days ago. They'd spoken with Powell twice already, including an interview at his condo, before bringing him in for questioning today. He said a witness claimed he saw someone resembling Powell and another man rough up a girl at the Point Fermin Park the night of Beauchamp's death. That witness had picked Powell in a photo line-up. Cousins said a car like Powell's was spotted at the scene too. He also said Powell had submitted to a swab test for DNA analysis.

I thanked the detectives and told them I was taking Powell out of there.

"Take him," Cousins said. "I dare say we'll be seeing him again real soon."

"Let's go, Walter."

Daylesford seemed to be suppressing the urge to detain Powell by force. I found myself wondering how many men Daylesford had smacked down who'd misread his dumpy heft as weakness. To me, he had a wrestler's menace: no ring craft, no twinkle-toed shuffle needed; just hand speed and big-armed strength. He'd have you in a resolute chokehold quick as a bear. And he looked like nothing would please him more than to grab hold of Powell's head and use the table to beat a confession out of him.

Sitting opposite me in my office, Powell's attitude didn't change in the slightest. He bore a kind of spoiled-brat nonchalance that all this tiresome nonsense would, and should, be removed from his presence without him having to raise a finger.

Hell knows he wouldn't be the first good-looking kid to be over-endowed with entitlement, but there was something inherently off-putting about him. His anvil-shaped jawline framed a thin-lipped mouth, which sat beneath a sharp, pronounced nose and piercing blue eyes. His blond hair was clipped short at the sides with a long fringe combed back and every strand gelled into place. With his light gray suit, tucked-in black T-shirt and thin gold chain, he looked like he'd stepped out of a George Michael video clip.

When Megan offered coffee, Powell asked if it was instant or filtered. Not only that, he asked what brand it was. Satisfied his basic standards would be met, he ordered it white with two sugars; level teaspoons, please, not heaped. He then crossed his legs, straightened his back and looked at me—down his nose, like Ashby—as if he was giving me permission to proceed at will.

I kept him waiting while I read through the Nicola Beauchamp police report, witness statements and the notes from Powell's police interview.

When Megan came in with the coffee, I looked up to see Powell touch her bare arm lightly as she turned to leave.

"Thank you so much," he said in a rich, baritone voice. He took hold of one of her fingers and ran his gaze up from her hand to her eyes. "I'm sorry to be so particular about my coffee. I'm a coffee snob, you might say. But what a gracious soul you are."

He released her hand and took a sip. "Ah, you have nailed it," he said.

He had a voice that was fit for radio ads, public speaking and making women go weak at the knees. But I had to wonder, given the touch of camp in his manner, whether it was girls' knees he liked to bend. "After the day I've had, you are a godsend."

"It's a cup of coffee, honey," said Megan, flicking her eyes over to me with a hint of cheek. "You should see me shake a cocktail. But I don't think we'll be mixing after hours." She took back her hand and turned to me. "Be careful with this one, Mr. Madison. Give him a treat and you'll never get him out of your lap."

After Megan left, I returned my attention to the documents. As the seconds dragged by, I could hear Powell shifting in his seat, sipping his coffee and exhaling loudly to remind me of his presence, in case I'd forgotten. In time, I dropped the papers and addressed him.

"Walter, I'm not a fortune teller, but my guess is you're going to get charged for this."

"That's absurd. Surely you won't let—"

"And you need to get what I'm telling you into your head. Right now you're looking at life without parole. Do I need to tell you how hellish that would be for someone like you? Even the straightest of hard cons might want to bust your cheeks, you know what I'm saying?"

Powell's smugness was replaced by abject horror. Good. I'd wanted to rattle his cage.

"Mr. Madison," he stammered, "I'm as heterosexual as you are."

"I wasn't taking a shot at your sexual preferences, Walter. You think they'll give a shit whether you like dick or not? And for the record, you know nothing about me."

I put my elbows on the table and leaned forward.

"Let's get this straight: I don't like you. That might change but I doubt it. And it's not really your fault. It's more the circumstances of this arrangement. But I'm a professional, Walter, and I don't let personal feelings affect either the quality of my work or my dedication to the cause. So, we have something in common that binds us together. We want the same thing. And that is to make sure your ass doesn't end up in jail. Okay?"

I stood up and walked to the window. I was feeling a little better the more I talked. In a sense, the more I applied my brain to Walter Powell's plight the more it became purely a case of law rather than some obligation I'd been forced into.

"Walter, I want you to tell me your story and I want you to be completely honest. Some defense attorneys aren't inclined to ask you straight out whether you did it or not. I can go either way. But in this case, I want you to tell me. And before you say anything, I want to remind you that attorney-client privilege is sacrosanct. Whatever you say will never leave these four walls."

Walter's head was dead still and his face expressionless. As he pondered what to say, the tip of his tongue emerged and ran along his thin top lip.

"No, Mr. Madison, I didn't do it. I had nothing whatsoever to do with Nicola's death."

"Then why are you a suspect?"

"I can explain."

"I can tell you why you are a suspect, Walter. Just as I can guess why the police will soon be charging you with murder. Just going by what I have in front of me. They have witnesses making you at the scene, your car."

"They can't convict me on that! What kind of lawyer are you? You're supposed to be in my corner."

"I guess I'm not in the mood to be bullshitted by some kid who's used to having Mommy and Daddy wipe his ass after he's made a mess of things." One of the documents Megan had brought me was a profile of Walter Powell she'd compiled using everything she could find online. He was raised in Boston and lived a life of luxury and privilege until his father filed for bankruptcy five years ago. Walter finished college soon after, relocated to LA and in time became Rubin Ashby's communications director.

"Mr. Madison, I don't know what I've done to upset you, but, please, I am innocent. I didn't kill Nicola. I could never do that. I love her. At least I did. Well, I still do, as a dear friend."

The cocksure, cashed-up white boy act was dropped. In its place was something more akin to what I wanted, something near to genuine. I felt better for both blowing off a little steam and adjusting his attitude.

Now we could get started.

CHAPTER 7

"She's your ex, right?" I said. Powell set his coffee cup aside.

"That's right. We were together for three years. But we grew apart."

"Who broke it off?"

"Me."

"No hard feelings?"

"Well, not really hard feelings. The truth was that Nicola found it hard to move on. We'd met at a function in LA. It was the launch of a tech start-up. A mutual friend, Samantha, was invited and Nicola came along for the free drinks. Samantha introduced us and we really hit it off. We had three wonderful years together, but it became clear we both saw the future differently. I wasn't ready for marriage and kids, but that was what she had her heart set on. We remained friends but it was hard for us both. By that I mean she always believed I would come around to her way of thinking and realize that we were meant to be together. I just grew more and more certain that that was not what I wanted. And that really took a toll on her. I don't know if you know, but she tried to kill herself."

"No, I didn't know that."

"Yeah, at the very same spot where she died. She went out there one night and she had called me earlier that day and I finally called her back and she was a mess. So I got there as fast as I could and took care of her for a few days."

"I see. It's interesting you say she'd gone there previously to kill herself because at first glance her death looked like a regular suicide. Then the toxicology reports showed high concentrations of alcohol and Rohypnol in her blood. The cops found drag marks in the area near the clifftop; they found that the tips of her shoes were scuffed up, strengthening the suspicion that she had gone over unwillingly, and a car matching the make you say you drive on behalf of Mr. Ashby was seen in the area. So, the police came looking for you. They don't think she jumped. They think you threw her over."

"Mr. Madison, I swear I had nothing to do with this. I'm devastated by Nicola's death."

"Have you got a photo of her?"

"Yes. Plenty."

Powell pulled out his phone and handed it to me. Nicola Beauchamp was very pretty and had a beaming smile.

"What do you think, Walter? Did she commit suicide or did someone kill her?"

"Of course, she suicided. Why would anyone want to kill her?"

I made a few notes. This could well be my first line of defense—preparing the case for suicide.

"Tell me how she reacted to you breaking it off with her."

"Well, Nicola was quite a vivacious girl. A real party girl. By that I don't mean slutty. She was just huge fun. She had so much energy, it was infectious. But I was one of the few people who saw that there was a flip side. I wouldn't say she was bipolar but she was in the ballpark. Behind closed doors she would swing from being the life of the party to being crushingly depressed before my very eyes."

"Was this related to alcohol consumption? Drugs?"

"Generally speaking, yes. She did like to drink and she'd never say no to a line of coke. But some of the mornings after got pretty dark. I'd spend the day with her just trying to get her up and out of bed and into the daylight."

"She leaned on you?"

"Yes. And to be honest that was one of the factors that drove me away. I was younger and didn't want to be in a relationship that was so emotionally taxing."

"What about friends? Who did she confide in, other than you?"

"A couple," Walter said after a pause. "Samantha for one. The girl who introduced us."

"I know the cops have asked about your movements the night she died. The LAPD was called out on November sixteenth at eight in the morning after a jogger reported seeing a body at the base of the cliff. Where were you on the night of the fifteenth?"

"I was at Mr. Ashby's place. It was a movie night. We ordered pizza and watched a couple of movies."

"Who else was there?"

"Who else? Just me, Mr. Ashby and Otto."

"Otto Benson?"

"Yes."

"What time did you get there?"

"Um, let me think. It was about seven, eight o'clock. Closer to eight, I'd say."

"And when did you go home?"

"Not until the next day. I spent the night there. We all did. I'd had a bit to drink and didn't want to drive home. Mr. Ashby has quite a few guest rooms, so I crashed there."

"What is your relationship with Mr. Ashby exactly, Walter?"

"I'm his communications director. I manage all the content we put out on his website and brochures. I do various other jobs for him as well, like driving him around."

"You're his chauffeur?"

"I'm his driver, yes. That's part of what I do."

"What's the car?"

"A two-toned Maybach. It's a high-end Mercedes."

"What's it worth?"

"About two-twenty grand."

"Jesus. And that's your set of wheels off the clock?"

"Yes. Mr. Ashby doesn't drive, so I keep his car on standby. I have security parking where I live, of course. But I'm more than his driver. I'm his protégé. Taking him where he needs to go during business hours allows me to be constantly learning from him. That man is a genius, and I'm glad to say that he's my role model and mentor. I want to be as successful as he is one day. I recommend you spend a little time researching him, Mr. Madison. You'll see he's much more than a property developer."

"Oh, I will be looking into Mr. Ashby, you can be sure of that. But what about you? You want to get into property development?"

"Well, more the tech start-ups, venture capital, cutting-edge side of things. That's where my interest lies. Mr. Ashby's newest development is something that I'm putting everything into."

"What's that?"

"Silicon Beach Plaza. He secured enough land in Santa Monica to build a huge IT hub, a hive of digital-technology businesses. It will attract the best digital minds and the hottest tech companies on the planet. It will be a gamechanger in the IT world. Forget Silicon Valley. The frontier of technology will be moving to the coast: Santa Monica."

"That site on Arizona and 5th?" I'd almost forgotten about the huge development I'd driven past so many times. Suddenly, I remembered that residents had fought the project strenuously only to lose out.

"That's the one."

"Well, you can't be focusing on that right now."

"Why not?"

"You're one step away from being charged with murder, Walter."

"But you're not going to let that happen, are you? The cops are out to get me."

"I can't stop the police from charging you. Keeping you from being convicted is where I come in. And why on earth would the cops have it in for you?"

"I can tell you. More to the point I can tell you his name."

"Who's name?"

"Dean Swindall."

"Who's Dean Swindall?"

"A cop who hates me."

"LAPD?"

"He is now, but he's a yokel bigot from Tennessee."

"Is that a fact? So how do you two know each other and why would he want to see you charged with murder?"

"Because Nicola dumped him to be with me."

I was not expecting this.

"And you're telling me this guy's got a grudge against you that is so strong he'd try to frame you for murder?"

"That's what I'm telling you. He's been threatening me for ages. More so since I broke her heart. And now I think he's got his opportunity to get his revenge once and for all."

I scoured the documents on my desk.

"I don't see Dean Swindall's name anywhere in these reports about Nicola's death. He doesn't appear to be part of the investigation."

"Maybe not. But his fingerprints would be all over it. I know this guy. He's actually threatened to kill me."

"He's threatened to kill you?"

"Yes. And now he's got a chance to do the next best thing. Mr. Madison, I can tell you now this guy is on a mission to put me in jail for the rest of my life."

For the first time, Powell let his emotions show through and they got the better of him. Tears formed in his eyes and he looked in equal parts scared and sad.

Maybe I'd misread him. Maybe that smugness was actually a Herculean effort to keep his emotions in check. The antipathy I held toward him began to dissolve. If there's anything I dislike more than a rotten client, it's a dirty cop who thinks he's a law unto himself.

Suddenly, I didn't know which way was north on the moral compass, but I was sure as hell going to find out. No client of mine, however unlikeable, was going to be locked away by a cop with a vendetta.

"Okay, Mr. Powell. That's enough for today. You can go on home."

He stood and we shook hands. As he held on, his left hand joined in to cup mine. He moved in too close for comfort.

"Thank you, Mr. Madison. It's a comfort to know I'm in such good hands. Mr. Ashby said you were going to keep me safe and I believe it now. I'm trusting you with my life, with my future, and I want you to know I will do whatever I can to help you. Just name it. Anything."

I retrieved my hand and stepped backward to get the door.

"Steady on, Walter. Let's not go out and buy matching rings yet. This is a marriage of convenience, and don't you ever forget it. When this is all done and dusted, we will ride off into the sunset—you going your way and me going mine. And as the credits roll, I'll be washing my hands of you and your boss. I never want to see either of you again. Is that clear?"

Powell was taken aback and looked slightly wounded. Then his facial features morphed back into his resting bitch face.

"Crystal."

CHAPTER 8

I spent the next morning punching and kicking the hell out of a heavy bag. It did me good to get some Ashby-Mitch-triggered fury out of my system.

Jack Briggs pulled up outside the gym in his brand-new Black Ford Raptor, his new "weekender." As far as private investigators go, Jack Briggs didn't fit the cliché of the retired cop keeping his toe in the law enforcement game by becoming a snoop for hire. Jack was barely in his forties, had made a fortune off tech stocks and was a genuine LA legend. He had movie-star looks, a judo black belt, a chopper pilot's license and enough charisma to light up Sunset Boulevard. Until recently, he was one of the city's most eligible bachelors, but after Megan introduced him to former Olympic downhill ski champion Chanel Palmer, it was all over. They were engaged within a month. And soon after, he sold his Camaro to make way for a more family-friendly ride—the Raptor.

I'd called Jack earlier, proposing we head out to San Pedro to check out the crime scene. On the way he could brief me on what he'd been able to dig up.

As I got in, he handed me a coffee.

"Here you go, sweetheart. Your favorite. Pumpkin spice mochaccino latte with cream. Damn, I forgot the shortbread."

I blank-faced him and grabbed the cup. *He'd better not have...* I inhaled the aroma and took a sip. It was good Americana.

"Asshole," I said as Jack chuckled. "I don't need any more hits on my manhood."

"Is this Rubin Ashby you're referring to?" Jack said as he pulled out.

I nodded and filled Jack in on everything that had happened. I told him how it sickened me to think of my parents struggling after all they had done for Mitch and me. They'd intended to travel overseas together, go on cruises and be able to fly to LA at the drop of a hat to spend time with their granddaughter. But then Dad's health had gone south and Mitch had led Mom into financial ruin.

"How are Claire and Bella?" Jack asked.

"Bella's great. I know you don't take much advice from anybody, but I'm telling you, being a father is the best thing ever."

"How are things with Claire?"

I looked out the window. Claire had remarried, and I'd found it hard to get used to the fact that my daughter was part of another family unit.

"She's great. She's happy. She's killing it with her jewelry business. Yeah and Marty's a good guy. He's good with Bella."

"Is that bugging you?"

"There's not much about my life that's not bugging me, to be honest. I've never felt so restless and so cornered at once. That son of a bitch Ashby has got me over a barrel."

"You're not the only one."

"What do you mean?"

"What I mean is that's how Rubin Ashby operates: he uses leverage, whichever way he can get it, sometimes by force of personality or persuasion, and sometimes by force, plain and simple."

I thought of how Ashby had behaved in my office. To see someone so convinced of their own power was kind of disturbing.

"Go on," I urged Jack.

"You know some people think he's a business guru, a visionary."

"Yes. Walter Powell practically worships the guy."

"Ashby is relatively new to LA. Came over here ten years ago from Philly. Made a mint there in his twenties working for his uncle's building company. He had a talent for finding projects that were ripe for redevelopment. You know, run-down apartment blocks that he'd manage to wrangle from the owners. Then they'd be converted into a prestige residential block and make him and his uncle very rich.

"There was also a case where he was accused of swindling an elderly farmer. During the course of the sale, the poor farmer had somehow handed over the title before receiving the full sum. He complained to the authorities that Ashby had deceived him but could not prove it. So, Ashby scored a one-and-a-half-million-dollar farm with nothing more than a five-grand deposit. No amount of appealing on the farmer's behalf had any effect on Ashby. To him, the farmer was to blame for his own negligence."

"He didn't take him to court?"

"Yes, he did. Well, at least he tried. He engaged a no-win-no-fee lawyer who soon backed out of the case and the farmer never tried again. From what I gather, the lawyer had second thoughts about taking Ashby on or else was threatened by him. The guy won't say either way."

"You spoke to him?"

"Yes, but only briefly. And he doesn't want me to call him again. He's scared shitless of Ashby."

"So why LA? Why did he come here?"

"A few possible reasons and they don't include sunshine and California girls. He no longer works for his uncle—he struck out on his own way back—but his uncle was known to have ties to Giuseppe Trimbole."

"Is that who I think it is?"

"Yes. Boss of the Philly mob. Now, I've got nothing solid on this, but if those ties exist, he could be washing cash for the mob. He certainly came to LA with plenty of money to spend. There's no reason the money couldn't all be his, but Trimbole isn't so secure back in Philly. Came off second best in a power play that left his future a little uncertain over there. So, he may be using Ashby to secure investments in LA ahead of him relocating here too."

"So is Ashby a mobster or not?"

"Strictly speaking, no. He's a property magnate, I guess you could say, and swings a pretty big stick around here."

"How so?"

"He's built up a network of political allies. Overtly, it's a standard donor-candidate relationship. Covertly, I hear he's cut some of them in on lucrative property deals. Nothing proven, mind you. This could all be mudslinging from rivals. But whenever he hits a roadblock on a project, he suddenly ends up benefitting from a rezoning or a code redraft. The word is that's how he secured his latest project, a property in the heart of Santa Monica."

"Silicon Beach Plaza, yeah I know. Good work, Jack."

Jack pulled into the parking lot adjacent to the San Pedro cliffs. "I don't know half of what this Ashby character is up to, but I can tell you right now, you don't want to be caught up in that spider's web."

"Too late now."

CHAPTER 9

Jack and I walked across the grass at Point Fermin Park holding copies of the police report and crime scene photos. Beyond the grass was a walkway with a wall separating it from the cliff. Standing at the wall, I could see it was just a few yards to the cliff's edge. We located where the body was found and examined the supposed launch point. I asked Jack to take photos and made notes.

Everything was peaceful on the coast. The sea was calm, the water clear and the sky cobalt blue. But it was not hard to see why this place had such a sad and tragic history. There were signs urging despondent souls to stop and reconsider and to call the national suicide hotline.

Casting my eyes around, I spotted an old RV in the parking lot.

"Jack," I said, "come on. There's something I want to check out."

According to the police report, the eyewitness who claimed he saw Powell was a man by the name of Jaden Ross. He said he saw Powell from his campervan.

The van we approached was one of those decrepit pieces of junk that kept people a fingernail away from being homeless.

It was hard to see how it could be registered, but it was. The paint job was wearing out all over, both tail lights were smashed and one headlamp was gone. I stepped up to the side door and rapped my knuckle on the thin metal.

There was no response.

I waited a few seconds and knocked again, harder.

This time the van rocked a little. There was movement inside.

"What the fuck?" growled a drowsy, disgruntled voice. A few seconds later, the door was unlocked and swung outward.

A large man filled the opening. He was about six-four and no less than two hundred and eighty pounds. He raised his hand to shield his eyes from the sunlight. The flab of his upper arm and around his belly jostled at the sudden movement.

"What do you want?" he asked indignantly.

"Apologies for interrupting you, sir, but you wouldn't be Jaden Ross by any chance, would you?"

"What if I am? I'm allowed to park here. There's no law against that."

Ross must have taken us for cops, given we were both wearing suits, though Jack had no tie.

"No sir, we're not here about parking, but I would like a word, if you don't mind."

"What about?"

His arm dropped to his side and his big right paw reached behind to scratch the corresponding love handle. A waft of stale air rich in body odor hit me and I leaned slightly back to dodge the draft. Ross was a slob, no other way to say it. His T-shirt was probably white many years and countless lap-eaten dinners ago. I doubted his gray tracksuit pants had ever seen the inside of a washing machine.

"My name is Brad Madison. I am a lawyer looking into the circumstances surrounding the death of Nicola Beauchamp."

Ross looked at me with a blank suspicion.

"I got nothing to say to you," he said and reached for the door. "Leave me alone."

I shot a quick glance around to assure myself no one was watching, took one step forward and grabbed hold of the big oaf's shirt and wrenched him out of the van, his shoulder ricocheting off the metal door frame as he came. His feet were not quick enough to make good his landing and I stood aside as he fell heavily onto the pavement.

"You're an asshole, you know that?" Ross said from the ground.

"You ain't seen nothing yet, pal. Get up," I said. "On your feet. Now!"

He first pushed himself onto his knees and then stood up but remained hunched over and timid. "Easy, man! No need to get rough. We can talk."

"I'm glad you think so. I assure you I won't take up too much of your time. But I need you to tell me what you saw that night the girl died."

"I already told the cops everything. It's all in my statement. There's nothing more to say."

"I want to hear it straight from you."

"The cops told me not to talk to anyone."

"Oh, I bet they did. But you're not getting back in your rat's nest until I'm done with you, you understand?"

"This ain't right. You can't do that."

"It is and I can," I lied, but I could not drop my bluff. Something told me this guy was familiar with the law, by that I mean being on the wrong side of it. No doubt he'd been shaken down by the cops more than a few times in his life. "Tell me again. What did you see that night?"

"I saw two men get out of a fancy car over yonder."

"What were you doing here, wide awake late at night?"

"I couldn't sleep so I stepped out for some air. There was a big storm coming, so I thought I'd watch it come in."

"You were parked here?"

"Yes, this exact same spot."

"And?"

"And I saw these two guys leading this girl toward the cliff. She could hardly walk, like real drunk or something. They were on either side of her, supporting her, like. And they got to the wall. And they stopped and turned around to see if anyone was watching."

"They didn't see you?"

"No, and I didn't want them to. But I thought if the lightning flashed, they'd see me for sure and they'd come for me too."

"So what did you do?"

"I slowly backed into my van and quietly shut the door."

"While they threw the woman off the cliff?"

I was expecting to see a hint of shame come across Ross's face, but none showed. He just looked at me with blank eyes and shrugged.

"None of my business. I didn't know that that's what they were going to do. I just didn't want to get involved."

"Okay, Mr. Ross. Thanks for your time."

"Is that it?"

There was more to Ross's story than he was prepared to tell, but I wasn't going to get it out of him now.

"That's it for today."

As Jack and I walked back to the car, Jack grabbed my arm. I was surprised to see he had a stern look on his face.

"Buddy, you need to get your shit together. You just assaulted what could be a prosecution witness. If you get busted doing that, you'll be disbarred. That future you're fretting so much about will be gone. You won't have any money to help your mom or anyone else out. And you'll have no one else to blame—not Ashby, not your brother, not your mom, not me and not some lying piece of shit like that slob back there. No one."

"Yeah, you're right, Jack." I turned toward the ocean and sucked in a few lungfuls of sea air. "I need to snap out of it."

"Yes, you do. Now, about this fat slob behind us. Are you thinking what I'm thinking?"

"Yep, he's full of shit. Totally. He's hiding something. And we need to find out exactly what it is."

CHAPTER 10

Something Ashby had said during our meeting had bugged me for days. He'd implied that Harold Krieger, of all people, had recommended me to him. That struck me as very odd if it was true. And if it was, I wanted to know why. Why would he do such a thing? Call me paranoid, but I had a nagging feeling that I was being set up. How exactly I didn't know. But there was one person I knew who might be able to help me make sense of it. Jim Rafferty.

I turned off from the Saturday morning traffic on Wilshire Boulevard and onto a driveway marked only by a white column and the number "10101". This was the entrance to Los Angeles's most expensive piece of real estate: The Los Angeles Country Club. The 3000-acre golf course may have been set in the heart of Beverley Hills but it shunned all things Hollywood. Showbiz types were religiously kept out, with the exception being a cowboy actor who salvaged his resume by becoming president: Ronald Reagan. Hugh Hefner could jump, as best he could, over the back fence of the Playboy Mansion and step onto the fourteenth tee if not for the fact that he'd never be accepted as a member. Bing Crosby, whose house backed onto the fourteenth fairway, had similar hopes of getting in: none.

Along with the Hollywood set, Jews and blacks were kept out, and only in recent years had this thoroughly WASP enclave loosened its bigoted collar to better match the times. Not too loose, mind. This was still the epicenter of gentile power in California, an even more concentrated form than Downtown. So, of course, this was where I'd find Jim Rafferty. At our lunch he'd let slip he had a nine-twenty tee time. And I'd played golf with Jim enough in years past to know that he never played a round without a thirty-minute warm-up.

I pulled the Mustang to a halt in the parking lot and looked over at the practice range. Sure enough, there was Jim getting his groove on with his seven-iron, sending each ball on practically the exact same arc and coming left, just so, with a satisfying draw.

"Still compensating for those candyass drives of yours, I see," I said, stopping just a few feet behind him. I always baited him that a retiree could get more distance from their one wood than Jim could. It was a joke, but still it played on his insecurities, which led him to hone his short game fanatically and to carry a balloon-headed driver in his bag.

Jim did not look happy to see me.

"What are you doing here, Brad? I thought we were done talking for a few weeks after our lunch. Or are you still hoping to revive that partnership offer?" He lowered his head, struck another ball and watched it sail sweetly toward the flag he was aiming at. "Because there's about as much chance of that happening as you becoming a member here."

"And don't you just love that you're one of the chosen few?"

Jim stepped up to me. "Brad, I'm serious. What do you want? My tee time's in fifteen." He looked eager to get whatever we had to deal with out of the way. But I suspected he was less concerned with getting back to his practice than getting me off the premises.

"Sorry but there's something I want to ask you; have you ever heard of a Walter Lindsey Powell?"

Jim shook his head, but he was always a lousy poker player. "No, can't say I have. How come?"

"Walter Powell. He's the ex-boyfriend of Nicola Beauchamp, that girl who was found at the bottom of a cliff last week."

"Nope. The girl's name I recall but not him."

"Well, Powell's boss is the property magnate Rubin Ashby, who's paying me to keep Powell out of jail. And Ashby told me that Harold Krieger suggested he hire me."

Jim stole a quick glance over my shoulder.

"I'm not his personal assistant. I don't have a clue what Mr. Krieger does unless he brings me in on it."

"No sweat, Jim. Just thought I'd ask. But it's odd, don't you think? I mean why would he recommend me when you say he's got a dartboard with my face on it?"

Jim edged closer and kept his voice low.

"I don't think anything. I don't give a damn whether he recommended you or not. Who gives a shit? Now, if that's it, get the hell off my course."

It was clear I was testing his patience. But something told me he was scared.

"What is it, Jim? There's something about Krieger you're not telling me."

Again, his eyes quickly scanned the space behind me.

"What's the deal with Krieger and Ashby? Am I being set up? Why didn't someone from your firm take Powell's case?

Bert Patterson, he's your senior partner on criminal law, isn't he? Why wouldn't Krieger want to keep it in-house and take more of Ashby's money?"

Jim's face was dead serious.

"Brad, I'm only going to tell you this once. After this, we can't be talking. But you need to watch yourself. Rubin Ashby is a seriously dangerous motherfucker. Just do your bit, take your pay and be on your way."

"What are you talking about? I am doing my bit. That's why I'm here, to get some insight on Ashby."

"Look, I've got nothing to say. Other than you are treading on dangerous turf."

"Funny that, Jim. I thought I was standing on the safest turf in LA, being a privileged white guy and all."

"I'm serious, Brad. Watch yourself."

Suddenly, Jim's face broke into an easy smile. He waved at someone over my shoulder and stepped out to greet them.

"Harold, you're cutting it a bit fine, aren't you? We're almost set to go."

I turned around to see a man in his mid-sixties who I assumed to be none other than Harold Krieger. He was average height with skinny arms and a desk jockey's paunch stretching out his pink-and-yellow argyle vest. He was freshly shaved and, with bright blue eyes and silver hair worn short on the back and sides, he looked like an older version of the newsreader Anderson Cooper.

"So, we meet at last, Mr. Madison," he said, holding my eyes resolutely as our hands shook. "Damn shame you decided against joining us over at CDK. Like I told Jim, we could well have used a lawyer of your skill on our team. What's even more of a shame is that I hear you've had a change of heart. Just goes to prove the old adage that you have to strike while the iron's hot."

"Perhaps it was all for the best," I said.

"Oh, I don't think there's any perhaps about it, Bradley. If I may call you Bradley."

"Sure."

"You see, the fact that you flip-flopped just makes me all the more certain things are as they should be. We don't like about-faces at CDK. We want to be utterly confident that everyone is doing their all for the team. Isn't that right, Jim?"

"Couldn't have said it any better myself, Harold."

"But what brings you here, Bradley?" Krieger asked.

"I just had some business to discuss with Jim here."

"Don't you know that golf and business don't mix? It's a game that exposes all your weaknesses. I've seen men reputed to be exceptionally calm and cool-headed in business throw their clubs in anger. And unless you can control your emotions, you will never be seen as someone worthy of recruiting, only as someone who is fit to be exploited. And Mr. Ashby tells me you have quite a temper."

Was I meant to be reading between the lines here? Maybe, but I wasn't going to let this guy get a rise out of me.

"Brad here wants to know why you referred Walter Powell to him. He says Mr. Ashby approached him on your recommendation."

I shot Jim a look. I never thought he would just sell me out like that. I now saw where our friendship lay—a clear distance below his relationship with Krieger.

"Is that so?" said Krieger. "Well, I can clear that up very quickly. I think Mr. Ashby may have been referring to something I said a good while ago. I may have once sung your praises, Bradley, but not anymore. Whatever esteem I once held you in has evaporated."

"Are you always so sore when you don't get what you want, Krieger? To think I wasn't even aware I'd broken your little heart."

I turned for my car, wondering whether or not Krieger was telling the truth. I wasn't convinced I was not being played somehow. But I had to let it go. Something told me I was going to need all the wits I could muster.

I had to move forward carefully. Suddenly, I sensed I had some very powerful enemies. One of which could well be my paymaster.

CHAPTER 11

"Whoa!" said Jessica Pope, waving at her mouth after draining the last of her Thai chili martini. "Never thought you could quench a thirst with fire, but there it is, right there. Man, what a blast."

She then gestured to the plate sitting between us.

"What's the matter, big guy? Scared of a little piggy tail?"

Without a doubt Jessica Pope was one of the most striking women I'd ever met, and I mean that in every sense. She had model-grade beauty, from the tip of her blond head to her Manolo Blahnik-clad feet via five feet six inches of pulse-driving curves. She had brains, being one of LA's best prosecutors—a real tour de force in the courtroom. And she had style. She was in her early thirties and single and knew what she wanted. And every now and then, I'm glad to say, she wanted me.

"I'm more of a pulled pork kind of guy."

Jessica and I hadn't ever dated in a regular kind of way. We'd hooked up a few times, but after enjoying each other's company we'd just go on with our separate lives.

"Yeah, tell me something I don't know. Eat up, princess, before these babies get soggy."

Yes, we were strictly casual, but I had to keep my emotions in check with Jessica because she wielded some serious power over me. And I don't think that worked just the one way. Every now and then I found myself thinking we both wanted more from the relationship than we were prepared to let on.

That said, I was a dozen years older, divorced with one kid and not inclined to have more—I always felt she would surely be angling for someone younger when it came time to settle down.

When I called Jessica earlier in the week to sound her out for a date, she leaped at the offer. She wanted to pick the venue and so introduce me to an incredible Thai restaurant in West Hollywood. It was not too far from her apartment so she was kind of a regular there.

I took up the piece of crispy fried tail and bit into it. My teeth hit bone and cartilage but that did not matter as the rest was like a mouthful of delicious pork belly with crackling. I nodded my approval to Jessica.

"Not bad, eh?" She smiled. "I love this place. It's like being back in Bangkok, the markets there. Most Thai restaurants in LA don't have that authentic street-food feel. But this place, oh man, I could close my eyes and be in Chang Mai, drinking Singha on a warm tropical night, the hustle and bustle of Los Angeles literally a world away. I could live there."

"Thailand?"

"Bangkok, most definitely. I've been three times and I'd have no problem calling that place home. At least for half the year."

A waiter brought two bottles of cold Thai beer to our table.

"I always thought you lived for the court, to the exclusion of everything else."

"Well, that was true. For a time. But things change."

For a fraction of a second, I saw Jessica contemplate whether she should let her guard down. She thought better of it. She took a swig of beer and cocked an eyebrow at me.

"So why aren't you with that gorgeous girl of yours?"

She meant Bella, my ten-year-old daughter. Although they had never met, Jessica knew plenty about her. There was what I'd told her but then there was the nightmare event of a few years ago when some madman kidnapped her. She was targeted partly because she was a rising social media "influencer" (how I hate that word) and partly because she was my daughter. But that's another story. The events of her kidnapping and rescue never made it into the media, but I'd told Jessica everything. It made me shudder to think about that horrible time, but it also made me acknowledge that Jessica was not just a booty call, she was a friend.

"Not my weekend. So, lucky you."

The topic moved on to Claire and Marty, and I confessed that only being able to spend two days a fortnight with Bella still hurt. It had been so long since I was able to see her every morning, have a hug, a chat, make her breakfast. Now this other prick got to spend more time with my daughter than I did.

"Do you want to get married again?"

I gave her a smile.

"I don't think about it," I lied. "I'm just happy being here with you."

"Ouch."

"Oh Christ, that sounded bad. I'm so sorry, Jess. That's not what I meant."

She kicked me lightly under the table. She was smiling.

"Just teasing. I get it. You want this?"

There was one last piece of pig's tail.

"It's all yours."

After she'd chased the mouthful down with some beer she leaned in close to me. "Now that you've got a couple of drinks into me, why don't you tell me what's on your mind?"

She had me. I knew there was no fooling her, but I could never let on in advance that I was eager to pick her brain on a work-related matter. But it was more than that: I wanted to tap her for any inside knowledge she felt she could share.

"You know me too well. There is something I wanted to talk to you about."

"You mean your case. Walter Powell. The guy who murdered Nicola Beauchamp."

"Well, so the cops think."

Jessica didn't say a word. The waiter cleared the table and returned with a plate of rice noodles and a duck curry. Jessica held up two fingers and said something in Thai.

I laughed. "You speak Thai?"

"Enough to order more beer and a few other things."

"I've got to admit, I'm a little surprised."

"That I can speak a basic phrase in another language? Jesus, Brad, what do you take me for?"

"No, not that. I mean I'm surprised you haven't shot down my client. Typically, you waste no time telling me I'm on a loser case. This time you didn't. Why not? Is there something you can tell me?"

"Look at you. Hell, isn't that your job? To figure this stuff out?"

"Yes, but—"

"I'm just messing with you, Brad. Relax. You're right. I'm not sure about the case against your guy. Having said that, you've got two things in your favor."

"What?"

"First up, Ted Haviland."

"Who?"

"Exactly. Assistant DA. You've met him. He left the DA's office three years ago to go run a consultancy or something but it seems he couldn't hack it, so he's back with us. The only thing that man excels at is being underwhelming."

"Lazy or dumb?"

"I wouldn't say either. I think he just lacks the wherewithal to be ambitious."

"And you're saying he'll be handling the case if there is one?"

"Yes, he'll be prosecuting your client, if your client is charged. I still can't figure out why we welcomed him back with open arms. And now he's as happy as a pig in mud. Pulling 150k a year with benefits and dragging his lame ass around our courts."

"You're not a fan?"

"No but obviously someone upstairs is. But he's not going to like you."

"Haviland? Why not?"

"Because something tells me you're the kind of guy who gave him one of two things, probably both—an inferiority complex and a wedgie."

"I was never a jock," I protested.

"Doesn't matter. You're plain old alpha-class male. Look at you. Tall, dark and handsome. Thriving private business. In-demand, hot-shot lawyer who can charge what he likes." I wasn't about to admit to my CDK rejection or my financial woes just now. "And what's he got? Tried to go it alone and ended up back where he started with his tail between his legs."

"So, you're saying he'll make it personal?"

"I'm saying if you two were on *Survivor*, he'd wouldn't sleep until he had you voted off the island. So yeah, I'm saying he won't like you. Not one little bit."

"Great. Just what I need, another enemy."

"What?"

"Never mind. Now, you said you weren't sure about this case. What do you mean?"

"I'm not convinced your guy's the one they should be gunning for."

"Why not?"

I sat bolt upright and leaned in closer.

"Geez, it's like I'm having dinner with Lassie. Promise me something, will you? We get business out of the way and then we drop it, okay? I don't want to sit around talking shop all night."

I sat back and nodded.

"I'm willing to try."

"Okay, so you know Nicola Beauchamp was a reporter at the *LA Times*."

"Yeah, she had a beauty column or something like that."

"She wrote lifestyle. But it seems she had ambitions to do more than write about the latest cafes and cocktail lounges."

"Seriously? How do you know this?"

Jessica lowered her head and shook it slowly before locking eyes with me.

"You didn't hear from me, got it? One bark for yes. Two for no."

I cracked a smile. "Are you just going to tease me?"

She dropped her voice to just above a whisper.

"One of our guys took a call a couple of weeks ago from a young woman. She sounded nervous and wanted to remain anonymous but said she was a reporter and had gotten a tip-off about some rogue cops involved in some dodgy deals. She wasn't sure exactly what to do with the info and before our guy could get anything out of her that made sense, she hung up."

"Is there such a group of rogue cops?"

"This is LA, sweetheart. It could well be true but internal affairs aren't looking into anything major right now. But when I look at who's involved in your case, I see some red flags."

"Such as?"

"Harrison Daylesford. Everyone knows he's a regular 'bad lieutenant' but no one's yet proved it. And then there's his buddy."

"Detective Cousins? I thought he was straight."

"No, not him. Swindall."

"Dean Swindall? Nicola's ex?"

"Yeah. From what I hear, Swindall and Daylesford are two peas in a pod. So, if I was going to kick off an internal affairs probe, I'd be looking at those two. Both of whom happened to have a stake in your case."

I sat back.

"Why are you telling me this?"

"Listen, Brad, just because I'm a prosecutor doesn't mean I'm any less committed to justice than you are. Or should I say than you *think* you are? God, is there anyone more self-righteous in the law than a defense attorney? Oops, did I say that aloud?"

"Yes, Jessica. Finish your point, please."

"Well, I'm not about to stand aside and let crooked cops get away with murder."

"Are you saying you think Dean Swindall murdered his ex?"

"I'm not saying anything. Right now, between your guy and team Swindall and Daylesford, it's a coin toss. But you're going to have to figure it all out with that clever little brain of yours."

We were silent for a few seconds as she allowed me to process what all this meant.

"Okay," she said at last. "Let's close up shop on this lawyer talk. From here on in we are one hundred percent off duty and out to have a good time. Understand?"

"Woof."

"Good boy."

She reached for my shirt and pulled me toward her and kissed me deeply. Her tongue worked its way inside my mouth, rousing my whole body, particularly the zone concealed by the table. She let go and sat down again then reached under the table to squeeze my thigh playfully.

"Play your cards right and we might find something to do with that bone of yours."

CHAPTER 12

Tempted as I was to stay in Jessica's bed all morning, all day even, Sunday was a day I'd promised myself to go for a surf. Now, with a hangover that could fell a horse, the remedy offered by the cold Pacific Ocean beckoned more than ever.

I took up surfing in my late twenties when Claire and I rented a house in Venice. I loved it so much I ended up surfing throughout the whole year, donning a suit of neoprene armor in the colder months. But being from Idaho and accustomed to enjoying the freezing elements aboard a pair of skis, I loved the invigorating power of the cold. And exposing myself to it was without doubt the best way to get rid of a hangover.

I could not have spent the day with Jessica even if I'd wanted to. She had plans and was up, showered, dressed and ready to go by eight o'clock. She kissed me, and I smelled her and wanted her to come back to bed that instant, but she pulled back and walked away.

"Let yourself out," she said. "And forget about what I told you last night, yeah?"

"Forget it?"

"You know what I mean. You didn't hear it from me."

"God, you're beautiful."

"You're not so bad yourself. Be discreet, Brad. Okay?"

I knew she was dead serious.

"Of course, babe."

"Babe? Aren't you sweet? See you, handsome."

I got out of bed straight away, got dressed and headed home to get my board.

An hour later, I was at Zuma Beach waxing down my eight-foot mini mal. The swell was small but clean and there were surprisingly few surfers out. After getting my wetsuit on, I tucked the board under my arm and headed onto the beach. I dropped my towel with the car keys wrapped in it on the sand, made for the water and paddled out.

As I punched through the first wave the freezing water on my face shocked me, prompting me to gasp for air. The water began seeping into my suit and while at first it was like being wrapped in a blanket of ice it soon warmed up to body temperature as I paddled harder to get through the set.

By the time I'd made it to open water, I was breathing hard, my body was warm and my head was clear. What hangover? Just like that, it was gone.

As I sat on my board, I felt a sense of calm relief come over me. It had been an extremely trying week. I'd felt humiliated to be locked into an arrangement I had no choice but to accept. When I started my own law practice, I did it primarily because I wanted to keep my freedom, my independence. I got to pick and choose whom I represented. Not the other way around. And not like a law firm where you got assigned cases.

I'd done that when I first started out in the law, working as an intern at a downtown firm, doing what I was told. Then I upped and joined the Marines to do my bit for my country, survived two tours of Afghanistan and then got out while I could. But I was not the same man as the one who had left, and no one knew that more than Claire and Bella. But I got my practice started and I did very well.

Professional independence suited me. Like most soldiers, the war never left me entirely and when those ghosts of the past took over my present, I could take a day off to chill and I had no one to write a sick note to.

The fact that I got to choose my clients didn't mean I had to like them. But I'd never felt so owned by a client as I did by Rubin Ashby.

And I didn't like Walter Powell. But after my conversation with Jessica, it did me the world of good to think that he was innocent. Suddenly I was convinced that in all probability I had an innocent client to defend. And that's a shot in the arm for any defense attorney. It lends affirmation to the notion that your career, your life, actually means something. You're doing something unquestionably good. The absolute money shot of the trial game is to save an innocent man from a wrongful murder conviction.

So out in the surf, I gave myself a little pep talk.

Set your paranoia aside and do your job. Put in the hours like you would normally. And if you win the case, everything works out.

I watched as a set approached. There was one guy inside me who had the right to the first wave and he caught it. I watched him get to his feet and drop down the glassy face with a hoot.

I hooted too. I was grinning from ear to ear. Surfers get a real kick out of seeing a fellow rider catch a nice wave. And now it was my turn. I paddled closer into the crest and spun the board back to the shore. As I stroked hard to get the board up to speed, I rose with the wave. At the instant I knew the wave was carrying my board along with it, I sprang to my feet. I looked down to my right as the face ahead lurched up and arced into a glassy wall and the board came around under me to trim along the face.

Like skiing, surfing is the closest thing I've come to flying.

I put in a few turns before stepping up to the nose to stay on as the wave's power petered out. The ride was just about fifty yards long but already it had made my day.

As I stood in the thigh-deep water and pulled my board toward me, something in the parking lot caught my eye.

A black van had pulled in beside my car and I saw two men dressed in black puffer jackets and sunglasses get out and start looking over my car.

I began walking out of the water.

The pair then positioned themselves on either side of my car, leaning against it—one with his arms folded, the other with his hands tucked into his jacket pockets. One of them pointed at me. Clearly, they wanted me to see them watching me.

I lifted my board up and began running out of the surf. I reached the sand and jogged toward them. They were about two hundred yards away. Both men slowly pushed themselves off my car and walked casually back to their van.

"Hey!" I shouted.

Who the hell were these guys?

My immediate assumption was that they were Ashby's men, keeping tabs on me. But why? And why on a Sunday? At the beach, for Christ's sake?

I was only halfway across the beach when the van pulled out and turned for the highway with a loud screech. They were too far away for me to read the plates.

I stood there on the sand, right back where I was the day before, deeply angry and feeling used and manipulated.

CHAPTER 13

On Monday morning, I called Powell on my way to the office. He said the cops hadn't contacted him since we met.

"That's a good sign, isn't it?" he asked. "Maybe they are actually trying to find the real killer instead of wasting time on me."

"Maybe," I said. I didn't want to tell him I thought that was wishful thinking. My take was that Cousins and Daylesford had only one suspect in mind: my client.

Megan and Jack were already seated at the table in the conference room, a space I shared with other tenants on my floor. I took a moment to enjoy the expansive view of LA. It was one of the things I liked about having my office in Two California Plaza. But I was not married to the place. Even though Ashby's money had come at the right time, I'd decided to go ahead and relocate. To where exactly, I didn't know.

"Right guys," I said, clapping my hands together. "I want to get everything we know on the table so I can work out the strategy going forward. Fresh information is key."

"You bet, chief," said Jack with overplayed enthusiasm. "Let's open the kimono and do some blue-sky thinking."

"Yeah, let's swing for the fences and take it to the next level," said Megan with a snicker.

"Action that," said Jack.

"Mr. Madison, you need this shovel-ready by end of play today, right?" asked Megan.

"Nice," said Jack as he high-fived Megan.

I may have initially been the butt of this joke for inadvertently lapsing into management speak, but when you can't beat 'em, join 'em.

"That's what I like to hear, Megan. Let's leverage the crap out of this thing. It's time for an ideas shower. Let's put on a record and see who dances."

The three of us were now giggling like school children. For me, the light relief was just what the doctor ordered and put my mind in a better place to judge things clearly.

I took a seat.

"Oh. Have we got coffee?"

"Yes, of course," said Megan. "I'll get you some."

"No, you sit tight. I'll grab it," I said, getting to my feet. "Anyone else?"

I poured three cups and returned to the table.

"Okay, let's start with the victim, Nicola Beauchamp," I said. "Jack?"

Jack pushed documents over to both me and Megan.

"I spoke to half a dozen friends and colleagues," he said. "Names and details are there in the files. Most of them thought she'd killed herself. It was common knowledge that she was still not over Powell, even a year down the track, and desperately hoped they would get back together again. He was her one and only, she seemed to think.

"One colleague, Samantha Boylan, said she and Nicola were good friends. She said Nicola admitted to being depressed but she didn't stick with her therapy. Making matters worse, she was unhappy at work. Other reporters didn't take her seriously. Only a couple of people knew she wanted to have a crack at serious reporting."

"What was the story she was going after?"

I didn't want to repeat what Jessica had told me just yet.

"Samantha said it was something to do with corruption at the LAPD."

"Did she have a journal? Did she keep a written record of her work?"

"Yes, but her notes are brief to the point of being cryptic. I asked Samantha if she could take photos of them. She managed to just before the police seized the diary. There was just one name mentioned in those notes."

"Who?" I asked.

"Detective Daylesford."

"When was this?"

"Two days before she died."

Now it was time to share what I'd been told.

"Okay, well, apparently somebody called the DA's office a few days before Nicola's death. It was a young woman who said she was a reporter but didn't give her name. She hinted that she was looking into LAPD corruption. And now it seems she may have called Daylesford, who's reputed to be a dirty cop. Why would she call him directly if she knew he might be exposed by her story?"

"Maybe she didn't know if he was dirty or not," said Megan. "Maybe that was a rookie error and a potentially fatal one."

"That's what Samantha thinks," said Jack. "She's convinced Nicola poked the bear—a big nasty bear with an LAPD badge."

"Okay, it's almost an open secret that Daylesford's as bent as a corkscrew. But we can't assume Nicola knew that. But apparently Daylesford's pretty tight with Dean Swindall."

"Who's Dean Swindall?" Megan asked.

"Nicola's disgruntled ex. Powell told me he threatened him." Then it dawned on me. "That's why Nicola called Daylesford! She must have confided in Swindall and he directed her to Daylesford."

"So, he thought Daylesford would be able to convince her there was no story," said Jack.

"But what if she didn't buy it or indicated that she was not going to back off, what would they do?" asked Megan. "Throw her off a cliff?"

"Is it too much of a stretch to imagine them getting Nicola out of the way and framing Walter Powell?" said Jack.

"That's what we need to follow up on," I said. "Jack, this Samantha Boylan. Do you think she'd help us out on this?"

"For sure. To her, the cops are the prime suspects."

With other parties to cast suspicion on, the case against Powell weakened. If it came to a trial, I needed this killer-cop theory to be as solid as a rock.

"Okay," I said. "Let's look at Powell and Ashby."

"But I'm not done with Nicola yet."

"What do you mean?"

"Samantha said another girl went missing shortly after Nicola died."

"Another girl? Who?"

"A friend of Nicola's called Erin Coolidge. She's a freelance photographer who had apparently agreed to work with Nicola on this investigative story of hers. She's been reported as missing, but Samantha thinks she's been murdered too. Both of them silenced. I haven't had a chance to follow this up yet, but Samantha said there was an address written in Nicola's diary alongside the word 'pics.'"

Jack flicked a printout at me.

"Jesus," I said, looking it over.

"What?"

"That's Silicon Beach Plaza."

CHAPTER 14

I briefed Jack and Megan on what I knew about Ashby's Silicon Beach Plaza project.

Did Nicola's note mean she had asked the photographer to go there? And if so, why would she send Erin Coolidge there if she was working on a story about police corruption?

Such questions would have to wait. We had a lot of other ground to cover before I knew which way to proceed.

"Jack, what updates have you got on Ashby and Powell?"

Jack picked out two folders from his pile and handed one to me and one to Megan.

"We've already covered Ashby's Philly ties, so I focused on his dealings here in Los Angeles and tried to get a bead on exactly where Powell fits into the Ashby network. So, as far as Powell goes, he worked for a commercial real estate company for two years in LA and jumped ship to join Ashby's company. On paper, he's clean—no rap sheet to speak of, not even a speeding ticket."

"He tells me he's Ashby's communications director and that he's a protégé to some kind of guru."

"He's not the only one who believes Ashby is a visionary. Ashby keeps an entourage of young men around him. And they all seem to believe he's their path to divine wealth."

"Is Ashby gay?"

"It appears so. He never says so openly from what I've read in the press, but when he moved to LA, he began to lead a very different life to the one he had in Philly. He quickly divorced his wife, though he still takes good care of her and their kids. Then he set out to turn himself into the person he wanted to be."

"You mean physically? Like plastic surgery?"

"Yes. He had a string of procedures done and he didn't care who knew it. We're talking hair transplants, nose job, chin job, lips, Botox…"

"It's like he doesn't think he looks the slightest bit freakish," I said.

"I'm sure he doesn't," said Megan. "It's classic BDD."

"What's BDD?" I asked.

"Body dysmorphic disorder. It's an obsession with correcting what you perceive to be flaws in your physical appearance."

"But he looks macabre. How can he possibly think he looks good?" I was baffled.

"It's a psychiatric condition, like anorexia. He wouldn't see himself as everyone else does. All he sees is what he can improve next."

"He's had more work done than Mickey Rourke," said Jack. "Check this out."

Jack handed me a photocopy of a newspaper clipping. It was a photo from a Philadelphia paper of a balding guy in a suit with a round nose, no chin, chubby face looking busy on the phone. I was at a loss as to who the person was. Then I read the caption.

"You're kidding me. This is Rubin Ashby?"

"Ten years ago. Yeah. That's the man the present Rubin Ashby is running a mile from."

"The catalyst might have been deep anxiety," Megan said. "You know, something like what Jack alluded to: repressed homosexuality. He wouldn't get away with what he's doing in Philly. In LA, though, no one's going to call you out for trying to look younger, slimmer, or prettier."

I couldn't help but feel a pang of sympathy for the man. But at the same time, I found it hard to believe Ashby was driven by self-loathing. He was someone who oozed power, confidence and absolute surety in everything he said and thought. And I was sure acolytes like Powell saw him as a brave, perceptive, heroic figure; half emperor, half soothsayer—Marcus Aurelius with a cosmetic surgery fetish.

"So, he has more work done than an aging Hollywood diva, surrounds himself with virile young men and has ties to the mob," said Jack. "You couldn't script this stuff."

"True. You know I'm not a fan, but I'll give him this: he wields a powerful charisma. The way he talks, I'm not surprised people believe he can read the future like a prophet."

"In the property game, the proof is there. He's been an astute forecaster," said Jack.

"How do you know?"

"Some deep research—an *LA Times* interview five years ago," Jack quipped. "He tipped the fall of this company, picked the rise of that company and basically provided a state-of-play scenario about what would happen in the property market five years ahead, and it's all come true. You know he does seminars on property investment and finance. Hosts them all over the country in the finest five-star resorts. Charges people ten grand a head."

"And Powell?"

"Powell, beyond his role as communications director, is the MC at these gigs; you know, introducing Ashby to the fans."

I thanked Jack and Megan.

Technically, I wasn't working a case; Powell hadn't been charged with anything. To my mind, though, it was only a matter of time.

What were the cops waiting for?

It had to be something other than the DNA result. Or maybe the DNA result had come up negative.

I didn't want to just sit back and wait. I wanted to get a bead on how their case was stacking up.

It was time to pay Ted Haviland a visit.

CHAPTER 15

As I made my way through the DA's office, it came to me that I had indeed met Assistant District Attorney Ted Haviland before. It must have been five years ago—a fraud case in which I rejected his plea deals and succeeded in having it thrown out of court. Besides winning, had I done anything to offend him? Nothing that I was aware of. I didn't even think about him, to be honest. But I did find out that he'd taken the loss to heart. And so he should, he needed to improve his lawyering.

I was surprised, like Jessica, that he was marked to get this case. His shortcomings may well have made my job easier, but I'd never count on that. Plenty of prosecutors prevail despite themselves.

I knocked on a dark-stained door with his name on it.

"Yes? What is it?"

He must have known it was me. I was right on time for our eleven o'clock. I pushed the door open and walked in with an outstretched hand.

"How you doing, Ted? Brad Madison."

He was seated at his desk with his back to me. His hands were rummaging through an open drawer of files. "Right with you," he said. His desk had a high stack of files sitting in a red wire in-box. Next to that was a paper day calendar and a black articulated desk lamp. It was a time warp; he looked committed to keeping everything in paper and ink. His laptop was a concession to modern times but even that looked antiquated. My memory of Ted Haviland the man suddenly gelled—a forty-something guy going on eighty.

It was a good minute before he spun around. Even then he didn't look at me. Of course, by this time my hand had dropped.

"Take a seat, Madison," he said while he jotted something down on a Post-it note. He then pressed the slip onto the first page of the file he'd just retrieved. Only when he'd closed the file and repositioned it on his desk did he deign to cast his eyes in my direction.

"Good to see you, Ted," I lied. "I thought you'd left the DA's office for greener pastures."

Ted just sat there looking at me with his big unblinking eyes. "Well, they wanted me back and I love it here. How could you not love putting scum behind bars? Any decent lawyer would."

Open mouthed, he let his ham-fisted put-down hang there. Haviland had an odd-shaped face—narrow and triangular. And in the middle of it sat a large, triangular nose you could almost use as a rafter square. Even his short, slicked-back hair seemed to be demarcated into wedges. His clean-cut look was straight out of the fifties.

To be honest, I didn't think he was happy here at all, in neither time nor place. He struck me as the kind of guy who should have changed his life's course straight after law school since he didn't have the sense to drop out midway through. But he just stuck at it. And what he got in return was some rearguard sense of purpose and the reassurance that he would have a good salary and benefits until the day he retired.

"Good for you, Ted. So, how's the Beauchamp investigation coming along?"

"In a word, excellent," he said and reached into the pile of folders and dug out a few. "I'm not sure what you've seen already, but this information is all current. Things are not looking good for Walter Powell."

"Are you actually considering other suspects or would that be too much to ask?"

"I place a great deal of faith in the abilities of our city's police force, Madison. And, as far as I can see, they have every reason to regard Walter Powell as the prime suspect."

"They haven't charged him yet."

"Oh, they will," he said chirpily, as though he was tipping the sun to break through the morning cloud.

"You will do me the courtesy of giving me advance warning if you do intend to charge my client, won't you?"

This was simply the done thing, not a special request.

"Who do you think you're talking to? You may enjoy favors from Jessica Pope, but I don't have to tell you a goddamn thing." *Was that a coincidental double entendre? Had to be. There's no way he'd know Jessica and I were involved.* "I'll have Powell arrested when I please. And that's when you'll know."

There was no point arguing. I took the files he offered and opened the top one. I'd already seen the bulk of its contents: the police report, the medical officer's report, crime scene evidence and eye-witness statements.

"Don't expect a plea deal, Madison," said Haviland. "I'm not going to go soft here. Walter Powell killed this girl. She was so incapacitated by drugs, a child could have pushed her off that cliff. But we have him at the site on the night of the murder."

I looked up from the files.

"That still leaves a motive, Ted. Why would he do such a thing? You have nothing that will convince a jury that he suddenly decided to throw his ex-girlfriend off a cliff. You have no DNA evidence to support your theory. Not a scrap of his DNA was found on the victim's body. He has a rock-solid alibi."

"Rock solid alibi?" Haviland scoffed. "That's a laugh. And as for DNA, you'll be hearing more on that shortly, I suspect."

I resumed reading until I found what I was looking for.

"Ah, I see you've already listed Dean Swindall as a prosecution witness. No ax to grind there. The jilted ex. That's going to be fun in court."

"He's an officer of the law, Madison. When he says Nicola Beauchamp told him she was going to meet with Powell the night she died and was extremely anxious about it, I believe him and a jury will too. He has more credibility when it comes to justice than a roomful of crime enablers like you."

I ignored the jibe.

"Is this how you're going to play this, Ted? Sing the praises of the LAPD and hope the jury sings along?

"As if I'd tell you my strategy," he said, taking me way too literally. "I'd never reveal my memos to you."

"When can I get the full forensics report and your expert witness evidence?"

"When I'm good and ready."

Obviously, he planned to hold on to key evidence as long as he could.

"If we go to trial, Ted, you'd better not keep me waiting until minutes to midnight to hand over your evidence."

I didn't care how he wanted to play it. There was no way this beige-souled bureaucrat was going to get the better of me.

Haviland allowed himself a smirk. I regretted giving him a small sign that he had gotten under my skin. He interlaced his hands in front of his face, poked his extended index fingers into his chin and fixed his gleaming bug eyes on me. "I can't wait for that DNA report to come in. You know—the bracelet found at the bottom of the cliff?"

"What are you talking about?"

"A man's bracelet. One of those leather ones with Aztec beads."

"Like your jewelry, do you, Haviland?"

"You bet. But not as much as your client. We'll prove it's his bracelet. Just like the one he's wearing in about a dozen Facebook photos. And it ends up just a few yards from Nicola Beauchamp's body."

"It could be anyone's."

"No, *you* could be anyone's. But this here is evidence. And I am confident we will have a match for your murderer. We'll have more than enough evidence to take this to trial if we have to."

"There's not going to be a plea deal. I can tell you that now."

"Good. Suits me just fine."

I bet it did. Haviland would be desperate for a well-publicized win. A tidy murder conviction that made the LAPD and the LA justice system look good would no doubt give his career some uplift.

"Me too. I can't wait to see the look on your face when the jury lets Walter Powell walk because you failed to make your case stick."

"Keep telling yourself that. You need to keep your hopes up somehow, I guess. But don't kid yourself; we're the good guys here, and you people, well, you just get in our way. That's all I've got for you now. Just leave your files. I'll look at them later. When I could use a laugh. Nice of you to drop by."

He had one palm extended toward his door.

"You're right about one thing, Haviland," I said. "This is going to be fun."

CHAPTER 16

Later, I drove to Powell's apartment. On the way, I mulled over my encounter with Haviland. I was sure that Powell's arrest was imminent. And if Haviland would grant me notice, the arrest could be done discreetly, beyond the eyes of the media. But I suspected that when Haviland gave the all-clear to arrest Powell, he'd just about put out a press release.

Powell greeted me with a reserved welcome. He summoned half a smile, but his face and eyes were, as usual, unwelcoming. I couldn't help but wonder at how such a seemingly cold, reserved character could manage to attract a vivacious beauty like Nicola Beauchamp. Maybe there was something reassuring about that bland countenance of his, something steadfast and loyal and predictable. Safe, in other words. And calm.

Was he her safe harbor?

The apartment's interior reflected Powell's character: subdued, plain and minimalist to the point of being sterile. It was fitted out with modern furniture and artwork, but the entire decor bore no lift of color or boldness.

"You want some coffee?" Powell asked as he ushered me inside. He pointed to a mug on the white marble kitchen counter. "I've just brewed some chai tea. Would you like some?"

"No thanks. I'm good. Let's grab a seat."

We sat opposite each other at the glass dining table.

"So, what do you think?" he said flatly.

"Of what?"

"Of my place."

"It's great. But I wasn't sure if it was yours. I don't see any personal touches. You know, photos of yourself, your family or friends." And the books, I didn't mention that; there were no books to be seen apart from one coffee table book aligned on a low glass table.

"Well, it is mine and I guess you might say I'm not a sentimental sort of guy."

I figured a place like this must be worth at least two million.

"Mr. Ashby must pay you well."

"What makes you think he has anything to do with it?" Powell snapped.

"I meant nothing by it, Walter," I said calmly. "You work for him. It's a nice place. But it's something your average wage earner would not be able to afford, particularly someone your age."

"I may be young, but I have learned a thing or two about building wealth."

He took a sip of his chai and waited.

"I've just come from a meeting with Ted Haviland," I said. "He's a prosecutor and he will be handling your case if you do get charged. I just wanted to fill you in on what I've learned and to talk about a couple of things."

"He thinks I'm guilty?"

"Of course he does. So do the cops, Walter. And, as much as I hate to say it, I think it's only a matter of time before they arrest you."

Powell seemed nonplussed.

"Did he tell you that?"

"Yes."

"Why would I kill Nicola?"

He stared at me, having delivered the question in a calm voice.

"I don't know, Walter. But you had better hope that they don't come up with a great answer to that question. In fact, I need to know is there anything at all that happened between you two that upset you?"

I stopped myself from saying anything more. Powell shook his head slowly. I waited, determined that he was going to be next to speak. About half a minute elapsed.

"I loved Nicola. You know, like I told you. I had no ill feelings toward her. After we broke up, she still wanted to spend time with me. I thought she was finally coming around to accepting that our relationship would stay platonic. I thought she was finally moving on. But then again, I could have been kidding myself."

"In what way?"

"She was very good at hiding her feelings, especially her deep-rooted anxieties. I always wondered whether she was coping as well as she made out."

"Did you ever ask her?"

"Yes, I did. Several times. But she always sounded so positive."

"Might she have feared that if she revealed too much she would push you away?"

"Yes."

"So, you suspected she was still in love with you?"

"Yes."

"Why would Dean Swindall say she was scared of you?"

Powell fixed me with a suspicious glare, as though just by asking such a question I'd betrayed him.

"Because he's a liar. He hated me for stealing Nicola from him, and this is his opportunity for payback."

"He says he spoke to Nicola the night she died and that she said she was going to see you and that she felt apprehensive about it. Is there any truth to that?"

"None whatsoever."

"Did you see Nicola the night she died?"

"No."

"Did you see her the day before she died?"

"We did meet briefly. In the afternoon."

"Where?"

"Here. We had one drink and she left."

"What time was this?"

"About five o'clock. She said she had plans for the evening."

"What were they?"

"I didn't ask and she didn't say."

"Do you think Dean Swindall has taken the opportunity of Nicola's suicide to frame you?"

"Yes. She's gone and he blames me."

I opened my briefcase and pulled out some files. I picked out a photo of the bracelet and presented it to him.

"Do you recognize this?"

"It's a bracelet."

"Yes. But have you seen it before?"

He paused for a few seconds before answering. I could see his right hand reach for his left wrist through the glass tabletop.

"Yes. I have one just like it."

"Where is it?"

"It's in my room," Powell said warily. "Why do you ask?"

"Can you get it for me?"

He paused again.

"Of course. Can I ask why?"

I tapped the photo in front of him.

"This was found at the foot of the cliff where Nicola's body was found."

Powell's jaw dropped slightly so that his lips parted.

"Is that right?"

"Yes, now would you mind getting your bracelet for me?"

Powell didn't move. He didn't say a word. He just looked at me, again, like I was not on his side.

"Walter, you know that you can tell me anything and it will be safeguarded under attorney-client privilege. It remains, and will always remain, between us."

"I know that."

He was clearly struggling to decide what to say next.

"What is it, Walter?"

"It's not here."

"What's not here? The bracelet?"

"Yes. It's gone."

"And you don't know where it is?"

"No, I don't."

"When did you notice it was missing?"

"I think the cops took it."

"Which cops?"

"Cousins and Daylesford. They came here, started asking me some questions and then one of them asked if he could use the bathroom. He was gone for fifteen minutes."

"Who went to the bathroom, Daylesford or Cousins?"

"I don't know."

I described Daylesford.

"Yes. Him."

"Right, so while Cousins questioned you, Daylesford was roaming around your apartment. Did Daylesford say anything to Cousins when he returned?"

"No, they just exchanged looks. Like Daylesford nodded that he had finished."

"Then what?"

"They wrapped it up and left. Oh, and they warned me not to leave town."

Powell licked his thin lips dryly, content to say nothing more. It was as though he saw no merit in helping me in any way more than was absolutely necessary.

"Do you think they took it?"

"They must have, mustn't they?"

"It will take some convincing for a jury to buy that."

"That's what we're paying you for, isn't it, Mr. Madison?"

There was another long passage of silence. I watched Powell take another sip of tea. Then he looked at me curiously. At length, he spoke.

"Do you think I did it?"

The way he asked it, it was like the subject of his question was someone else. It only reinforced that my client was not all there, not in a mental sense but in that he was someone who would never reveal themselves in full to the world. And all I could think of was that this emotional distance he maintained was not going to sit well with a jury.

Not well at all.

Powell was a client I'd have to save in spite of himself.

CHAPTER 17

"She's late," I said to Jack, spinning the remnants of my whisky before necking it.

"No, she's not. If she was a German train, you might have a point. She told me she can't just up and leave work the minute her shift ends. Ah, here she is."

Jack directed a wave over my shoulder. We both got out of the booth and stood.

"Hey, Samantha. Thanks for coming," said Jack. "This is Brad."

Jack had briefed me a little about Nicola Beauchamp's friend and colleague. She was a news reporter when Nicola arrived at the paper, and in the four years since, she had moved into features. Boylan, who looked to be in her early thirties, was about five feet two in her high-heeled boots. Her dark curly hair was pulled back in a ponytail. She unwrapped her scarf and pushed it down the table to the wall then hopped into one side of the booth. She was eager to get started on our task: getting justice for her friend.

"What can I get you?" asked Jack as I slid into the booth across from Boylan.

"I need a beer," she said and looked over Jack's shoulder to read the blackboard list of craft brews. "Let's see. I'll have a pint of Bohemia."

"You?" said Jack at me.

"What's Bohemia?" I asked Boylan.

"A very good pilsner."

"Sounds German," said Jack. "You should like that, Brad."

Boylan's eyebrows knitted in confusion.

"Ignore him," I said to her before addressing Jack. "A pilsner would be great."

As Jack made for the bar, Boylan reached into her shoulder bag and laid a pile of printouts, a thumb drive and her laptop on the table.

"I photographed the recent pages of Nicola's diary and printed them out here. The photos are all on the drive, as well as all the files I could get off her desktop and hard drive before the cops came. I've already had a look through, and there's not much of interest. But maybe something will catch your eye."

"Thank you."

Boylan clasped her hands together and fixed her gaze on me.

"Okay, besides files, what do you want from me?"

"I'd like to know more about Nicola and her foray into investigative reporting. Did you know about that?"

"Only a little. We were pretty close, so she kept it real quiet. I had no idea she was aiming at something so ambitious."

"Exposing serious corruption in the LAPD?"

"Yeah. But since she was murdered, it kind of makes sense to me."

"What does?"

Jack came back with the drinks. Samantha picked up her pint and lifted her glass at us before taking a sip.

"Well, after she died and I saw her notes, I guess a very likely explanation began to gel in my mind. And now I'm convinced of it."

"Convinced of what?"

"That the cops killed Nicola and they're trying to frame Walter for it."

"Why would they do that?"

"Because I think he's the one that gave her the tip about the crooked cops."

"What makes you say that?"

"It only occurred to me recently, but I remember Nicola being kind of excited. She said she had a story idea and that it had sprung from something Walter had said. We were having a few drinks and I kept pushing her, but she refused to get into specifics. Then, later, she asked if I knew who broke the Rampart story and whether they had won the Pulitzer."

The Rampart scandal was the explosive exposure of deep-rooted corruption within the LAPD anti-gang unit operating around Rampart Boulevard in downtown LA.

"You're convinced she was looking into some sort of police corruption?" I asked.

"Well, yeah. After she mentioned Rampart, Nicola sort of bit her lip—you know, 'Whoops, I shouldn't have said that.' And as much as I tried, I couldn't get anything more out of her. But this wasn't a joke. You could tell her brain was spinning something quite serious around."

"And that's all she said?"

"Yes. And even then she thought she had said too much."

"And do you think she would sound Dean out about it?"

"I honestly don't know if she would have trusted him. But then she might have taken a chance."

"What do you make of Dean Swindall?"

"I met him a few times when he and Nicola were together and he was just kind of off. I mean he was from the boondocks and all, but he was so un-PC it was shocking at times. I think part of the reason Nicola came to LA was to get away from Dean, but he followed her up here and she was too sweet to cut him off. I mean there was a nice side to him and he was so sweet on Nicola, but he would say something racist or offensive and think it was funny when no one else would be laughing. He was like a teenager really, someone who still didn't know right from wrong when it came to social etiquette. And I'm not talking tea with the First Lady, I mean just social discourse 101. He was tone-deaf to other people's sensitivities."

"It might have been nothing with the guys back home but…"

"Yeah, but here it was. I mean wake the fuck up, dude. And the scary thing was he's a cop!"

"Did he ever talk about his job in a way that concerned you?"

"What do you mean?"

"Did he tell you something he did on the beat that wasn't lawful?"

"No. Nothing he said suggested he had committed a crime or abused his position. But I think that only shows he wasn't entirely stupid. I'd put money on him being bent. If he didn't kill Nicola, I'm sure he knows who did."

"And you believe they're trying to frame Walter?"

"Yes. They're trying to cover either their asses or someone else's. And not just Nicola's murder, they're out to frame him for Erin's murder too."

"You think they are connected?"

"I wasn't sure Erin was dead until the cops came around asking after her."

"They came and saw you?"

"Yes."

"Who?"

"Let me see, I wrote down their names." Boylan picked out a notebook from her bag and flicked through it. "Here it is. Detectives Harrison Daylesford and Brian Cousins. They came into work and asked me all these questions about Erin and Walter, about Nicola too, but they were focusing on Erin and Walter. I think they want to pin both murders on Walter."

"Dean Swindall says Nicola was afraid of Walter."

"Of course Dean would say that. He hated Walter."

"Because Nicola loved him hopelessly?"

"Yeah. The only crime Walter was guilty of was breaking her heart. And he tried to remain her friend, all the while knowing she was in agony."

"Walter said they had grown apart."

"That's probably fair to say. But she couldn't see it or if she could, she didn't want to accept it. Man, she could pick 'em."

"What do you think of Walter?"

"He could be aloof, but he was pretty decent. He did like to shoot his mouth off a little after a few drinks. He'd kind of boast about being in the know about all the wheeling and dealing going on in the construction game, like he knew how the city really worked and we reporters didn't. He'd say there was stuff going on we wouldn't believe but that it would never see the light of day because the media would never touch it."

"What kind of stuff?"

"Nothing too specific but it would be like he was telling ghost stories, enjoying giving us a little scare."

"You don't look like someone who scares easily."

"I'm not. But Walter would say some pretty odd things. He would go, 'Just remember, I know where the bodies are buried.' He said this a few times, like, to let us know he had some kind of inside information on LA's dark underbelly. I mean we all know the construction game can be a real dirty business, but once I remember he got quite serious about it. He warned us both, not that he took either of us seriously as reporters, not to go poking around into the nefarious world of construction or we might find ourselves buried in the foundations of Silicon Beach Plaza. He laughed after he said it, but there was a disturbing sincerity about it. It was creepy."

"Did you ever meet his boss, Rubin Ashby?"

"Oh, yeah. I met him once. And, like I told Nicola, I was sure he was in love with Walter."

"Really?"

"You don't think so? Jesus, it looked obvious to me."

"Do you think the feeling is reciprocated?"

"No, but it sure as hell bugged Nicola. She hated Ashby."

"Why?"

"Because Walter idolized him and spent every waking hour either working for him or singing his praises. As far as Nicola was concerned, she would never be able to get Walter back as long as he was devoted to Ashby. I mean, to her Ashby was her rival. She *loathed* him."

CHAPTER 18

A row of large, sepia-toned photos extended all along Arizona Avenue between 4th and 5th Streets. They were plastered onto boards that concealed the Silicon Beach Plaza construction site. Trying to find an opening, Jack and I passed the enlarged prints, each depicting a scene from Santa Monica in the 1800s—an aerial of the beach showing a cluster of houses near the shorefront, bathers wearing neck-to-knee costumes, a steam train delivering land speculators from LA, and so on. At that time, Santa Monica's population was less than five hundred. The purpose of the nostalgic display was obviously to connect the old with the new in a positive light, but I found myself wondering whether, when it came to development here, sanity had ever prevailed.

I wasn't alone in thinking this. Resistance against development had hardened in the minds of many Santa Monica residents and they'd fought tooth and nail to stop Ashby's Silicon Beach Plaza from going ahead. It took him several years to buy all four buildings on the block, but he struck a hurdle in the city-owned parking lot. Yet despite the outcry and protests from a strident residents' group, who wanted the whole lot turned into a public park and who declared they'd be robbed of sunlight and sea breezes, the city council members voted to sell it to him.

In the business world, the move marked Ashby as a genius. In other circles, it marked him as the devil incarnate. What was for certain was that the Santa Monica displayed on those boards was gone for good. Like it or not, Ashby's vision for Santa Monica's future had won.

The final two boards at the corner of 4th were devoted to that vision. An artist's impression depicted an admittedly stunning looking building featuring office space, market-price apartments plus some affordable housing. The accompanying starry-eyed text put Ashby's vision into words: "Bringing the epicenter of global technology to the coast," from which the whole city would profit. Shiny Silicon Beach Plaza would be where the future of the world would be shaped. Venture capitalists would be shoulder-to-shoulder with cutting-edge tech research that could future-proof humanity, providing solutions to everything from the ozone hole to overfishing.

Media coverage of the project was almost as fawning. Various articles lauded Ashby's vision for seizing on the current trend of well-paid tech professionals choosing to call LA's beachside suburbs home.

It was late afternoon and the tree-lined 4th Street was in shadow. About forty yards up ahead from the corner, a dump truck laden with earth pulled out of an access gate. We moved to this vantage point and Jack proceeded to take photographs.

Work was still in its early stages. The demolition was done and the rubble removed. Now it was little more than a large rectangular patch of tracked-out dirt with two white portable cabins positioned side by side on the southern flank.

I wanted to take a look at the site because it had cropped up in various elements of Walter Powell's case, the most curious being his warnings to Nicola Beauchamp and Samantha Boylan. The cops would also come sniffing around here too after seeing Nicola's work diary, wondering why Erin Coolidge was sent here and whether that had anything to do with her disappearance. So, at the very least, I had to be aware of, as much as possible, everything that the cops were likely to know.

As far as building sites in Santa Monica went, Silicon Beach Plaza was huge, taking up an entire block. As one of the articles put it, "How Ashby managed to steer it through a maze of obstacles is a modern miracle."

"Got to hand it to the guy," I said to Jack.

"He paid a hundred mill for all the properties he's just knocked down," said Jack while taking photos. "And when the paint dries on this project, he'll have about two hundred and fifty apartments worth an average of three million each, office space and retail leases spread out over fourteen stories with a bunch of affordable housing as loose change. I wouldn't be surprised if he doubled his money."

"Hell, what wouldn't he do to get that, huh?"

"You said it. The question is would he seriously stop at nothing to get his way?"

"Meaning?"

Jack dropped his camera from his eye and began checking his shots. "The council was split three-three on whether to sell him the parking lot. And God knows what not having that parking lot would have cost him. It's almost a quarter of the footprint."

"So, what happened?"

"They got him to shave off some office space, which basically reduced the project down from fourteen to twelve stories. Next thing you know, the vote got passed."

"That would have taken a dent out of his bottom line."

"Yes and no."

"What do you mean?"

"Straight after he got the council's approval, he hit them with a viability assessment that claimed he could no longer make a competitive return. So, he reduced the affordable housing component, upped the market-price apartment component and got his potential profit back to where it was previously."

"And they were okay with that?"

"The project had already been approved and viability assessments are private. They had to take his word for it."

As Jack and I talked, I noticed a vehicle pull up across the street. I could not be sure, but it looked a hell of a lot like the black van that had parked beside my car at the beach.

The driver's side window dropped down to reveal a man in dark sunglasses watching us. It was the same guy from the beach, no question. Even from the distance that day, I saw he had Carrera-type sunglasses and a pronounced M-shaped receding hairline.

"Son of a bitch," I said and began marching toward the van.

"What are you doing?" asked Jack.

"That van. His fucking goons are following us. They tailed me the other day."

As I said this I broke into a jog. I could hear Jack firing off some shots as I ran. The driver put the van into gear and pulled a screeching U-turn right in front of me.

I stood in the acrid smoke and memorized the number, for what it was worth. But I already knew exactly who that car, or at least the gorilla driving it, belonged to. And it was about time I gave that bastard a piece of my mind.

As I walked back to where Jack was standing, my phone rang.

"Brad, it's me, Walter. I've been arrested." There was no emotion in his voice whatsoever. It was like he was delivering an absent-minded order over a fast-food intercom. "This is my one phone call. Over to you."

Normally, I'd go straight away, but something more urgent had come up.

"Hang tight, Walter. And keep your mouth shut. I'll be there as soon as I can."

CHAPTER 19

The Westwood offices of Ashby Realty Corporation had an entrance befitting a five-star hotel—high ceilings, wood-paneled walls, huge bouquets of flowers and even a fountain. Two receptionists stood behind a huge marble counter. I ignored them and marched toward the elevator.

"Excuse me?" one of them cried. "Can I help you, sir?"

"No thank you," I said without looking, pressing the elevator button. "I know where I'm going."

"But you need to..."

The door opened and I stepped in. I knew by the time I reached Ashby on the fifth floor she would have transmitted her alarm upstairs.

When the doors opened, I found myself toe to toe with the van driver. He was early fifties and looked every bit the kind of guy who met all his troubles head-on, with his face. His features were about as orderly and appealing as a half-eaten hospital meal. And I bet he'd seen a few of those in his time. And it was no surprise he was jacked. Thick arms, thick neck: big muscles, no speed. I'd bet he'd telegraph a punch a mile off, and I was itching for him to try.

"Step aside, asshole."

He didn't move other than to shift his scarred chin up slightly.

"If you don't move in two seconds, you're going to be feeding yourself through a tube," I said, preparing to deliver an uppercut to that chin with my right elbow. At such close quarters, it was a powerful opening shot and one of the least expected.

"Vinnie!" a voice called from behind. "Move! Let him past! Now!"

It was Ashby. I could hear his steps on the tiles as he approached.

"Do as your master says," I said. Vinnie stepped back. "Nice work. You've earned a biscuit."

"You're a lucky man," Vinnie snarled at me. "This time anyway, pretty boy."

Pretty boy? Hell, this guy needed to learn a thing or two about books and their covers. Luckily for him, he backed away and Ashby stepped up.

"What's this about, Bradley? What are you doing coming in here disrupting my office?"

"Don't pretend you don't know, Ashby. Why have you got your pit bulls following me?"

He held up a pacifying palm and with the other showed me to his office.

"Let's take this inside, shall we?"

I walked in ahead of Ashby to find myself in a spacious office overlooking Beverly Hills. I turned away from the view to see Otto Benson standing next to Ashby.

"What's he doing here?"

"Whatever you want to say to me can be said in Otto's presence."

Benson stood with his feet planted, arms folded and a cocksure smirk on his face.

Ashby didn't offer a seat.

"You're upset about my men."

"Damn right I am. Why are you having me tailed? Is this how you treat your business partners?"

Ashby clasped his hands behind his back and paced slowly across his office. He then addressed me in a quiet, curious voice.

"How is Walter? I haven't heard from him today."

"That's because he's been arrested."

A look of shock and pain came over Ashby's face. He obviously cared deeply for Powell. Maybe Samantha was right.

"He called you?"

"I'm his lawyer, aren't I?"

Ashby snapped a damning glare at me.

"Then what in the hell are you doing here? You need to be with Walter!"

"Priorities. You and I need to sort this out first. Call your men off or you can get another lawyer for your boy."

"I understand why you are upset"—his words may have been sympathetic but his tone was stone cold—"and I'll let you have a little cry about it."

What?

"But here's the thing, Bradley. Nothing is going to change." He stepped closer to me, his macabre face conveying contained fury. "I think you're about to tell me that what I'm doing exhibits a lack of trust toward you. Right? Well, you have only demonstrated that it is patently obvious that I need to keep a close eye on you. What the hell do you think you're doing, snooping around my site?"

He came closer, tilting his head as his eyes bore into me. "What were you doing there? Are you investigating me? Is that what you're doing?"

"I'm investigating Walter Powell's case. And certain elements deemed it appropriate that I take a first-hand look at the site. And that's exactly what the cops will do if they haven't done so already. That's part of my job, Ashby, to know what the opposition is doing."

Ashby huffed and waved his hands impatiently in front of his face before turning away from me.

"You know what, Bradley? I don't care. And by that I mean I don't care what your excuse is. I have hired you to defend Walter and I don't know what exactly it is you call it but you don't seem to be living up to your end of the bargain."

"I'm doing due diligence on this case. If you don't trust me, fine. Go get someone else."

"I'll do no such thing. You are going to see this through and you are going to make sure Walter walks free of this charge. Which begs the question: what are you doing wasting precious time having a tantrum in my office?"

"I'm not going to work for you if you don't back your gorillas off."

"Is that a fact?"

"Try me."

He stepped one pace closer and lowered his voice. "Well, you try this. I'm not just keeping tabs on you, my friend. My reach extends much further than that. You've got a family to think of. A young daughter, Bella. What a charming girl and she appears to be quite popular at the Crossroads School. Then there are your parents in Boise who I know you care deeply about."

Anger was not the word. I wanted to tear this arrogant bastard's head off.

"You son of a bitch."

"Call me whatever you like. Have a swing if you like, Bradley, but nothing will change the fundamentals of our arrangement. Walter's fate is very important to me. He is irreplaceable as a friend and as an employee, and I want him back on my team as soon as possible. Do you understand? There's more at stake in this matter than you could possibly imagine. If Walter ends up in jail for this girl's death, I will hold you personally responsible and I will unleash hell upon you and those you love."

How many times had I had to bridle the explosive anger Ashby roused in me? But, again, I knew I was trapped. And, again, I vowed to myself that this was not going to be a one-way street.

"There's a reason you want Powell off and I'm going to find out what it is," I said.

"Be careful what you wish for," said Ashby, opening the door to see me out. "Now just so you understand perfectly, I will not be calling Vinnie off. Get used to it. I'm hiring you, Bradley, but I don't trust you."

This was not a case; it was a cage fight.

On my way out I stopped in front of Ashby. "The feeling's mutual, Ashby. And you are going to get far more from me than you bargained for."

Yes, I was going to play the committed attorney to the hilt. I'd do my job. I'd get Powell off. But that wouldn't be the end of it. Not by a long stretch.

I wasn't going to rest until I'd made sure Ashby could never lord it over me or anyone else ever again.

And in the end, he would know—I swore to God—that hiring me had cost him a lot more than money.

CHAPTER 20

Ted Haviland had seized on a positive DNA result to have Powell arrested. At the bail hearing, Haviland convinced Superior Court Judge Sondra Kemp that his evidence might just be strong enough to secure a murder conviction against Powell and so declared it would go to trial.

I believe I showed Judge Kemp that Haviland's case was full of holes, but she was not swayed by my arguments. To make matters worse, she proceeded to deny Powell bail.

Both Ashby and Powell were furious. They'd expected Judge Kemp to dismiss the charges and set Powell free then and there. I had to remind them that with the eyewitnesses and the DNA results, the prosecution was essentially given the benefit of the doubt. I told them that this was normal, that defendants were typically at a disadvantage during the early stages of criminal prosecution.

Ashby scoffed at this, but I reiterated that the judge's decision to send it to trial was little more than an acknowledgment that Powell was strongly *suspected* of committing the crime. Come the trial, I assured them both, the advantage would swing back in our favor because it takes a hell of a lot more than a "strong suspicion" for a jury to find a defendant guilty of murder. A jury had to believe that Powell was guilty beyond reasonable doubt, and that was a much, much higher standard than most people thought.

I think it was all Ashby could do to refrain from abusing me.

"You'd better be right, Bradley," he said.

Powell cast a sullen and silent figure as he was escorted away to take up residence in Men's Central Jail.

It was time for me to push Ashby, Powell and Co. to the back of my mind for a couple of days.

I was getting out of LA, and I couldn't leave soon enough.

CHAPTER 21

Going back to my childhood home in Boise always used to do me good. For one, it was such a wonderful counterpoint to LA. As soon as I walked in the door, I was no longer just a city lawyer. It was like I'd shed a husk, and I became so much more at ease, my spirit humming with a calmer, more collected sense of self. This was why I'd always wanted, when Claire and I were together, to leave Los Angeles and come back to practice in Boise. But Claire grew more and more wedded to LA; then we got divorced and so Bella wasn't moving either. That meant I was stuck there.

But this homecoming was different. Looking at the "For Sale" sign in front of Mom and Dad's home made my heart sink. There was no turning back now. Memories of us as a family flooded my mind. Just the simple things: watching *MASH* in the evenings or the Seahawks on weekends with Dad and Mitch, mowing the lawn, riding our bikes out of the garage to go fishing. The only thing I have now that comes close to that is the time I get to spend with Bella.

I squeezed her hand as we stood in front of the sign. The sale was prompted more by Dad's illness than Mom's financial loss, but it was a sad sight nonetheless.

The old house was built on top of hot underground springs and was one of the first in the country to use geothermal heating. The water was drawn in, piped through the house and then returned to the Boise City canal. We thought it was cool to live on a natural jacuzzi. An added benefit for my parents, who were both keen gardeners, was that the warm water created a tropical microclimate in our backyard where they could grow exotic plants. It was as green and lush as the Amazon out there.

Dad, being a real outdoorsman, relished our exotic "jungle." If not for the call of medicine, he'd have loved to have been one of those rugged biologists who spend weeks out in the wild studying bears and wolves and fishing for their own supper. As a pediatrician, he'd had to restrict that love of the great outdoors to weekends and holidays. But in the process, he taught Mitch and me how to fish, shoot, ski and camp.

Most times when I went back, I'd look forward to casting a fly with the old man, reassuring him that his knowledge was in good hands. And he did get to watch on with pride as Bella took to fishing like a natural, whipping the line out into the South Fork of the Boise River with adept flicks. But there'd be no more fishing with Dad. Those days were gone.

"Don't take it personally if Pa doesn't remember your name, sweetheart," I said to Bella. "It's not that he doesn't love you. It's just that his memory is getting rusty."

"I know, Dad," she said. "You've told me Pa has Alzheimer's disease. Can I still give him a hug?"

"You bet. But we'll have to wait till he's at ease with us and pick your moment, okay?"

"Does it mean that you'll get Alzheimer's one day, Dad? Will I?"

The question took me by surprise. From what I'd read after Dad was diagnosed a few years ago, I had about a ten percent chance of getting it, which were okay odds, I guess. Dad's first signs were so benign they didn't impact how he lived his life at all. At sixty-seven, he was recently retired and so wasn't forced out of his beloved medical profession. What concerned him was being a burden on Mom. Next I heard he was forgetting things and could no longer be trusted to even BBQ steak for their Sunday dinner.

"No, darling," I said. "There's a genetic factor but it's a very long shot. I'll never forget who you are, I promise."

"You'd better not."

I gave the front door a courtesy knock before turning the handle.

"Hello?" I called as we stepped in.

"In the kitchen," cried Mom.

Bella beat me there and I entered to see her and Mom embraced in a loving hug.

"What are you cooking, Grandma?" Bella asked. "It smells delicious."

"You didn't think I'd let you come without making your favorites, did you?"

"Brownies! Are they ready?"

"Almost," Mom said, coming toward me. "Lovely to see you, dear."

"Where's Dad?" I asked as we hugged.

"He's out on the deck," she said. "He likes to listen to the running water of the canal. Every now and then he swears he hears a trout rise."

"How is he?"

"It's been a good day today. He's so looking forward to seeing Bella. And you, of course."

"Is it okay if Bella goes out to him? You know..."

Mom knew exactly what my reservation was. "He'll welcome her with open arms. As I said, he's having a good day."

I squeezed Bella's shoulder lightly.

"Sweetheart, why don't you go say hi to Pa?"

Bella's face beamed and she skipped out the back door.

As soon as she was gone, Mom grabbed my forearm.

"Now dear, I want to tell you that I haven't brought your father into this financial mess. For one, I don't want him to be worrying about anything. He frets enough as it is. He doesn't need to know what he can't fix; you understand?"

"Yes, of course, Mom. But like I told you I'm going to fix it."

"Now listen, dear. It's not as bad as you think. Once the house is sold and we're settled into the new apartment, we'll be fine. We'll have to take a drive down there and I'll show you—it's beautiful."

Unfortunately, Dad had sought my opinion on an investment a few years ago so I was well aware of how much they had in the bank. And there was no way they could afford to take a million-dollar hit. Mom was just trying to alleviate my concern and, no doubt, to diminish the enmity I held toward my brother.

"Mom, I'm not going to stand by and watch you lose a million dollars. Sorry but that's just not happening."

"Thank you, dear, but I don't think there's much you can do. Bert Caldwell had a look at the contracts and he said there was no way I could get my money back. He said, 'That's what you get when you back the wrong horse.'"

Caldwell was a local accountant friend of Mom and Dad's.

"Bert Caldwell's an idiot. Don't listen to him." It irked me that she would consult him. "I've told you what I'm going to do and that's that."

I walked over to the fridge and found a beer. Mom shuffled over to the oven to check on the brownies. The oven door squeaked as it opened then loudly slammed shut after she let go.

"Well, I don't want you blaming Mitch. I'm a grown woman. He didn't talk me into anything."

"Except buying two half-million-dollar properties that turned out to be worthless."

"Brad. Enough. Please, I don't want this to spoil your visit. This will be one of the last times you stay here."

She let her words sink in.

"You've found a buyer?"

"Not yet but the agent is confident it won't last long on the market."

There was a mix of emotions in her voice—a mix that I shared.

"Well, that's great news, Mom. You and Dad can move on to your next chapter."

Mom reached for a handkerchief in her pocket and wiped her eyes.

"I'll miss this place terribly," she said.

I put the beer down and gave her a big hug. "We all will, Mom."

"Brad," Mom said with her head rested against my chest. "I want you and Mitch to get along. Before long, there'll only be the two of you left in this family. And I want to see my boys look out for each other again. You used to be so close."

"That was a long time ago, Mom. And my relationship with Mitch is just fine. You can't force real affection. He and I love each other as brothers, that's it. We're too different to be true friends."

Mom pulled away and held my arms as she looked up at me.

"I'm your mother and I know otherwise. Something's not right between you two, and I'm not talking about my investment. Things changed drastically when you were in college. I don't know what happened, but I'm asking you to fix it. You're the older brother. I want to leave this world knowing that my sons don't hate each other."

I shrugged.

"I just can't make that promise, Mom. I can't. I'm going to go out and see Dad."

The back of the house had a series of decks connected by wooden paths. The canal flowed between two decks connected by a wooden bridge. Steps from the outer deck led into the garden.

The whole arrangement was shrouded in greenery, but I noticed most of the flowerpots had been removed. Must have been to allow Dad to hold on to a rail everywhere he walked. As I turned for the bridge, I heard Bella's voice cry out.

"Dad!"

I broke into a sprint but quickly found them. Dad was lying on the ground near the steps and Bella was trying to help him up.

I got Dad to his feet and helped him back up the steps and onto a bench. He looked a little rattled.

"What happened, Bella?" I asked.

"I think his hand missed the railing," she said.

"I'm fine. I'm fine," said Dad, breathing hard. "Damn this stupid business."

"Bella, why don't you go grab Pa a glass of water?"

"Okay," she said and darted off. I turned to Dad.

"Dad, what happened?"

"I did have a grip on the damned rail, but suddenly it gave way."

"Has this happened before? I mean have you had a fall before?"

He looked irritated and stared at the ground ahead. "Just the once. Upstairs in the bedroom. That was when we decided to move our things into the lower bedroom so that I can stay on the one level."

"Mom told me you'd switched rooms. She never said you'd had a fall."

"It's been very hard on her. And it's only going to get worse. It's a good thing we're selling. The apartment will do very nicely until I move into a home. But at least she will be comfortable. After that she'll be able to get a nice place in town for herself and have plenty left in the bank. I've been urging her to travel, you know."

"No, I didn't."

"She should. We can pay someone else to take care of me and she can go and see more of the world, just like we planned to do after I'd retired."

"You know she won't do that, Dad."

He let out a big sigh. "I know, Son. I wish your mom and I had done more traveling together. She desperately wanted to go back to Europe. We talked about spending Christmas in Kitzbuhel. That has a ring to it, doesn't it?"

"Christmas in Boise is pretty nice too, Dad. You've got a very special part of the world here."

"You're preaching to the converted. But what about you? I thought you wanted to move back."

"I did. Still do, but the divorce screwed that. I'm staying near Bella."

"What are you doing raising a kid in Los Angeles? Boise has everything—great schools, great fishing, the mountains."

"I'd be back in a heartbeat, but it's not going to happen. Not for a long while at least."

He looked at me.

"Claire's remarried, right?"

"Yes."

"So some other guy is playing at being Bella's father."

"Not much I can do about it. But I don't feel entirely threatened; Bella and I are very close."

"And what about you?"

"What about me?"

"Are you ever going to spend long enough with another woman to put a ring on her finger?"

"Dad, you don't know what I've been—"

"I know more than you think. Roger keeps me posted."

Roger Russell was one of Dad's best friends. He was also my godfather and mentor. Roger and I caught up every couple of months, and while I did feel comfortable telling him about my love life, I was very discreet about what I said.

"Roger only knows what I tell him, Dad."

"You need a steady relationship. Bella needs to see that too. You don't want your kids worrying about how you're living your life. I realize that might be a tall order for you."

Dad was referring to PTSD.

"I'm not going to let my past mess up my future, Dad. I'm doing fine. I won't be scaring anyone away, at least not because of my PTSD."

"You're in a good place then?"

"Yes."

"From my experience, a good place is better with fine company. Take it from me. And speaking of which"—Dad's eyes lit up as Bella returned—"here's my darling."

He reached out and squeezed her arm.

"You're getting more and more beautiful, sweet Bella. Oh my, you're going to break so many boys' hearts."

"Grandpa, boys are stupid. Except for you and Dad, of course."

CHAPTER 22

I was sleeping in my old room. Although Mom had long ago changed the linen to be more appropriate for guests, my framed autographed Glen Plake poster was still on the wall, the mohawked extreme skier standing on the roof of an old Cadillac speeding through the desert with the skis mounted onto the racks. "Brad, keep those tips up!" Plake wrote across the top in black ink before adding his signature. Even though there wasn't a snowflake in sight, that image captured what skiing meant to me: the speed, the freedom, the exhilarating immediacy of a highly adrenal activity. I'd never call it a sport. It was, for a time, simply the recipe for the best way to live.

As I stood in front of the poster, memories of the mountains came flooding back. Inevitably, a tragic day that changed my life became lodged in my mind. I thought of Mitch at the race track and what we'd said to each other. This reflection gave me pause to park my resentment and anger toward him.

I slid the mirrored wardrobe door aside and saw the boxes of my things were still there. It didn't take long to find what I was looking for.

Inside an old journal was a newspaper cutting that had yellowed with time. As I opened it, the events contained in the story felt as close as yesterday.

BOISE SKIER DIES IN AVALANCHE AS BROTHERS SURVIVE

Boise local Adam Goodman, 18, has died after being caught in an avalanche in the mountains of Washington state. Mr. Goodman was skiing with brothers Mitch Madison, 18, and Brad Madison, 20, when the avalanche struck, sweeping him to his death.

A search and rescue team responded to a radio call from the brothers. An hour after the crew arrived a rescue dog located Mr. Goodman buried in snow. He was unresponsive and attempts to revive him were unsuccessful.

It is understood Mr. Goodman was not wearing an avalanche beacon, a device that can help speed up the location of victims.

The Madison brothers were uninjured but were taken to the hospital in shock. It is understood they tried desperately to dig for their friend, but their efforts were in vain.

It is not clear whether the skiers triggered the avalanche themselves or were simply caught in a random act of nature.

The avalanche occurred on Mount Herman near the Mount Baker Ski Resort.

By the time I'd finished reading my eyes were filled with tears.

The article had gotten the basics right, but many elements of the story remained known only to Mitch and me. And we'd never since revealed our secret to a soul.

So, no one but us knew it was my idea to ski out to Mount Herman.

No one else knew it was me who said the steep slope, beckoning with glistening fresh powder on a bluebird day, would definitely hold and that we were in for an epic run.

No one else knew that Mike was the least convinced. He had just completed basic training with the Marines and had come home to join his high school buddy Mitch and his elder brother, the "sensible one" studying law at Stanford, on a three-day backcountry ski trip.

No one knew that I was the only one not wearing an avalanche beacon. Back then, though, everyone was looser about that kind of thing.

No one knew that, for some unknown reason, Mike suddenly took off his beeper and threw it at me.

No one knew that as I caught it, dumbfounded, he said, "See you at the bottom." And then he dug his poles into the snow and slid out onto the slope and began a traverse.

No one knew that as I immediately set out to follow him, Mitch shouted out Mike's name and gripped my arm violently.

No one knew that Mitch had suddenly felt certain that the slope would go and had resolved to stop both me and Mike. But he was too late for Mike, who heard Mitch's cry and brought himself to a stop before he'd even put a turn in. Behind me, Mitch called out to Mike again, waving him back. Mike then carefully flipped his skis around and pushed himself back toward us.

No one knew our horror when we heard the snow above Mike crack like a cannon shot and felt the ground shake beneath our feet.

No one knew what it was like to see Mike swallowed whole by the white torrent, his red jacket barely staying visible as the cascading snow and ice swept him down. As Mitch made a radio call I skied down alongside the now ragged slope, in some places stripped back to bare rock, trying to find where Mike had ended up.

No one knew how we shouted and screamed his name frantically.

No one, not even Claire, knew that Mike Goodman was why I joined the Marines. Yes, I wanted to do something for my country in its time of need and hour of grief following 9/11, but it was mainly to repay a debt I felt I owed. I'd denied them Mike, so I offered myself in his place. It was the very least I could do.

And no one knew that I owed Mitch my life.

That secret changed our lives and our relationship. Afterward, we fell out and went our separate ways and were glad to have little to do with each other. But I didn't have to stay in touch with Mitch to know this about him: he blamed me for Mike's death, and he never wanted me to forget that he saved my life. And it wasn't just his damaging profligate ways that roused my anger toward him, it was the resentment that he held that over me.

All of it looked like such foolishness now.

I sat down on the bed and wept, grieving for Mike and hating Mitch, almost as much as I hated myself.

CHAPTER 23

If spending time in a cell was getting to Walter Powell it didn't show. Greeting him across the bare metal interview desk once again, I was struck by his utter lack of emotion. I couldn't help but wonder if he actually possessed what you might call normal feelings. But I'd concluded that while he must surely be fretting somewhere deep inside, he was wired differently to most people. Being charged with murder, being thrown behind bars and being put on trial in a few weeks did not rouse in him anything other than his now-familiar reserved indignation. In some cases, you might think it admirable or tough or stout. But with Walter Powell, it was just plain odd. Defense attorneys often advise clients accused of murder to show no emotion. There was no need to tell Powell that.

"How are you doing, Walter?" I asked.

He remained still, leaning back in his chair. That air of confidence was still there like he was certain that this was all going to be a temporary inconvenience. "It's not where I want to be, but what can I do?"

"Walter, I want to talk about Nicola," I said.

"Haven't we covered this enough already? I've told you everything about her, about our relationship and about—"

"Why didn't you tell me about the tip-off?"

"What tip-off?"

"The one that you gave her. An idea for an investigative story."

"Oh that. I can hardly remember what I said."

"Well, I want you to try and remember."

"What does it matter? Who wants to know?"

"I want to know!"

"What does it have to do with the case?"

"Do you not want to tell me?"

"No, it's not that. I would just like to know the context of things; what does this have to do with my case?"

"Are you for real? This *is* your case. Everything about your relationship with Nicola is about your case. And that tip-off might relate in some way to why she was murdered. Is that a good enough reason for you?"

"Yes."

"Why are you being evasive?"

"I wouldn't say I'm being evasive. I simply want to understand where you're going with this."

"We're not going anywhere with this right now. We're going in circles. What was the information you gave her?"

"It wasn't a tip-off. I just mentioned something I'd heard about some members of the LAPD who were on the take."

"What information?"

"This is confidential?"

"Just between you and me."

"So you cannot tell anyone the details of what I reveal to you?"

"Not unless it helps your case and not without your consent. You know I'm bound by lawyer-client privilege."

"I just want to be absolutely sure because if this comes back to me, I'm dead."

All of a sudden, it seemed Powell could convey something of what he felt—he looked scared. I gestured to an imaginary dome above us.

"This is a cone of silence. You are my client. I am your lawyer. The strictures of that relationship, the safeguarding of that confidentiality, are bulletproof, forever. Even after you are no longer my client. Your safety rests on the integrity of that confidence and so do my reputation and my career. So, please. Elaborate."

"I never had any names—I need to state that right now—but I had it on good authority that some police officers were intimidating local politicians into helping certain property developments get over the line."

"Which ones?"

"The Trident complex in Century City. Then there was a Paul Spears project a year or so back. The cops would step in and find ways to convince certain council members to play ball."

"What kind of ways?"

"Blackmail. Threats. Pull them over and say they found drugs in the vehicle."

"And what did they get in return?"

"Your average cash backhanders and then some. From what I heard some were getting brand-new apartments."

"And you don't know any names?"

"No."

"So Dean Swindall isn't part of this group?"

"Swindall? Nicola had told me he didn't mind bending the rules but no, I never heard his name mentioned. I never thought he was involved. If I did, I would have had second thoughts about saying anything to Nicola."

"Why?"

"Why? Because he would have come straight for me. Hang on, are you saying he was involved?"

Powell seemed genuine.

"I have no idea whether or not Officer Swindall was involved."

"Well, I wanted to help her out. I knew she wanted to write some kind of story that made her feel like she was doing meaningful journalism. But I didn't want to put her life in danger."

"How do you mean?"

"Well, Nicola was desperate to find a story that she could break on her own and prove that she had what it took to be an investigative reporter."

"She told you this?"

"Yes. Why?"

"She hardly let on anything about this to any of her other friends, Samantha Boylan included."

"I can't explain that. But she wasn't like that when we were together. She was as happy as a pig in mud writing about food and drink. But after, you know, she became single again, I think achieving credibility as a journalist became more important to her. When I got this information, I spoke to her about it."

"You told her everything you told me?"

"Yes."

I shook my head in disbelief.

"Walter, why on earth didn't you tell me this before?"

He didn't blink.

"You never asked. And I didn't want to tell. As I said, I didn't want it to become known that I was the source of that information. And then there was my other fear."

"What fear?"

"That she died because of what I told her; that I was pretty much responsible for her death."

I struggled to respond. I wanted to shout at him that he had to learn to trust me and that his fears were not necessarily reality, but I didn't see the point. I decided to move on.

"What was her reaction when you told her about cops helping out on property deals?"

"She didn't say anything about it, really, other than that it was interesting. But I could see she was giving it some thought. Do you think this is related to her death?"

"We know from her notes she contacted Detective Harrison Daylesford. Then soon after that she is seen having an argument with Swindall. A few hours later and she's dead. Who gave you this information about the dirty cops?"

"I don't want to say."

"Come on, Walter. Was it Ashby?"

He hung his head.

"Yes."

"Rubin Ashby told you certain cops were working as goons for hire to intimidate council members into green-lighting development projects?"

"Yes. Well, he didn't tell me directly. I just heard him talk about what some of his rivals were up to. So, I thought I could help both Mr. Ashby and Nicola at the same time."

"And not long after Nicola acts on your tip-off, she gets thrown off a cliff."

Powell looked at me ruefully.

"See? You *do* think I'm to blame."

I stayed silent for a moment. As far as I could tell, the thought pained him.

"Why did you do it?" I asked.

He snapped his gaze at me, alarm written over his face.

"What do you mean? I didn't do it!"

"The tip-off, Walter. Why did you give her the tip-off?"

"Oh… I just… I just felt sorry for her."

"You didn't think it would lead her into very dangerous territory?"

"I didn't think too much about it, to be honest. I presumed she would not be operating alone, that she would have the support of her editor and other reporters; you know, someone giving her the right advice about how to approach things. For me, the info I gave her was just a starting point."

"Well, it seemed she took it on all by herself."

If what Powell said was true, it lent weight to the theory that cops killed Nicola Beauchamp. And the only cops in the frame as far as I could see were Daylesford and Swindall.

If I was going to attach any substance to this theory, I had to find the link between Swindall, Daylesford and suspicious development approvals.

On my way out of the jail, I took out my phone and called Jack.

CHAPTER 24

"Do you get a discount here?"

My question took Officer Dean Swindall by surprise, given I'd just suddenly appeared at his shoulder in a downtown food mall queue. But he gave me an easy smile and shook his head.

"No, sir. I'd be glad if they did, but the truth is I'd be happy to pay twice what they charge. Best place to eat in the city, if you ask me."

His opinion didn't surprise me since we were lined up at Howlin' Ray's Nashville chicken joint.

"What do you recommend?"

"This is your first time?"

"It is."

"Then go for the chicken sandwich and don't be a hero when it comes to the heat. Medium is plenty hot, even for people who say they like it hot. Above that, you start getting into ruin-your-day kind of territory."

"Thanks. I'll take that on board." The people ahead shuffled forward a couple of steps. Swindall followed. "Must be nice for you to get a taste of home, Dean."

Acutely aware that the nameplate pinned above his right breast pocket only displayed his surname, Swindall's face fell flat. He turned himself around to face me square on. Not threatening but wary. He sensed he might have a situation.

"How do you know my name, stranger? We haven't met."

I put out my hand.

"Brad Madison, attorney at law. I'm representing Walter Powell in the Nicola Beauchamp case."

Swindall looked at my hand as though it held a bribe he wasn't going to be seen accepting.

"What do you want?"

"Just a few minutes of your time."

"What say I don't have it?"

"Come on, let's just chew the fat while we wait for our lunch."

"I'm not interested in talking to you." He turned back around. Then he addressed me over his shoulder. "You've got some nerve following me."

Jack had been tailing him all morning and directed me here.

"I just want to ask you a couple of questions."

"Go read my statement. Whatever I've got to say about the case is in there."

"Yeah, that's the thing; I have read your statement."

"Well, that's all you're going to get. You want to ask me questions, then depose me. We'll invite my lawyer, a court reporter, set up a camera, the whole works."

He stepped forward one pace as the line moved.

"Okay. So, you're willing to testify that Nicola was apprehensive about seeing Walter the night she disappeared?"

"Seriously, is that your question? Maybe you're not as smart as I took you for."

"What were you arguing with Nicola about?" I'd been told this by one of Beauchamp's neighbors who'd refused to testify, not that I'd ever tell Swindall that. Swindall kept looking ahead, like the only thought swimming around inside that brain of his was whether or not he was going to have fries and a peach tea with his sandwich. I kept at his shoulder. "You were seen arguing with Nicola the day she died. That's what one of her neighbors is going to tell the jury."

"It was nothing."

"Really? I know you couldn't accept that she chose Walter Powell over you. And you kept hanging around. How many times did she have to tell you it was over? Or did you think you were back in the frame after Walter broke up with her?"

"You writing a romance novel, Madison? You've got the imagination for it."

"We're going to be covering this on the stand, you know."

He turned to face me, his nostrils flaring slightly.

"You know what. Ask away. Yeah, we argued that day but only because I was trying to make her come to her senses about Powell."

"So you were telling her to move on? From the sounds of it, you're not the best person to be giving that advice."

"We were friends. Yeah, I wanted more and she didn't. But more than anything I wanted her to be safe."

"What I don't understand is why she would have to fear Walter Powell. What am I missing? Or are you just wanting to do whatever you can to see my client take the fall for Nicola's death?"

"You mean her murder."

"Yes, her murder. What could she possibly have to fear from Walter Powell?"

"Why don't you ask him?"

"I'm asking you because I'm not convinced by anything you say. And I'll tell you this right now: if I'm not buying what you're selling, it's going to be an absolute breeze for me to make sure the jury doesn't buy it either."

"Is that a threat?"

"No. It's not, Dean. It's the law, the court side of the law, the side where I get a big say in how the show runs. And if I find out you are making up this stuff about Nicola fearing Powell, then I will expose you as a fraud and a liar for all the world to see. I'm being straight with you. I just want you to have a think about how things might fly if your story isn't solid as Plymouth Rock."

He turned to face me again. It looked like I might have gotten through to him.

"Yes, she still loved him and she wanted to be back with him. And I didn't like that at all. I believed we still had a chance. We had a good thing going back in Tennessee. There was a job at the Jackson station. We talked about moving there, having kids, that kind of stuff. But she felt she was too young and made a career move to come to LA."

"And you followed her."

"Yeah. And if you hear from some people that I was no good for her, they're lying."

"So why should she fear Walter Powell?"

"She never said, but she sure as hell was apprehensive about seeing him. It was like she knew something really bad was going to happen."

"Is this what you two argued about?"

"Yes."

"It had nothing to do with her contacting Detective Daylesford?"

Swindall's eyes suddenly lit up, but he managed to keep his bearing relaxed.

"What are you talking about?"

"You don't know that Nicola had decided to investigate information she'd received about corruption within the LAPD?"

Swindall's eyes narrowed into gunslinger slits.

"You must have your wires crossed, attorney. Nicola wrote about beauty products and some such. She wasn't interested in—"

"Oh, but she was. She had ambitions to be an investigative reporter. Are you telling me that's news to you?"

"Yes."

"You had no idea she had contacted Detective Daylesford after she had received a tip about a bunch of crooked cops?"

"No, I did not."

"Well, isn't that interesting? The day after she calls Daylesford, you go pay her a visit. You're seen, and heard, arguing with her."

"I had no idea Nicola was looking to do a story on the LAPD. And I don't believe you. If she was, she would have told me."

"I guess that's my point."

Swindall was furious now, and he conveyed a silent message that he'd love to smash my teeth in.

"Didn't Nicola have more to fear from you than Walter, Dean?"

"Now why would you go and say a thing like that?"

"Just giving you some food for thought." I pointed over his shoulder. "Speaking of food, the line's moved. You better go get served. I think I'm going to skip lunch today. Good talking with you. See you in court."

I turned and walked and felt Swindall's eyes on me as I exited the mall.

CHAPTER 25

"How did your chat with Swindall go?" asked Megan when I got back to the office.

"Good. I think it dawned on him that the trial may not play out the way he expected. He knows he's in my sights. What he doesn't know is that I just don't have the evidence to bury him, or at least discredit him."

"Apart from jealousy as a motive."

"Apart from that, yes."

Jack arrived and took a seat. He looked distracted and bothered, as though a heavy thought was lodged in his head.

"What's up with you?" While I was up in Boise, I'd asked Jack to tail Ashby. But first I wanted to hear what happened to Swindall after I left him.

"Nothing," he said brusquely and waved me off. "Let's get on with it. You want me to start with Swindall?"

"You bet. What did he do after I left?"

"Well, he decided he wasn't hungry," said Jack. "Once you were out of sight, he pulled out his phone and made for the exit looking greatly perturbed. He got to the street and waited. It was clear a pick-up was happening, so I ran and got my bike. I came around just as he was getting into a black-and-white."

"A prowler. Did you see who was driving?"

"No. So it—"

"Where'd it go?"

"If you let me finish, I'll tell you!" Jack snapped.

"Sorry, Jack. Please, continue." Something was up with Jack, but I thought if he wanted to tell me, he would.

"The car heads over to Twin Towers, stops out front and Swindall gets out. The squad car takes off, and five seconds later, another car pulls up beside Swindall and he gets in."

"Patrol car?" I half expected Jack to snap at me again. He seemed to have accepted he'd overreacted because he dropped the attitude.

"No. An unmarked Ford Fusion. Metallic light blue. Non-government plates."

"CID, you think?"

"I'd put money on it."

"So, the Fusion takes off?"

"Yep, but it just does a circuit, pulls up at the pick-up spot, Swindall gets out, and straight away the squad car swings by to collect him."

"Who did you follow after that?"

"I figured I'd best tail the Fusion."

"Good."

"It sets off and ends up round the back of Union Station. And then this guy gets out and goes into Starbucks."

Jack showed me a photo on his phone. I knew who it was immediately.

"Detective Harrison Daylesford. So straight after getting a visit from me, Swindall reports to Daylesford. We need to see what we can get on these guys. Megan, how did it go with the cases I showed you?"

I'd asked Megan to follow up on the two clients of mine who'd claimed they knew victims of Daylesford's abuse of power.

"Good. Well, your former clients were of no help, but I did some digging and found out that right now three prisoners are seeking to overturn convictions in cases linked to both Swindall and Daylesford." She placed a folder in front of me. "Each one is being handled independently."

"Nice work," I said.

"I think only one of them has a chance of getting anywhere though."

"Why's that?"

"Because he has a decent lawyer. The second has hired a drunk and the third's got a cut-and-run specialist who'll find the quickest way out if he doesn't see a big payday coming his way."

"Now why doesn't that surprise me?"

"You should take their cases, Mr. Madison."

"I've kind of got my hands full right now, Megan."

"I know. It just pisses me off, you know? If what these men say is true, then they shouldn't be rotting away in jail, and they shouldn't be prey to some shameless, selfish lawyer who will probably screw their chance at getting free."

"I hear you, but my hands are tied right now. Is that all you've got?

"On those cases, yes. But I also wanted to show you this."

"What is it?"

"A small article from the *Los Angeles Times* from six weeks ago. It says a twenty-three-year-old woman was assaulted in the

Point Fermin Park area. She says the man tried to abduct her and pull her toward his van. Bonnie from the downtown sexual assault response team looked into it for me and found out the woman reported the assault to a medical center down in San Pedro. She said there had been a few assaults believed to be by the same man, but the cops have done nothing."

"And...?"

"Look who has a series of sexual assault priors." She slid a photocopied document toward me.

"Jaden Ross," I said. "My God."

I began pacing the room, my mind racing with a string of new possibilities about the fate of Nicola Beauchamp.

"What is it, Brad?" asked Jack.

I stopped.

"Jaden Ross said nothing when he was first questioned by the cops. Then he turns up to give a statement to Swindall, saying he saw someone who looked like Powell with Nicola Beauchamp at the cliff."

"And?"

"What if Jaden Ross is more than just a witness?"

"What do you mean?"

"I mean he could be the killer."

Suddenly, Jack slammed his fist on the table.

"Damn it, Brad! Is that your next move? To find evidence against Ross? Because if that's your plan then count me out."

I was stunned. "What the hell's gotten into you, Jack? Something's been bugging you since you walked in here today. What's going on?"

"I'll tell you what's going on: you're getting played. The way I see it, Ashby wanted the girl dead and Powell helped him do it."

"What makes you so damned sure?"

"I can't prove it, but nothing else makes sense. Your client is someone who gets whatever he wants and he's prepared to do whatever it takes."

"But look at the evidence. It's weak. It's inconclusive. And you know what? You might be able to afford to be morally selective about the work you do but I can't."

"Ashby forced it on you! You know that. You're just another one of his errand boys. That's why you feel so shit about yourself. There's more than one way to get your mother's money back, you know."

"Well, it's not quite that simple. But let me break it down for you. My job is to defend my client to the best of my ability, and to that end I'll leave no stone unturned. And I don't give a damn if you think I entertain some crackpot ideas along the way."

"It's not right. I hate Rubin Ashby and I hate Walter Powell."

"I'm not their biggest fan either. But it's my professional duty to ensure Powell gets a fair trial. I don't have the luxury of just working for the innocent. The onus is on Ted Haviland and the State of California to prove Walter Powell is guilty. And I'm going to make their job as difficult as I possibly can."

Jack stood up. "Good luck with that."

"What do you mean? Are you out?"

"Right now, I'm so pissed I think it's best if I hold fire on telling you that."

"Take the weekend. Take longer. But let me know. I don't want to do this case without you, Jack, but I understand the way you feel. I can quickly bring someone else in if it comes to that."

Jack nodded. "Okay, I'll let you know." Then he walked out the door.

I'd lied. Yes, I could get another investigator, but they wouldn't be half as good as Jack. And they wouldn't be my best friend.

CHAPTER 26

"Knock. Knock."

I knew the voice without looking, and at eight-thirty on a Tuesday night, it was as welcome as summer. I stood up and met Roger Russell with a handshake and a hug.

"Not too busy are you, Brad? I know the trial starts next week."

"You'd never guess, the damned prosecutor just dumped a heap of material on me that I'd been hassling him for for ages."

"Ah, that old trick."

"He thinks I won't know it all like the back of my hand come trial. Well, he's in for a surprise, I can tell you."

"That's my boy. But listen, if now's not a good time…"

"Hey, you are a sight for sore eyes. I've hated having to stand you up these past few months."

I must have put off our regular dinners three times by then.

"That's no problem. That's why I just came by, actually. I figured if I didn't, I would be waiting until after the trial for you to buy me a meal."

"I've been absolutely snowed under."

"I can imagine."

"Please, have a seat."

"I'm not keeping you."

"You know, Roger, until you walked through that door, I didn't know that a visit from you was exactly what I needed."

"What can I say? I have a sixth sense about these things," he said, taking a seat with a laugh.

"Let me get us a drink."

I went to the liquor cabinet and cracked open a bottle of Talisker 18, a very decent scotch I reserved for very decent company. Roger and I may have been a generation apart in terms of age, but we were kindred spirits. It was one of my father's greatest gifts, bringing Roger and me together. We began getting together for regular dinners back when I was at law school. I could talk to him about anything. And although I'd said precious little about Mike's death, I think Roger suspected my decision to join the Marines had something to do with it. Not that he ever said anything explicitly.

Throughout college and beyond, Roger was there for me as a source of wisdom and fount of law knowledge. Often our dinners ended up as a lecture of sorts, as Roger led me by way of the Socratic method into a deeper understanding, appreciation of and respect for the profession. I was proud to report my successes as a student back to my father, but to earn Roger's pride meant more because he was the man I aimed to emulate professionally. Although he'd been a distinguished trial lawyer, he was now a named partner at one of the top law firms in the city, where they benefited not just from his brilliant mind but his great character.

"You know what's at the top of my bucket list?" Roger asked as I poured.

"To get your hands on a never-ending bottle of this?"

"Close. A tour of Scottish distilleries."

"You're too young to have a bucket list."

"Don't flatter me, Brad. I'm nearing seventy and I have the good fortune to have both mind and body well intact. A bucket list is highly fitting for me. Call it a side hustle."

"Side hustles are meant to be hobbies that at least have the potential to earn you an income."

"So maybe I'll buy into a distillery or buy a couple of casks that have exceptional promise. There's a new Islay distillery that might fit the bill. But I don't want to part with any money until I try the wares."

"Then let's do it. I'll come with you."

"Really? That would be wonderful."

"We'll go after I'm done with this case." As soon as I said those words, I knew that getting Powell off was only half the job I'd assigned myself. My determination to cut Ashby off at the knees had not abated. Every meeting with him had only strengthened my resolve to prove to him emphatically that I was no mere underling. How I would achieve this was not yet clear, but the opportunity would come, I'd make sure of it. "Actually, we'll have to wait a while longer, Roger. There are some other things I have to see to before I can jet off to Scotland."

Roger stared into his glass, preparing his next words carefully.

"You know why I came here tonight, Brad?"

"Thirst?"

"Ha. Not quite. The truth is I am a little concerned about you."

"How so?"

Roger shifted but he wasn't uneasy. He never shirked from talking straight with me.

"I know what's going on at home, Brad. And I know about your mother's financial troubles. As if that sweet woman doesn't have enough on her hands with your father taking a turn for the worse."

She confided in Roger?

"I didn't think she had spoken to anybody about that," I said, "save for that idiot accountant."

"Brad, Jane and I have known your parents for forty years. We've done so much together. Jane may not be around anymore, but I still keep in regular contact with your folks. I spoke to Carol soon after the news broke about her investment property. I knew something was up but she wouldn't tell me. So, I went to see her. How are you feeling about the case?"

"Confident. It's a trumped-up charge. The police have been hell-bent on pinning this murder on Walter Powell, and the jury is going to see through their shoddy deeds."

"Maybe, but I don't believe convincing a jury of police misconduct will be easy, even though we're talking about the LAPD. Despite what they see in the media, your average citizen has an ingrained desire to believe the police are the good guys. The odds are not in your favor."

"They can't get their way every time. And this time they won't."

"Okay, so let's assume you've succeeded in freeing Rubin Ashby's employee—what's his name? Walter Powell. What about Rubin Ashby?"

"What about him?"

"Brad, I know you. You are planning to get revenge of some sort on that man. Something tells me you didn't take this case on the best of terms. I mean why would you assist the man who has cost your mother a small fortune? My guess is that he has you over a barrel, is that right?"

"Yes."

"You have a deal with him, correct?"

"Yes."

"You get Powell off; Ashby repays your mother?"

"Yes."

"I see. And you do not want it to end there?"

"How can it, Roger? What about all the other people he has screwed? Not just on the Costa Rica deal but on others. That man has built an empire on other people's misfortune and he needs to be stopped."

"And you plan to stop him how?"

"I'm working on it." That was not entirely true. I had nothing that resembled a strategy to take Ashby down.

"Okay. Do you mind if an old friend offers you some advice?"

"Of course, Roger. I respect you more than any man I know."

"Once you're done with the case, forget about Ashby. Bank your money, enjoy your win, and ensure that your business benefits from your success. And after that, focus on your family."

"My family?"

"I don't mean your daughter, Brad. I have no concern about the strength of the bond between you two. I'm talking about your most immediate family. For the sake of your mother, you need to get things right with Mitch."

"Jesus, Mom really told you everything. Look, Mitch and I have a history. We'd have happily stayed out of each other's lives if Mitch hadn't brought this fiasco upon us. He is greedy, self-centered and has no moral spine. His failings have brought my family together. That's the bond we have, Roger."

Roger sighed.

"Just think about it, Brad."

"I will but I can't promise I'll do anything other than make sure Mitch and I never see each other again. I just can't let go of that anger."

"And the same goes for Mr. Ashby, no doubt."

I nodded.

Roger drained his glass.

"Take it from a wise old man: let go of your hate and lust for revenge."

"How can I? And why the hell should I?"

"Well, for one, Rubin Ashby is a very dangerous man. And for another, there are things going on right now that may mean you won't have to play any part in his downfall."

"What are you talking about?"

"The word is that he will be the sole target of bribery charges. Several Costa Rican officials have come forward to say he offered cash bribes to get his land deal over the line. They have tapes."

"I would have thought that was just business as usual."

"It is. But he's put so many noses out of joint there that the Costa Rican government appears set to throw him under a bus."

"What does he care? He'll never go to jail there. There's no way they can extradite him. It'll just be a speed bump. He'll just go back to screwing over people here in the US or somewhere else in the world."

Roger paused.

"I wouldn't be so sure. The way I see it, Ashby's living in a house of cards and Costa Rica could well be the first to fall but others will definitely follow."

"Interesting, Roger. But it's just a theory."

"I think it's more than that, Brad. I think, as far as Ashby goes, he'll get what's coming and you won't have to lift a finger."

"So just let it go?"

"Yes. Exactly. Let it go." Roger put his glass down and stood up. "And I'll send you an itinerary of my ideal Scottish tour. Feel free to add or improve as you see fit. Then I'll book the flights."

As usual, after time spent with Roger, I felt a little more at peace with myself and with the world. Maybe I could just let go of Ashby, leave him to his own fate, whatever that may be.

The thing was I didn't believe in karma. I didn't believe that the universe balanced the scales of human justice and inequality. That was society's responsibility. And if karma didn't claim Ashby by way of a Costa Rican takedown, then I'd be waiting to step in.

And maybe, I thought, I could enlist a little extra help. I picked up my phone and tapped on a contact.

"Hello," the person answered.

"Hey, it's Brad. Sorry, I know it's late… Is your passport up to date?"

CHAPTER 27

After I passed through the court security scanner, my phone lit up as I retrieved it from the tray. It was a message from Jessica.

"Kick ass, handsome. But may the best case win." She signed off with a heart, a kiss and a wink emoji.

"Spoken like a true fence-sitter," I typed back with a smile. "May God give you splinters."

I pocketed the phone and lugged a thick pile of files toward the court for the second time that day. In the morning, Haviland and I had conducted the voir dire on the jury pool to whittle them down to the final twelve.

What pleased me about the morning's voir dire was that I thought Haviland did little to win jury members over. His questioning was abrupt, his manner officious and his attempts at empathy forced. While I'm not saying I Clark Gabled them with old-school charm, I think I was able to connect on a fundamental level.

Unlike most trial lawyers I know, I've served on a jury. I was summonsed two years ago and while most attorneys find a way to excuse themselves, I relished the opportunity to get into the trenches so to speak. It was a murder trial that resulted in a conviction. And while I'm proud of the work we did and the verdict we reached, I believe I came away from the experience a better lawyer.

I got to experience first-hand how heavily the concept of justice weighs on the mind of a juror. In our case, there were the families to think of, both the victim's and the defendant's. For both sides, the verdict would impact them every day for the rest of their lives. That responsibility was immense. Anyone who doubts the profound effect the role has on ordinary people has clearly not sat in a jury or known someone who has. They are rarely given their due.

Haviland was raring to go. He must have hoped that the flood of material he dumped on me the past few days had thwarted my preparation. Although I hadn't had much sleep the past three nights, I did my best to appear cool, calm and confident, and I could see Haviland was disappointed that I seemed so fresh. Put it down to adrenalin and coffee.

Once the jury was picked, Judge Kenneth Austin called a ninety-minute recess, which I spent sharpening up my opening statement before downing more coffee and heading back to court.

When I entered, Haviland was already seated at the prosecution table with all his papers in order. Dressed in a brown suit, white shirt and black tie, you wouldn't say he aspired to any sartorial heights. He was a champion for a world in which plain talk, plain conduct and plain expectations were society's hallmarks. He sat looking straight ahead, his hands resting on his knees under the table. It wouldn't have surprised me if he'd brought an apple for Judge Austin.

Ah, Judge Austin. Now there was a piece of work. He was famous in law circles for being as unpredictable as the weather in Kansas City, from where he hailed. Arguing before him, you could never assume you had his support for any length of time. While he may have sustained your objection one minute, he might overrule another based on similar grounds the next.

You could say he was capricious. But I'd say he was calculating to the point of being devious. It was widely known that he had a difficult relationship with the bottle. Not that his drinking diminished his faculties. He was the kind of man who, when it came to handling his booze, had both Winston Churchill's fortitude and sharpness of tongue. It was my belief that Austin knew exactly what he was doing. It was his court and he liked to keep you on your toes, dancing to his tune.

The bailiff announced Judge Austin's arrival. The judge took his seat, tapped his gavel and called the case. A few minutes later, the jury entered. All the while, when I glanced at him every now and then, Haviland did not move. I wasn't sure whether to take this as a sign of confidence or nerves. Even when his right leg started to shake, it wasn't clear. For all I knew, he might have just been eager to get started. Maybe we were more alike than I realized. Maybe we were equally excited, equally charged, equally thrilled to be in court again.

"Are you ready for opening statements, counsel?"

Both Haviland and I stood in unison, buttoning our jackets. "Yes, Your Honor."

"Good then. Mr. Haviland, let's proceed with opening statements, shall we?"

"Yes, Your Honor."

As I sat down, Haviland stepped out from behind his desk and moved toward the jury. He started out a little scratchy. Not to be harsh, but you could tell it had been a while since he had done this. Maybe the leg jiggling I'd noticed earlier was a sign of nerves after all. But you don't have to be a brilliant orator to connect with a jury. And over the course of Haviland's statement, I could see he succeeded in bedding down the tenets of his case.

Haviland argued it was clear from the medical examiner's report that Nicola Beauchamp did not die of her own hand and of her own free will. She was murdered. Of that there could be no doubt. How did we know this? Drag marks at the scene. He promised the jury that they would see with their own eyes photos of this evidence and they would be visiting the scene themselves. He cited the medical examiner's report that Nicola Beauchamp's blood contained a high level of alcohol and traces of the date-rape drug Rohypnol. And in the medical examiner's expert opinion, the amount of Rohypnol in her system would have rendered her all but unconscious.

He said the jury would no doubt hear from the defense that Nicola Beauchamp was a suicide risk and had come to this very spot to kill herself before, only to think better of it. But the blood tests alone ruled out suicide. How does a woman in such a state of inebriation that she can hardly stand climb over a wall to leap from a cliff? It's not what happened. She was murdered. And she was murdered, as the State will prove, by that man there: Walter Lindsay Powell.

Haviland said the jury would hear from eyewitnesses who saw Mr. Powell and another man with a distraught woman that night. He said he would show the jury that Mr. Powell had substantive reasons to kill his former girlfriend. For one, she was investigating a story that may have implicated the company that Mr. Powell worked for. He said it would be evident that such exposure would have been catastrophic for the man the defendant was devoted to—Mr. Rubin Ashby.

I knew Haviland would use this as the motive. Daylesford would have told him that corrupt property developers were the thrust of Nicola's phone call to him, not police officers.

Haviland said he would show the jury that a man fitting Mr. Powell's description was spotted at the scene. And at the bottom of the cliff, just a few yards away from Ms. Beauchamp's body, police found a damning piece of evidence: a bracelet that DNA testing proved belonged to Mr. Powell.

After appealing to the jury to ensure that justice was done for the family and friends of Nicola Beauchamp, Haviland returned to his seat, sat down, looked straight ahead and returned his hands to his knees.

I never assumed I could take Ted Haviland lightly. Now I was particularly attuned to the threat he presented. He may have been as plain as a town-square pigeon, but that didn't mean he could not pack a punch.

I used my opening statement to cut through to the bare facts that favored my client. I pointed to the fact that Walter Powell had an alibi. I touched on the relationship between Walter and Nicola Beauchamp, how even though he'd broken up with her he'd remained her good, trusted friend.

I said the prosecutor mentioned that Nicola Beauchamp might be considered a suicide risk because she'd come to the same spot to kill herself before. And who did she call on that night? Walter Powell. And who raced to her assistance and talked her out of her desperate actions? Walter Powell.

The prosecution, I said, mentioned the fact that Nicola Beauchamp had aspirations to become an investigative reporter and to that end had begun looking into a story about corrupt land deals in Los Angeles. But what the prosecutor did not tell them was that it was Walter Powell who gave her that tip.

I insisted the evidence would show that Mr. Powell was an innocent pawn in a game of injustice, that he was being blamed for a crime he did not commit and that he had been brought before this court on weak evidence. I said I was sure that when the jury came to their final assessment of all the facts, they would agree that Mr. Powell should never have been put through this trial and should be able to resume his life as a free man, albeit one who had lost a dear friend.

To finish, I hammered the point home about reasonable doubt.

"Members of the jury, 'reasonable doubt' is the cornerstone of this trial. It lies at the heart of the question you must answer. And that question is not, 'Is it possible that Walter Powell killed Nicola Beauchamp?' That question is, 'Do you believe *without reasonable doubt* that he killed her?'

"Remember: our starting point is presumed innocence. You must presume from the outset that Walter Powell is an innocent man. And once all the facts have been presented to you, you will need to decide if the prosecution has convinced you of Walter Powell's guilt so powerfully that you simply cannot doubt it.

"But, no matter what the prosecution claims, there is no certainty when it comes to the supposed case against Walter Powell, only doubt upon doubt upon doubt. Yes, we are examining the death of a young woman, but never lose sight of the fact that we are determining the future life of a young man."

After I thanked the jury, I returned to my chair feeling that the jury was with me.

I was even surer when I looked Haviland's way to see both his legs were jiggling furiously.

CHAPTER 28

Haviland opened by calling Dr. Arnold Nguyen, the forensic pathologist who performed the autopsy on Nicola Beauchamp. I guess Haviland wanted to crush the suicide theory from the outset. He stood with his hands clasped in front of him as Dr. Nguyen was sworn in. Then, without moving from that position, he established the doctor's credentials and experience.

Dr. Nguyen estimated he'd performed hundreds of autopsies and had found the examination of Ms. Beauchamp's body to be straightforward.

"Could you please tell us how Ms. Beauchamp died?"

"She died as the result of severe blunt force trauma to the head, neck and upper body, consistent with that of landing head first on rocks at high speed."

"The sort of injuries you would expect if someone jumped off a cliff?"

"Well, no."

"No?" Haviland said, flicking wide eyes at the jury.

"She landed head first. It is highly unusual—no, I would say rare, hardly ever—for suicides who jump from great heights to land head first. They almost always land feet first. Even in such desperation they do not dive. That would be too—how should I say?—exuberant."

"Dr. Nguyen," Haviland said, "you reported there was a medium-high level of alcohol in the victim's blood, is that right?"

"Yes, it was twice the legal driving limit."

"Were traces of any drugs besides alcohol found in the victim's blood?"

"Yes. There were positive results for cocaine and flunitrazepam."

"Flunitrazepam?"

"Most people know it as Rohypnol."

Haviland took a sheet of paper and walked it over to Dr. Nguyen.

"This is exhibit five-seven. Dr. Nguyen, is this the medical report you prepared after completing your examination of Nicola Beauchamp's body?"

"Yes, it is."

"Could you please read what you entered for the concentration of flunitrazepam found in Ms. Beauchamp's blood."

"It was fifty-seven micrograms per liter."

"Is that a lot?"

"It's more than twice what you would find in someone who has been prescribed the drug as a sedative. Anything more than fifty micrograms per liter and the drug begins to seriously impair motor skills, judgment, coordination, and reaction time balance."

"It reduces your capacity to fend for yourself?"

"Most definitely. That's the very reason it is used as a date-rape drug."

"Now, you found a concentration of fifty-seven micrograms per liter. How much time had passed between Nicola Beauchamp's death and your examination?"

"About twelve hours."

"Twelve hours. I see. But the concentration of the drug would have been higher at the time of Nicola Beauchamp's death, wouldn't it?"

"Yes."

"What would the concentration have been?"

"Based on the known half-life of the drug, the concentration at the time of death would have been up around ninety micrograms per liter."

"Is that high?"

"Very. Once you get over a hundred, you're looking at overdose."

"Can you please help us understand Nicola Beauchamp's state at the time of her death?"

"A blood concentration of ninety is enough to incapacitate some people. Knock them out, essentially."

"Could she have walked freely by herself?"

"Objection," I called, getting to my feet. "Calls for speculation."

Haviland shot me a hot glance. "Your Honor, Dr. Nguyen is eminently qualified to surmise the degree to which Ms. Beauchamp would have been in control of her body at the time of her death."

"Overruled," barked Judge Austin. "You may answer the question, Dr. Nguyen."

"Certainly, Your Honor. With that combination of drugs and alcohol, Ms. Beauchamp would have struggled to stay awake, let alone stand on her own two feet."

"Struggled to stay awake," said Haviland to the jury. "Is the idea that she climbed over a four-foot-high wall and jumped off a cliff of her own free will unlikely?"

"Unlikely to the point of impossible."

"No further questions, Your Honor."

"Your witness, Mr. Madison," said Judge Austin.

"Thank you, Your Honor," I said as I rose. "Dr. Nguyen, you say there is just about no way Nicola Beauchamp jumped to her death by her own choosing."

"Yes. That's correct."

"You say she was intoxicated to a high degree due to the alcohol and flunitrazepam. But she also had a high concentration of cocaine in her blood, didn't she?"

"Yes."

"And isn't it true the cocaine would have acted as a strong stimulant?"

"Yes."

"Strong enough to offset some of the stupefying effects of the flunitrazepam?"

"To some degree, yes."

"So, it is possible that Nicola Beauchamp had the physical wherewithal to walk and to get herself over that wall, isn't it?"

"As I said before, it would be highly unlikely."

"But given the stimulants in her system, can you rule it out?"

"No, I don't suppose I can."

"No further questions, Your Honor."

CHAPTER 29

Next came Haviland's second expert witness, a physics professor named Simon Lutsky. His report was among the lump of discovery files he dumped on me at the last minute. But I had read it through carefully and committed some salient points to memory.

Professor Lutsky, a resident academic at the University of California, Berkeley, was about sixty. The band of hair circling his otherwise bald scalp sprang outward in such disarray you'd guess it had never felt the touch of a comb. He had a narrow face divided by round, wire-framed glasses that tilted at a slight angle. The shirt beneath the blue blazer he wore was unironed. In short, he was the very image of the absent-minded professor, someone so consumed by intellectual pursuits that everyday considerations like appearance were easily overlooked.

With his initial questions, Haviland covered the professor's academic qualifications, achievements and awards. Then there was the previous trial Professor Lutsky had been called upon to lend his expertise to. Three years ago, his research was pivotal in clearing the name of a young man blamed for the death of a twenty-year-old woman who fell from a high-rise balcony. By the time Haviland had covered all this, no one in the courtroom could have doubted Lutsky's ability to illuminate the court on Nicola Beauchamp's death.

"Professor Lutsky, you conducted multiple experiments in order to reach a conclusion, didn't you?"

"Yes, that's correct. Close to fifty in all."

"Could you please describe those experiments to the court?"

"Well, first I visited the site where Ms. Beauchamp died. I studied the access to the cliff; I recorded the height of the cliff and also the point at which she landed. Then I carried out several experiments to replicate the various ways in which she could have met her death. Well, the three ways, really."

"You mean suicide, mishap or murder?"

"Yes."

"Continue, please."

"First, we could rule out mishap. If Ms. Beauchamp had merely slipped accidentally at the top of the cliff, she would not have fallen straight into the air. She would at first have slid then hit some rocks on her way down."

"But there was no evidence of this, was there?"

"No. The injuries to her body were limited only to the areas that hit the rocks she landed on. There were no traces of dirt under her nails, no scrapes to her fingers, hands or forearms or lower body, no scratches or cuts on her legs and no dirt from the cliff on her clothes."

"And what did you conclude?"

"That her death was no accident. It was either suicide or murder."

"What were your findings on the possibility of suicide?"

"I found that it could not have been suicide."

"Why not?"

"If we could use the diagram."

"Oh, yes, of course." Haviland brought an image up on the large courtroom monitor. It was a side photo of the cliff with various markings superimposed on it."

"May I use this laser pointer, Your Honor?" Lutsky asked Judge Austin.

"Of course."

From his seat, Lutsky aimed the pointer at the screen, where a bright red dot appeared. He proceeded to walk the jury through the physics of Nicola Beauchamp's fall. The key point was that the impact point was almost ten yards out from the top of the cliff. Another key point was that there were just over six yards of flat terrain between the wall and the edge. He told the court he'd conducted various tests at the university pool's diving tower and found that even the most athletic women among his volunteers could not jump out to a landing spot more than seven yards from the cliff.

"We know Ms. Beauchamp was not what you would call athletic," said Lutsky. "Therefore, it would have been impossible for her to reach that landing point under her own steam, so to speak."

"So, it is your contention that she did not kill herself?"

"This was not a suicide."

"Were there any other salient findings from your research, Professor Lutsky?"

"Yes, we looked at how the body could get that far from the cliff on such a short run-up. We asked one male student, who is one of Berkley's strongest athletes, a football player, to throw a young woman of Ms. Beauchamp's height and weight off the diving tower. And no matter how hard he tried, he could barely throw her beyond five yards out. The other male volunteers we tried came up even shorter. Then we tried with two men of average strength with a four-yard run-up, and that's when we started to approach the distance of ten yards."

"And your conclusion?"

"My conclusion is that Ms. Beauchamp was thrown to her death by two men."

"Thank you, Professor Lutsky. Nothing further."

"Mr. Madison," Judge Austin called. "Your witness."

I stood up and nodded to the judge.

"Thank you, Your Honor."

I had no doubt Lutsky was diligent and well-meaning, but my job was to ensure that nothing from the prosecution got through to the jury without me giving them pause to think. It was my duty to keep the verdict alive at every point, so the jury members could not accept anything adverse against my client without reservation.

"Professor Lutsky, so you replicated the incident that occurred on a stormy, windswept night in the confines of the Berkeley University pool?"

"That's right."

"Would you say your experiments accurately reflected what happened that night?"

"It's the best that can be done. I stand by that."

"Was it sophisticated enough?"

Lutsky was clearly annoyed by the inference that his work was somehow amateurish.

"It was as sophisticated as it needed to be. We are talking about applying basic physics here—run, jump, dive, fall, land—not quantum mechanics."

"Point taken, professor. So, on the subject of basic physics, what was the height of the diving platform?"

"It is ten meters high."

"I see. It's metric because it's built to international competition specs, right?"

"Yes."

"Which makes it about eleven yards high. And what was the height of the San Pedro cliff Nicola Beauchamp fell from in meters?"

"Thirty-four meters. Or thirty-seven yards."

"Thirty-seven yards. I take it you had to extrapolate your figures to reach your conclusions, is that right?"

"Yes, of course."

"Right. So, when you say two men were able to throw a body of Ms. Beauchamp's weight a distance of ten yards, you took the distance of where your volunteer had landed then used a calculation to estimate the outward distance from a greater height?"

"Yes, that's a very basic way to put it," huffed Lutsky, growing irritable at having to persist with justifying his work.

"Professor Lutsky, what is the degree of accuracy for your tests?"

"The results are about ninety-five percent accurate."

"But that's your estimation, is it not?"

"That's right, but it can be validated easily by someone else."

"But only you conducted these tests, right?"

"Yes."

"So, we just have to take your word for it then, I suppose. Yet, even then, if you are ninety-five percent accurate there's still a five percent chance that you are not. Isn't that right?"

"Yes, but that's very much academic."

"Yes, it is academic, Professor Lutsky. Isn't that the problem?"

"Objection," cried Haviland. "Mr. Madison is badgering the witness."

"Sustained," said Judge Austin. "Rein it in, counselor. I won't have witnesses mocked in my court."

"Your Honor, I was merely pointing out that there is a big difference between a tragic real-world event and the artificial environment used for the professor's experiments."

Judge Austin glared at me.

"Counselor, I'm not going to repeat myself."

"Yes, Your Honor."

My provocation had gone exactly to plan. Haviland's objection had allowed me to make a statement that cut to the chase about why there should be fundamental reservations about the professor's work.

I gave Judge Austin a slight bow of the head and turned my attention back to the witness.

"Professor Lutsky, in all your tests you used a female volunteer who was about the same size and weight as Nicola Beauchamp, correct?"

"Ah, yes. A volunteer."

"Did this young woman in your tests struggle?"

"No, she was asked to remain limp. I was advised that the victim would have been close to being unconscious, given the drugs in her system."

"But the court has already heard that it is by no means certain that Ms. Beauchamp was unconscious or anywhere near it. So, what if she was struggling? What if she was trying to grab hold of her would-be killers?"

"I'm not sure what you're getting at."

"If she was struggling for her life, could she have dragged one of her assailants with her?"

"Maybe. Maybe not. Maybe all she got a hold of was a bracelet," said Lutsky.

Damn. I'd walked into that one. I heard a faint, victorious hiss to my left. Haviland was no doubt pumping his fist under the table.

"Professor Lutsky, the students you employed in your tests to throw your victim into the pool, did they ever end up falling in the pool themselves?"

The professor breathed deeply looking at me with cold disdain.

"Yes. That sometimes happened."

"How many times?"

"I cannot recall."

"They are recorded in your paper. On page seventeen you wrote…"

"We used the two male students twenty-four times, and in fewer than ten attempts, one or both of them fell into the water."

"That's right. You wrote that one or both boys attempting to throw the female volunteer fell into the water nine times out of twenty-three."

"Yes."

"But isn't it true that the boys fell in mostly during the early attempts?"

"Yes, that's true."

"In fact, after fifteen attempts, the boys did not fall into the water at all. They had gotten better at throwing the girl into the pool. Is that right?"

"Yes."

"Which means that in the first fifteen attempts, one or both boys fell in the water in two out of every three attempts?"

"Yes, that's correct."

"And that's from the university dive tower. With no struggling from the girl. Wouldn't a wet, windy night on top of the San Pedro cliffs have been far more precarious for anyone attempting to throw someone off, Professor Lutsky?"

"I would have to agree."

"So strictly from your testing of the scenario, we should have found two or three bodies at the bottom of that cliff, shouldn't we?"

Lutsky was sullen and reluctant to answer.

"Professor Lutsky?" I said.

Lutsky coughed. I could tell he was weighing up all the words he wanted to use to defend his testing but resigned himself to one: "Yes."

CHAPTER 30

The following day, Haviland called two witnesses who said they saw a car matching the basic description of Ashby's two-toned Maybach that Powell drove. I had, of course, read their statements and I believed their testimony did nothing to strengthen Haviland's case.

In my cross-examination, I was able to make it clear to the jury that, unlike what Haviland would have them believe, his two witnesses did not narrow the car seen down to a field of one. Both of their descriptions were generic; neither knew the make and neither could confirm for the court whether the car's darker panels were black, blue, gray or deep purple.

Next came Tony Casparian, a man in his mid-forties who said he was out on a late-night stroll when he saw two men crossing Point Fermin Park, heading toward the parking lot. It had been recorded in his statement that when Daylesford and Cousins had run him through a photo line-up, he'd said Powell "maybe" was one of the pair. But in the time since making that statement, Casparian's memory had gotten sharper, and that "maybe" had become "definitely".

I had, of course, had Jack look into Casparian's background. The details Jack delivered left me thinking Casparian was a bad witness for Haviland to use. This quiet loner seemed too obliging, a bit too eager to please the law. I believed he was one of those invisible men, who go through life unnoticed by other people, whose advice is never sought, whose company is never missed. I suspected he might be seizing a golden opportunity to be listened to. This suspicion was confirmed when I dug around some council records.

"Mr. Casparian, you were walking along the coastal walkway in a southerly direction when you say you saw the two men, is that right?"

"Yes."

"And what time was this?"

"It was after midnight, about half-past."

"But somewhere between midnight and one o'clock?"

"Yes. Definitely."

"And how far away from the two men were you?"

"I'd say about seventy yards."

"I see. And from that distance you felt confident in identifying the defendant as one of the two men?"

"Yes, I did."

"It was a dark night, wasn't it, Mr. Casparian? All the more because the quarter moon was blocked by cloud."

"Yes, it was."

"So how was it you were able to see the features of a man seventy yards away so clearly?"

"Well, there are street lamps all through the park."

"I see."

I brought up on the monitor a map of the park I'd prepared. It was an aerial photo of Point Fermin Park in daylight. I'd added a mark showing where Nicola Beauchamp fell.

"Mr. Casparian, would you mind stepping forward and telling us where the two men were when you saw them?"

Casparian left the witness box and pointed to an area of grass. "They were here," he said.

"Are you absolutely sure?"

"Yes."

I pressed a small blue sticker to where Casparian had pointed.

"And where exactly were you?"

Caspar pointed again and said, "I was here."

After again asking if he was sure and receiving his full confidence, I marked the spot with a small red sticker.

"Now, as you can see here, there is one street lamp in the vicinity of the position the two men were in. Do you agree, Mr. Casparian?"

"Yes."

"You can see from this photo that it is a lamp. And if there was an element of doubt that it was a street lamp, we can identify it as such from its distinctive shadow seen here." As I said this, I zoomed the image up on the shadow. "Isn't that right, Mr. Casparian?"

"Yes, that is a street lamp."

"Thank you very much, Mr. Casparian. Please, if you could return to the stand."

As Casparian resumed his seat, I went to my desk.

"Your Honor, I have a record here from Southern Californian Edison, the company that maintains the street lights in that area. Exhibit two-six-three."

Judge Austin looked at Haviland who offered no objection.

"Now, the lamp here in question can be identified by a metal plate that displays its ID code. Could I direct your attention to the screen, please, Mr. Casparian? Please watch carefully."

Once he was looking, I played a video I'd shot earlier at Point Fermin Park. The first few seconds panned around the park and came to rest on a single lamp.

"This is the lamp you say illuminated the two men on that dark night, correct?"

Casparian was not so forthcoming now. He sensed a trap.

"Yes, that's the lamp."

I hit the play button again and the camera zoomed in on the lamp's ID plate. "Mr. Casparian, could you please read the ID code on that lamp?"

"Ah, P-T-zero-zero-one-one-four."

"P-T-zero-zero-one-one-four, correct?"

"Yes."

I replaced the video with a photo of a document on the screen and spun around to address the jury.

"Mr. Casparian, on the screen is the exhibit I just mentioned. It is a document from Southern California Edison that lists all the street lamp outages on the night of Ms. Beauchamp's death. Now, as the court has heard, there was a terrific thunderstorm that night. And before it even hit the coastline, the intensity of the lightning knocked a few street lamps out. Now, the lamps along the coastal walkway were unaffected because they had been upgraded two years ago. But many of the lamps in Point Fermin Park had not been upgraded. They are more than fifty years old and several were blacked out by the first lightning strikes that occurred at ten thirty-four that night. And we know this how?"

I brought up a photo of the blacked-out lamp.

"Now, a citizen who noticed the outages took this photo and submitted it to Southern California Edison via their email report system. And this report was submitted at eleven sixteen that night."

Casparian's face was turning pale.

"So, Mr. Casparian, I have one last question for you. The street lamp you said helped you identify one of the two men as being Walter Powell was not in fact working at the time you say you were there. So, how could you have identified them by the light of that street lamp?"

The witness was lost for words.

"Would you care to revise your testimony, Mr. Casparian?"

He hung his head before returning his gaze to me.

"I don't know. I was sure that was the man I saw. Maybe it was the lightning."

"Maybe it was the lightning," I repeated. "But that's not what you told us so confidently a few minutes ago, is it, Mr. Casparian? What is the jury supposed to believe?"

"I don't know." Casparian bowed his head.

"A man's life is at stake here, Mr. Casparian."

"I don't know if it was him."

"Sorry, are you now saying you are not sure if one of the men you saw was the defendant Walter Powell?"

"Yes, that's right."

I almost felt sorry for Casparian. And I could almost hear the air seeping out of Haviland.

CHAPTER 31

Detective Harrison Daylesford was one of those cops who made testifying in a courtroom in front of a judge, jury, an adversarial lawyer and a full public gallery seem about as intimidating as sitting for a driver's license photo. He took the stand with the assuredness of a man with nothing to hide and something to tell.

After he'd taken the oath, the big detective faced Haviland with a ready-when-you-are lift of his chin.

"Detective Daylesford," Haviland began, "could you please recount for the court what you saw when you arrived at the scene of Ms. Beauchamp's death?"

"I got a call at approximately four forty-five in the morning and I went out straight away. It's about thirty minutes from my home, so it was about a quarter past five when I arrived. My partner Detective Brian Cousins got there ten minutes later. We sealed off the area and inspected the top of the cliff. We had to use our torches. But at first light—which was right on six—we started to get a full picture of what had happened."

"Detective, how many suicides by falls have you attended?"

"Taking a stab at it, I'd say at least forty. I've seen more of that stuff than just about anybody on the force and far more than I ever wanted to."

"And on first inspection, did you think Ms. Beauchamp's death was a suicide?"

"No way."

"Why are you so sure this was not a suicide?"

"First off, the distance the young woman's body was from the edge. She'd have a shot at the Olympics if she could jump that far out."

"Anything else?"

"She landed head first. Her body had fallen into a hole in the rocks and we found her with her legs sticking up in the air. I'm sorry, there's hardly a nice way to put that."

"We understand, detective. But what does that tell you?"

"Suicides almost always jump feet first. That means they land feet first. So, it was my view from the outset that she was thrown off that cliff with some force."

I kept my eyes on the jury during this exchange. I knew this was where I'd have to cease all references to suicide. I would not mention it again, otherwise the jury would see me as hanging desperately on to a false theory. It was now time to move into the next phase of my strategy.

"Detective, was there any other evidence that bolstered your first impression that this was a case of murder?" asked Haviland.

"Yes. At first light, we scoured the lawn between the parking lot and the walkway wall and we found drag marks on the grass."

Haviland brought an image up on the screen. "This is exhibit number forty-two. Detective Daylesford, what are we looking at here?"

"The photo on the left shows a close-up of the drag marks we found on the grass. The middle photo shows that those drag marks lead directly to the wall right at the very spot where Ms. Beauchamp went over the cliff. The photo on the right shows soil and grass marks on the toes of both her shoes. We had forensics take a look, of course, and they found the grass and soil taken from Ms. Beauchamp's shoes were a perfect match for the lawn where the drag marks were."

"What does this evidence tell you?"

"That Ms. Beauchamp put up as much of a fight as she could but she was nonetheless dragged to her death."

"Detective Daylesford, later that morning, you were able to inspect the area at the foot of the cliff, is that right?"

"Yes, we were airlifted down to the impact area."

"What evidence did you find there?"

"This was where we recovered Ms. Beauchamp's footwear, as well as items that had apparently fallen from her person at some stage of her ordeal."

"What were these items?"

"Her purse, her jacket and a necklace."

"Her jacket? Did it come off during her fall?"

"No. We believe the jacket and her purse were separated from the victim before her fall. The jacket was torn, indicating it had come off forcibly."

"Please elaborate."

"The jacket was found a good fifteen yards from the body. It would appear that this item of clothing was recovered from somewhere on top of the cliff and then thrown down after the body. And the purse was found near the jacket, not the body."

"I see. So, you quickly believed there was foul play?"

"Very quickly, yes."

"Detective Daylesford, when did Mr. Powell become a person of interest?"

"Again, very quickly."

"Why?"

"Well, as I said, we decided—myself and Detective Cousins—that this was a murder scene. And as soon as we were able, we looked at Ms. Beauchamp's phone records and began calling the numbers. Before long, I found myself speaking with Mr. Powell. I informed him of Ms. Beauchamp's death and that his number was one of the last on her phone."

"What was his response?"

"A little unusual."

"How so?"

"He didn't ask one thing about her. This was his girlfriend of three years not too long before, and he didn't express any sadness and he didn't ask me one question about how she died and when. In fact, his exact words were, 'She's finally done it.'"

"He implied that she committed suicide?"

"Yes."

"Was there any evidence linking Mr. Powell to the murder?"

"Well, near Ms. Beauchamp's body we recovered a man's bracelet."

"How do you know it was a man's? A photo of exhibit two-zero-six, the bracelet, is on the screen now."

The courtroom monitor showed an image of the bracelet laid out beside a ruler.

"You can see there it's eight inches long," said Daylesford. That's the standard length for a man's bracelet."

"Is there anything else of note about this bracelet?"

"Yes, you can see it's been yanked off the wrist."

"I have the close-up photo here," said Haviland.

"Yes, that makes it clear," continued Daylesford. "The steel clasp at the end is distended, indicating that it's been wrenched off."

"In some kind of struggle?"

"Objection!" I called out. "This question calls for a conclusion."

"Sustained," replied Judge Austin immediately.

Haviland didn't mind. He just wanted to say the words for emphasis. It's easy to erase something off the court transcript—the written words never to see the light of day. The same can't be said for the picture that those words paint in a jury's collective mind. You just can't unhear that.

"Detective Daylesford, who does the bracelet belong to?"

"It belongs to Walter Powell."

"Did he admit this?"

"He told us he owned a bracelet just like it, and after we ran a DNA test, we got a positive for Mr. Powell. That's when we charged him."

"Do you have evidence to suggest Mr. Powell had a motive to kill Ms. Beauchamp?"

"Yes. About a week before her death, I actually received a call from a woman who refused to give her name. She said she was a reporter and was following up on some information she had received relating to some criminal activity carried out by property developers in conjunction with, she claimed, members of the LAPD."

"What was the nature of this criminal activity?"

"Her source claimed that property developers and the police had colluded to influence council decisions on certain land deals."

"Why did she call you?"

"She was assured that I could be trusted. And she was told, I believe, that I could offer some off-the-record insight into whether or not this could possibly be true."

"What was your response?"

"I told her these were very serious allegations and that I knew nothing of such activity."

"Did you speak to her again?"

"No."

"So, if you thought it was not a story, then why would her actions prompt Mr. Powell to kill her?"

"Well, she actually mentioned the name of one developer suspected of corrupting councils."

"What company was that?"

"Rubin Ashby of Ashby Realty Corporation."

"That would be the company Mr. Powell works for, correct?"

"Yes. The founder Rubin Ashby is Walter Powell's boss."

Ted Haviland had good reason to resume his seat with evident self-satisfaction; you didn't have to know juries as well as I did to know that this one had lapped up Daylesford's testimony with knife, fork and spoon.

Now it was my turn. I needed to give the jury some indigestion.

CHAPTER 32

"Detective Daylesford. Do you pride yourself on being thorough?"

He seemed almost miffed to be asked such a lightweight question. "Of course, I do." The dry note of his reply signaled a change. Gone was the good-natured rapport he shared with Haviland, and in seeped the disdain.

"And when it comes to collecting evidence at a crime scene, it is vital to be very thorough to ensure the integrity of every piece of evidence, isn't it?"

"Yes, it is."

"You must have a very efficient process of gathering and cataloging evidence at a crime scene, do you not?"

"Of course we do."

"But I mean you, personally, detective. Do you have high standards when it comes to managing crime scene evidence?"

"It's something I pride myself on. The crime scene must be kept untainted until we have extracted everything we possibly can as far as evidence goes."

"Because if you miss something, it could ruin the case, could it not?"

"Yes. You often don't get a second chance."

Haviland was on his feet. “Is this going somewhere? Surely Detective Daylesford doesn’t need to be here testifying in court about his work ethic.”

“I’m inclined to agree,” said Judge Austin.

“Your Honor, I’m just establishing the detective’s professional standards.”

“Get to the meat of it, Mr. Madison.”

“Certainly, Your Honor. Detective Daylesford, you say this bracelet that you found points the finger of guilt straight at my client. Have I got that right?”

“It’s one of many pieces of evidence that make Walter Powell the prime suspect in the murder of Nicola Beauchamp.”

“I see. When did you first speak with the defendant about Ms. Beauchamp’s death?”

“Detective Cousins and I went to Mr. Powell’s residence the afternoon after the body was found.”

“So, you spent the morning, as you say, at the cliff and then you went to see Mr. Powell that afternoon?”

“Is that a question?” Daylesford grumbled.

“Yes, it is.”

“As I said before, we followed up on the phone records and that led us to the defendant.”

“I see. Your Honor, I would just like to show Detective Daylesford this document, if I may.”

With Judge Austin’s nod of approval, I approached Daylesford and handed him three sheets of paper stapled together at the top left corner.

“This document is the transcript of the interview you and Detective Cousins had with Mr. Powell that afternoon, correct?”

“Yes. It is.”

"A document that both you and Detective Cousins have signed."

"Yes."

"Could you then please explain to the court why you never raised the subject of the bracelet with the defendant?"

Daylesford stalled almost imperceptibly. You could almost hear his brain whirring.

"I was not asking the questions, as it happens, so I can't explain why the subject was not raised."

"I take it that means Detective Cousins conducted the interview. Am I right?"

"Yes."

"And what were you doing during the interview?"

"I was present."

"For the entire interview?"

"For most of it."

"The transcript is time-coded, Detective Daylesford. Two minutes and twelve seconds after the interview begins, you excuse yourself to go to the bathroom. You ask the defendant for directions and then you leave. Your return is acknowledged by the defendant, who asked what took you so long. This question is asked of you fourteen minutes and twenty-three seconds after you excused yourself."

"What can I say? I was a little stuck. It happens." Daylesford's face made light of it, but his eyes glowered.

"During that time, Detective Daylesford, did you search Mr. Powell's bedroom?"

"Objection!" cried Haviland. "This is a slur that is meant to impugn the character of a distinguished detective."

"Overruled. Please answer the question."

"No, I did not search the defendant's bedroom."

"Detective, are you sure that's not where you found the defendant's bracelet, rather than at the bottom of the cliff?"

"Objection, Your Honor! Again, this is a malicious attempt to malign the character of the witness."

"Sustained. Watch yourself, counselor."

"Of course, Your Honor. If I may continue?"

"So long as you exhibit your best behavior, Mr. Madison."

"Yes, Your Honor. Detective Daylesford, the bracelet that is believed to belong to my client, did you find it the first morning you were there?"

Daylesford paused.

"Yes."

"And like the other pieces of evidence—the jacket, the purse, the shoes—you bagged it and then labeled the bag with the case number, is that right?"

"Yes."

"And that evidence would have all been submitted back at the station for filing, would it not?"

"Yes."

"So why didn't you hand the bracelet in with the other pieces of evidence found at the scene?"

Daylesford's mouth twitched, a little I-want-to-smash-my-fist-through-your-face twitch. He was clearly someone not used to being challenged. "I can't really answer that, except to say we had been up most of the night and it was just an oversight."

"Just an oversight?"

"Yes."

"And when did you hand the evidence over to the lab for DNA testing?"

"It was a few days later. I had forgotten about it, but I had to restock my evidence kit bag, and when I did so, I found the bracelet and handed it in straight away."

"Weren't you just telling us how impeccable your standards are when it comes to gathering evidence?"

No answer.

"Seems kind of sloppy, doesn't it, Detective Daylesford?"

No answer.

"Detective Daylesford, handing in a key piece of evidence days after it was claimed to be have been found, is that good police practice?"

No answer.

"Your Honor, I think the question warrants an answer."

"Answer the question, please, detective," said Judge Austin.

Daylesford cleared his throat. "No."

"Could you please speak louder?"

"No," Daylesford said firmly with eyes fit to kill.

"But if we go purely by the records, no bracelet was found that morning. Isn't that true, detective?"

"Yes."

"And there was no mention of it when you and your partner questioned my client, was there, detective?"

"No."

"Neither you nor Detective Cousins asked my client anything about a bracelet, did you?"

"No."

"Did you actually tell your partner Detective Cousins that you had found a bracelet?"

"I'm not sure."

"But you didn't think to tell your partner to grill Mr. Powell about it?"

"No."

"You didn't jump in to question Powell about the bracelet yourself?"

"No."

"Really? A detective of your experience, who, as you say, just a few hours earlier had found a bracelet that would incriminate Walter Powell, yet when you go see him you don't pursue any line of questioning whatsoever about it."

"Is that a question?"

"It's a big question, Detective Daylesford, and it deserves an answer. Why didn't you tell Cousins to ask Walter Powell how the hell his bracelet ended up at the bottom of a cliff next to his dead ex-girlfriend?"

"We did ask him."

"No, you didn't. Not that day you didn't, Detective Daylesford. Not on the day you say you found it. You and your partner said absolutely nothing about it."

"We did ask questions about it. After we got the DNA results back."

"Come on, detective. That was days later. Now, are you sure you didn't find the bracelet in Mr. Powell's apartment?"

"Objection! Again, Your Honor, badgering the witness!" Haviland was on his feet, yapping.

"Overruled," snapped Judge Austin with a crack of the gavel. "Answer the question, please, detective."

"That is a lie."

"If you say so, Detective Daylesford."

Daylesford slammed his fist on the witness box railing.

"I *do* say so! You piece of..."

I didn't look at Daylesford as I made my way back to the defense desk.

"Counsel, are you finished with your cross-examination of the witness?" asked Judge Austin.

From my desk I set my eyes calmly upon Daylesford.

"Yes, Your Honor. I'm done with him."

CHAPTER 33

Dean Swindall sauntered his tall, lanky frame to the stand wearing one of those affable smiles that looked like a wince. His manner and ease of limb could either come across as friendly or sly. Maybe it was the nod he gave the jury, along with a quick, glint-toothed grin. He was, or at least wanted to appear to be, southern cordiality personified. But it was somehow just a bit off-key and I wondered if the jury sensed that too. To me it was less the air of a kindly cop and more that of a used car salesman. *Good,* I thought. *Just give this guy enough rope.*

Haviland had obviously given a lot of thought to how to play Swindall. And he seemed to modify his tone of voice and bearing to match those of the witness. For starters, I was surprised to see him lean his thigh against the prosecution desk with both hands in his pockets. He did indeed look relaxed if a little forced. And in asking his initial questions, he adopted a slight have-a-chat way of talking. It wasn't just me who'd noticed. Not only were all the eyes of the jury on him, but a few raised eyebrows were too.

When he'd say, "Officer Swindall," he'd end the surname with a rising inflection. Then with the following phrase—say, "Could you please tell the court"—Haviland's pitch would peak at "you" before steadily descending. I half expected him to throw in an "if you wouldn't mind so much" for good measure. I could only assume that Haviland's objective with all this was to create a trusting bonhomie between him and Swindall, and by extension between Swindall and the jury.

And Swindall, for his part, slipped into the role sweetly. He laid on the treacly accent with a spoon and wrapped his phrases up with utmost politeness. His words rang with an honest-to-goodness tone and were delivered with fresh-eyed candor, as though he was simply confiding in Haviland and didn't mind who heard.

Asked why he became a police officer in Los Angeles, Swindall declared it was to be with the love of his life, Nicola Beauchamp. He said they'd been high school sweethearts in Memphis, had gone to the prom together, attended church together and enjoyed the most wonderful, enriching times together. He said that he and Nicola had spoken about getting married and him getting work in Jackson and that they talked of children and dogs and long, contented summers.

Then he said Nicola had not so much had a change of heart as a burst of ambition. She decided she didn't want to be one of those mothers who looked back and wished they'd established a career first, something solid that could be rekindled later on in life. Nicola had always loved to write and was hired by the *Tennessean* after college. She looked up to her Auntie Sue, who'd founded a successful home and lifestyle magazine in Nashville. Nicola thought so long as she got a start she could work from anywhere as a freelance writer. But she wanted to have big-city experience on her resume, so she set her sights on California.

Three months later, she was off to LA, having landed a job as an *LA Times* lifestyle writer. Swindall said they couldn't stand being apart, so he up and followed her and was soon hired by the LAPD. Then, he sadly recounted, things had not worked out. They'd broken up and he'd moved out of their shared apartment.

With his soft circling done, Haviland stiffened his tone. It was time, in his mind, to start burying Walter Lindsay Powell.

"Officer Swindall, you met with Nicola the day she died, didn't you?"

"That's right. I most certainly did."

"Could you please explain the nature of that meeting?"

"Well, I hate so much to say it, but we'd had a disagreement."

"About what?"

"First, I called her that morning to see if she wanted to have lunch. We weren't boyfriend and girlfriend anymore, but we were still friends. And I guess I still felt that in a sense I was looking out for her. I do know that my being in LA was of some comfort to her family. But she said she did not want to have lunch. She sounded upset."

"What was she upset about?"

"She wouldn't say on the phone, so I decided to drop what I was doing and go on over."

"You went to her apartment?"

"Yes."

"Did she welcome you?"

"Of course she did. But she didn't want to open up about what was troubling her."

"Was she in tears?"

"No, she was just, you know, agitated."

"What was she agitated about?"

"Well, she wouldn't say at first, but eventually she revealed that she was seeing Walter Powell that night and that there was something she was nervous about. Apprehensive, she was. That's the word. Very apprehensive."

"Why was she apprehensive?"

"At first, all she said was that he might not take it well."

"What did she mean?"

"I can't say exactly. Powell had broken up with Nicola a year or so before then, but she still liked to hang out with him occasionally."

"As you did with her, I take it?"

"Yes, sir. I mean we're all adults. We can't be holding grudges against people who add something special to our lives."

"And Nicola thought Walter Powell was something special?"

"Yes. Personally, I could never work out what she saw in him, but that was her choice."

"So, you said at first she wasn't inclined to say anything."

"Yes, but I kept pushing her."

"And?"

"Well, she said it had something to do with a story she was pursuing. A story that was outside of what she normally did. That's when I found out her ambition was bigger than even I had ever imagined. She told me she wanted to be an investigative reporter."

"And what did that have to do with the defendant?"

"Well, eventually she opened up more. She told me that Powell had given her a tip-off about some shady dealings by property developers. It seemed he had hoped the story, if it ever came to light, would adversely affect the rivals of Rubin Ashby, his boss.

But Nicola said to me that she had realized that the story may well in fact backfire on Mr. Powell. Badly."

"In what way?"

"She said it would not turn out too good for Mr. Powell's boss, Rubin Ashby."

His direct examination completed, Haviland returned to his seat looking quite self-satisfied and with good reason: his plan had worked. It seemed the jury had warmed to Swindall.

Now it was my turn. I had to make Haviland's success fleeting.

CHAPTER 34

"Officer Swindall, you said you and Nicola remained good friends after you broke up, is that right?"

"Yes."

"Did she break it off, Officer Swindall?"

"Yes."

"And you were not happy about it?"

"No, I was not happy. You could say I was heartbroken. But, as they say, time heals all wounds."

"Did you seek to maintain a friendship with Nicola Beauchamp?"

"Yes. I didn't see why we could not remain friends."

"Was it a case of you refusing to accept that things were over?"

"No, that's not right."

"Objection, Your Honor. Argumentative."

"I'm merely establishing the relationship, not just between Officer Swindall and Nicola Beauchamp but between Officer Swindall and the defendant."

"Overruled," said Judge Austin.

"Officer Swindall, Nicola dumped you for Mr. Powell, did she not?"

He tried to find a way to deny it, but it eluded him.

"Yes."

"And you found that awfully hard to accept, isn't that true?"

"Of course I did. Any reasonable person would. It happens all the time."

"Officer Swindall, is it true that you became angry with Nicola at her decision to leave you for Walter Powell?"

"For a while, yes."

"Is it true Nicola asked you to keep your distance after she broke up with you?"

Samantha had told me this. Swindall gave his answer some thought and decided not to deny it.

"Yes."

"But you refused to leave her alone, didn't you?"

"If you're suggesting I was some kind of stalker, you've got it all wrong."

"So, you gave her plenty of space, did you, Officer Swindall?"

"Yes."

I held up a document.

"Exhibit sixty-two, Your Honor. Ms. Beauchamp's phone records." I held them aloft as Judge Austin nodded his permission to hand them to Swindall.

"Officer Swindall, is that your cell phone number highlighted there in Nicola Beauchamp's phone records?"

"Yes, it is," Swindall said glumly without lifting his eyes from the pages.

"Now, these records indicate you phoned and texted Nicola Beauchamp several times a day. For two years. The vast majority of calls went unanswered, as did the vast majority of your text messages. And in many of the text messages you sent, and in the voice mails you left, you expressed an intense dislike, a hatred even, of the defendant Walter Powell, is that true?"

"I felt it was my duty as a friend to let Nicola know what I thought."

"Your duty, you say? Did she seek your opinion on relationship matters?"

"Sometimes."

"Really?"

"Yes."

"Did she ever seek your opinion about the man she chose over you, the man she loved?"

Swindall's face went red and he clenched his jaw in an effort to restrain his tongue.

"I wouldn't say she asked me directly, but we were still friends and I was looking out for her."

"Would it be more accurate to say that Nicola Beauchamp wanted you out of her life but didn't have the heart to tell you?"

"Objection," cried Haviland. "Assumes facts not in evidence."

"Your Honor, these records, as I said, show that Nicola Beauchamp ignored the bulk of Officer Swindall's calls and texts. And, as far as Officer Swindall's enmity toward Walter Powell goes, perhaps I should play some of the messages in which Officer Swindall makes his feelings explicitly clear.

Haviland shook his head.

"Overruled," said Judge Austin.

"Officer Swindall, did Nicola Beauchamp ever tell you that you should go on back to Tennessee?"

Swindall paused to shape his answer. "She did suggest that. But she wasn't the only one who wanted to advance their career in Los Angeles. I got myself a good job and I like it very much."

"I mentioned earlier that in your voice messages and texts you had very unkind words to say about the defendant Walter Powell. You don't deny this?"

"No. I made no secret of the fact that I did not like him."

"You were jealous of him, right?"

"No, I just didn't like him."

"Officer Swindall, did you ever threaten Mr. Powell?"

"Not personally, no."

"Okay. Not personally. By that do you mean not in person?"

"Yes."

"But what about in other ways? Did you threaten Mr. Powell in a text message?"

Swindall didn't answer.

"One of your texts is actually printed out on there on page three. Actually, there are several." Swindall flipped to the appropriate page and read. "Officer Swindall, do you accept that these are text messages sent by you to the defendant?"

"That is my phone number."

"But did you send those abusive messages?"

"What do you think?" he said flatly.

"That's the purpose of my question, Officer Swindall. I'll ask you again: did you send these abusive messages to Walter Powell?"

"Yes."

"Please read the first one highlighted there, Officer Swindall."

"I am going to take you down, you piece of shit."

"And the second?"

"I will make your life a living hell." Swindall slammed the page down. "He provoked me into saying these things!"

"How so, Officer Swindall?"

"He rubbed my nose in the fact that Nicola loved him and then he broke her heart."

"Ah, that's what I was coming to. These messages you have just read were sent to Walter Powell after he broke up with Nicola, isn't that right?"

"Yes."

"Did you ever feel obligated to seek revenge on account of two broken hearts, Officer Swindall?"

"They are just words."

"Words indeed," I said as I returned to the defense table.

CHAPTER 35

As I left the building, I was surprised to see Jack standing out front. I hadn't seen or heard from him since he'd stormed out of my office. I was pleasantly surprised to see he was holding coffee. And a Howlin' Rays food bag. But maybe I was jumping the gun. Maybe he'd come to let me down easy so, work-wise, we'd part on good terms.

"Good to see you, Jack," I said with a smile. "But I hope that's not a farewell coffee and burger you're holding. If so, I don't want them."

Jack smiled and held out a cup to me.

"Take it. I'm still going to ride shotgun with you on this. The deep reservations I have about Ashby and Co haven't gone, but I understand that you're hitched to their wagon and, for your sake, let's just say it's business as usual."

This was a huge relief. I knew how much it would be eating at Jack's conscience if he was helping someone get away with murder. He'd always warned me that he'd draw a line on any case that he worked on. Unlike me, he wasn't bound by a professional obligation to ensure that a person, whether guilty or not, got a fair trial. But in his own way, he was supremely committed to the cause of justice. He just had to believe. And in this case, with a client like Ashby and a defendant like Powell, he was having real trouble keeping the faith.

"Great to hear."

We headed over to a bench in Grand Park and sat.

"I didn't just get lunch," Jack said as he dug into the bag, pulled out a burger and handed it to me. "I've got some news."

Jack said he'd been busy looking into Erin Coolidge's disappearance. After a few attempts, he'd built up the trust of Erin's boyfriend, Luke Wells.

"You know, it's odd," said Jack. "The cops seem to have given up on finding Erin Coolidge."

"Does the boyfriend know what they are doing?"

"He said they don't seem to be trying very hard. But like Samantha, he had a couple of visits from Daylesford and Cousins a while back and then heard nothing."

"My guess is that they're working on blaming Powell."

"Luke Wells is convinced they think he's involved."

"Why?"

"He said they were almost belligerent in the way they treated him. He thought they were convinced he was hiding something. He said Daylesford was particularly intimidating. They have interviewed him twice. Second time, they grilled him on any slight variation he had on his initial story."

"He's not a serious suspect, is he? They'd have to have Powell in their sights, surely."

"Yes, but Luke said they reckoned his alibi was weak. But how can it be rock solid when no one knows when Erin went missing and what happened to her afterward?"

"You said they interviewed him twice."

"Yes."

"Is there any good reason to regard him as a suspect? Has he got any priors? Any history that would give them cause?"

"No. And by all accounts he and Erin were madly in love. He is convinced Erin has been murdered and that the cops think he did it. The kid is a mess."

"Seriously, why would Daylesford and Cousins be putting heat on him?"

"He swears they're following him."

"Really? How stable is this kid? You don't think he's just being paranoid?"

"No, he's a pretty solid character. But the cops do have him rattled. And that pisses him off. He's wondering why they're wasting their time following him around when the real killer, assuming Erin is dead, is still out there."

"Why? Exactly."

"But I showed him the photos I had of Daylesford's car and he was certain that that was not the car he saw on his tail."

"Daylesford could use a different car every day if he wanted."

"That's right."

"So they could be going after him once they're done with Powell."

"Possibly."

I realized I'd been holding my unopened burger all this time. I peeled the wrapper back and bit into it. As I chewed, I felt the heat build in my mouth. For a second, I thought Jack might have pulled a prank on me by ordering the hottest grade, but the heat peaked at a level that I could cope with. Or so I thought. Suddenly, I had to exhale some air fast to cool my mouth down.

"Hell, what level is this?" I said as I breathed with an open mouth.

Jack laughed. "That's the hot, one above medium. I couldn't let you off too easy."

I tried to chew and breathe at the same time, my face covered in beads of sweat.

"No, I'm good," I lied. I saw a water fountain nearby and, to the tune of Jack's laughter, scurried over and drank thirstily. When I returned, I held off on eating and attempted to continue the conversation. "Okay, if we assume that in both cases the suspect is completely innocent, what does that tell you?"

"My guess would be that Daylesford and Cousins actually know who the killer is."

"Yes, and they are doing their utmost to protect them by framing someone else." I shook my head. "The thing is everything I've heard about Cousins is that he's as straight as they come."

"Me too," said Jack. "Just because they are partners as cops doesn't mean they are partners in crime. Daylesford could be operating in the shadows."

"And he could have help in Dean Swindall."

I looked over at the park. These cops were playing a dirty game, I was sure of it. And despite Dean Swindall's performance on the stand, it would be an uphill battle getting the jury to entertain the idea that cops were protecting a double murderer. But Erin Coolidge was not my case. The fate of her and Luke Wells would have to wait until this trial had ended.

"What's next?" I asked Jack.

"I'm going to follow up on a thought I had about Jaden Ross."

"He's going to be on the stand tomorrow. Whatever you are hoping to get, I'll need it today."

Jack stood up and tapped me on the shoulder. "Don't sweat it, boss. I'll have something for you in a few hours. And if it is what I think it is, I think it will come in real handy."

I would have asked Jack to elaborate, but I could see he didn't want to raise my hopes and not deliver, so I kept my mouth shut and my hopes up.

Then I remembered there was something I needed to ask of him.

"Hey, when you're done with Ross, there's something I'd like you to do if you're up for it."

"Sure. You name it and I'll do it. On one condition."

"What's that?"

"You've got to finish that burger."

CHAPTER 36

"Your Honor, I would like to call Jaden Matthew Ross to the stand," said Haviland. This would be his clincher. He no doubt felt he had yet to swing the jury comprehensively in his favor. This, he must have hoped, would do the trick.

Ross had done his very best to look presentable for his court appearance. I actually did a double-take when I laid eyes on him. Not only was he showered and shaved, but he'd also had a haircut and wore a clean-looking sports coat over a pair of beige chinos. Beneath the coat was a light green vest, collared shirt and tie. He came across as a sort of quiet man you'd expect to occupy the same comfortable chair in the library every day to read the newspaper. I wondered how long the image would last, how soon his true nature would reveal itself.

By answering Haviland's opening questions in a quiet, sometimes inaudible voice, Ross appeared meek and mild. He was a drifter of sorts, he admitted. Technically homeless, if not for the van that he'd been living in for more than a decade. Before that he'd been employed as a clerk at the Housing Authority but suffered a breakdown after the death of his mother, with whom he'd lived. After falling behind in the rent, he found himself with nothing but his van. He took it to the coast and proceeded to beg and scrounge for money and fuel.

"Mr. Ross, where were you on the night of Nicola Beauchamp's death?"

"I was in my van."

"Yes, and where was your van parked?"

"Oh, yeah. I see. I had my van up at Point Fermin, the park there."

"Please speak up, Mr. Ross," said Judge Austin. "Big, clear voice, please."

"Yes sir!" said Ross too loudly, prompting him to shrink quickly.

"Somewhere in between would be ideal, Mr. Ross," said Judge Austin.

Ross nodded.

"Mr. Ross, did you see Nicola Beauchamp that night?" asked Haviland.

"I believe I did, sir."

"Please tell the court what you saw."

"Certainly. Well, about an hour before midnight, I got out of the van. I don't sleep too well and I heard thunder coming from over yonder and I thought I might watch the storm come in. I like to do that. It's quite a sight to see, a lot of thunder and lightning over the ocean."

"Did you see anybody in the park while you were admiring the storm?"

"Yes, sir. I saw a woman with two men."

"What were they doing?"

"It wasn't good. The woman was not walking right. At first, I thought she was drunk and they were helping her. You know, getting her some fresh air."

"Did you hear what they were saying?"

"Not a lot, but the wind carried some to me. And I heard her crying."

"What else did you hear?"

"Well, I heard something that sounded like a slap. But I was turned around. I was thinking of getting a blanket from the van because I was cold, so I was turned around when I heard that sound so I don't know what that was but—"

"Okay, Mr. Ross. Can you describe how the men were treating the woman?"

"They were kind of holding her up and marching her toward the wall with force."

"Did you get a good look at these two men?"

"I only got a decent look at one of them. The other guy always had his back to me. I couldn't tell you if he was black or white... I mean—"

"Mr. Ross," Haviland cut in. "The man you did get a look at, is he in this room?"

"Yes, he is."

"Could you point to him, please?"

Ross lifted his right forearm almost vertical then flicked his wrist down to leave his index finger pointing straight at Powell.

"For the record, are you pointing at the defendant Walter Lindsey Powell?"

"Yes, I am," Ross said firmly, looking straight at Powell.

"What else did you see, Mr. Ross?"

"Well, I was feeling a bit unsure about what was happening or what the two men were doing to the woman. I thought they were going to, you know, have their way with her. But I didn't want them to see me or else they might come and beat me up."

I stole a glance at the jury. The faces of each woman morphed into an expression of revulsion.

"I mean I'm not proud to say so—I know I'm a coward—but I thought if the lightning struck while I was standing there, there was every chance they could see me. So I got back into my van as quickly and quietly as I could."

Despite the jury's disgust toward Ross, his words had a ring of truth to them. The fact that he labeled himself a coward only added to his credibility.

I was in no doubt that the jury believed his testimony.

Haviland had every reason to think the case had swung his way.

And I was thinking the same. I hadn't heard back from Jack. That morning, he'd texted me to say he was still busy chasing that lead on Jaden Ross. Well, it was time for my cross-examination, and I readied myself to proceed.

That's when I felt a tap on my shoulder.

CHAPTER 37

"Mr. Madison … Mr. Madison!" Judge Austin bellowed. I looked up to see him looking extremely annoyed at being ignored.

"Yes, Your Honor?"

"Do you wish to cross-examine the witness?"

I stood up.

"Yes, Your Honor. I do."

My mind was racing along several paths at once, but I had to rein it in and focus on the present. The information Jack had just delivered was fantastic, but I wasn't yet sure whether I should introduce it myself or try to extract it out of Ross.

I decided to wing it, to trust myself and allow the benefit of all my experience to kick in. In jazz, you'd call it improvisation. That may sound foolhardy or unprepared but it's anything but; you can't improvise for shit if you don't have a huge bank of experience and skill and the wits to put it all to good effect. I'm no Miles Davis of the law but I'm no kazoo player either. This is what I live for.

Just then I had a moment—something I wished my younger self could see. Here I was standing in the courtroom defending a man charged with murder and feeling like it was my wheelhouse.

"Mr. Ross," I began when I reached the lectern, "everything you have said reflects exactly what is here in your witness statement. Not word for word but close enough."

It was not a question but he felt compelled to answer. "Yes."

"This is your statement here, is it not?" I walked to Ross with Judge Austin's permission and handed him the document.

"Yes."

"Could you please tell the court when you gave this statement to the police?"

"I'm not sure."

"The date is up the top, Mr. Ross."

"Oh, so it is. Ah, it was November the eighteenth."

"Which was two days after Nicola Beauchamp's body was found. Was this the first time you spoke to the police about this incident?"

"Ah, no."

Ross seemed to think this would suffice as an adequate answer.

"I think the court would like to hear more details about your first conversation with the police. Detectives Daylesford and Cousins came to your van on the morning of November the sixteenth, didn't they?"

"Yes."

"And what did they ask you?"

"They asked if I had seen anything suspicious the night before."

"And what did you tell them?"

"I told them I didn't hear or see anything. I told them I was in bed asleep. I told them I didn't like storms."

"Which isn't true, is it, because, as we've heard, you actually stepped outside your van to enjoy the spectacle of the storm that night, didn't you?"

"Yes. Like I told Mr. Haviland."

"Okay but when the police first came to you, you said you saw nothing. Then, two days later, you went and volunteered a different story to the police, the story you're telling us today."

"It's the truth."

"If that's the case, why did you lie to the detectives?"

"Well, first off, I wasn't proud that I did nothing to help the girl. And second, I was scared they might think I had something to do with her death."

"And then, two days later, you had a change of heart, is that right?"

"Yes. I read about the girl and I felt bad that I hadn't said anything about what I saw."

Now it was time to use the information Jack had dug up.

"Mr. Ross, between your conversation with the detectives and your appearance at the police station where you gave your statement, did Officer Dean Swindall pay you a visit?"

"Yes."

"Did Officer Swindall tell you to make a statement?"

"No!"

"It's very convenient, don't you think, Mr. Ross, that your statement damns a man of committing murder, a man that Officer Swindall hates?"

"Objection!" hollered Haviland. "Mr. Madison is testifying!"

"Officer Swindall admitted that to the court," I countered.

"Overruled. Please continue, counselor," Judge Austin said to me.

"Officer Swindall told you to make that statement, didn't he, Mr. Ross?"

"He told me to tell the truth!" yelled Ross with indignation.

"I suppose all he had to do was ask you nicely. Is that so, Mr. Ross?"

"Kind of."

"Kind of. What did he have over you, Mr. Ross? Was it the fact that you were a suspect in a number of sexual assaults reported in the San Pedro area?"

"No!" Ross shouted. "He didn't force me to do anything! And he sure didn't throw me to the ground like you did!"

The courtroom fell silent for a few seconds, Ross's words hanging there for the judge, the jury and the entire gallery to ponder what they meant. I mean there was not much to interpret about the gist of his words but more the veracity of them. This was not something for me to open up for discussion. I needed to close up shop.

"No further questions, Your Honor," I snapped and sat back down.

I was furious with myself. I'd allowed Haviland back in with that last outburst from Ross, but I also expected that Ross was no longer the key to me winning this case. The telling blow I hoped to land was yet to come, a blow that rested on the mission I'd sent Jack on. I hoped like hell he wouldn't return empty-handed.

With court done for the day, I had a quick debrief with Powell, packed up my things and left the courtroom. As I entered the foyer, someone came and stood in front of me. It was Otto Benson. He wasn't looking happy.

"What the hell was that?" he said.

"What are you talking about?" I went to walk past him. He grabbed my arm. "Get your fucking hand off me."

He let go. "Madison, Mr. Ashby sent me. He suggested it was time for the two of you to discuss where the case stands. He would like you to join him for dinner tonight."

"I'm busy. I'm in the middle of a trial and have witnesses to call tomorrow."

"He won't keep you long. The dinner will be downtown, just a few minutes from your office."

"Fine," I said and began to walk toward the elevator.

"The reservation has already been made. 71Above. Seven thirty."

I pressed the elevator button. The door opened almost straight away. Benson moved to follow me. I turned and raised my palm.

"Get the next one."

He gave a cocky half-smile and acquiesced without saying a word.

I lifted my head, watching the numbers count down as I descended. *Soon this will be over,* I told myself. *Soon Rubin Ashby, Walter Powell and Otto Benson will be out of my life.* Roger's advice was starting to make a whole lot of sense. Forget about payback—just take the money and be on your way. Let Ashby and his slimy entourage slink back into the swamp from which they came.

CHAPTER 38

It was seven thirty sharp when I approached Rubin Ashby at his table. Positioned against the window a thousand feet off the ground, 71Above presented diners with a spectacular rotating view of LA. But despite the visual feast on offer, Ashby had his back to the glass. I saw him lift his gaze from his phone when a waiter placed his steak tartare in front of him, the egg yolk a bright orange bulb atop a disk of raw meat. He only noticed me when I got to the chair opposite. By then he had a fork in his hand and the waiter had topped off his glass of red.

"Bradley. I hope you don't mind me eating. I am ravenous. Please, take a seat."

I did as he asked, and the waiter went to lay my napkin in my lap. I waved him off.

"Take a look at the menu. Everything is fabulous," Ashby said through a mouthful. "Here, try this." He took the wine bottle in one hand and my glass in another. "This is a delightful Cabernet Franc. It goes perfectly with the steak tartare."

"I'm not hungry and I've got a pile of work to do tonight. So, can we get down to it? What did you want to discuss?"

He replaced the bottle and glass to their previous positions.

"I thought it appropriate for us to have a run-through on how the trial is going, seeing we are almost at the halfway point."

"I'd say it's evenly balanced at the moment. Ted Haviland has failed to land a telling blow and I have managed, I'm sure, to dilute what he hoped were potent witnesses. But, as you say, we are halfway there and I am not one to count my chickens before they're hatched."

"Are you not concerned that Jaden Ross got the better of you?" he asked before taking a sip of wine.

"He didn't get the better of me."

"From where I sit, first impressions count but last impressions stick. And the last impression of your encounter with Jaden Ross was one of you falling flat on your face."

"That's not how I see it at all."

"I'm not concerned with how you see it, Bradley. You can see it any way you please, but what matters most is the way I see it. I'm paying you to ensure Walter Powell walks free. And as far as I'm concerned, you fucked up." Ashby spun his glass slowly on the table. "You couldn't help yourself, could you?"

A burst of rage erupted in me. I wanted nothing more than to tell Ashby to go to hell and to take Powell along with him.

"Rubin, listen—"

"No. You indulged in your ego in that courtroom and that concerns me a great deal. Now—"

"If you think I'm going to take pointers from you about running this trial you've got another think coming."

"If you'll allow me to finish, I'm not going to tell you how to handle the case. I'm just going to remind you that I won't tolerate you losing. Do you understand?"

I stared at him, silent.

"My mother did everything for me, Bradley. She was a poor woman who did all she could to shield me from hardship. She ate like a mouse while ensuring that my belly was full. She made sunshine in my life when hardship and poverty were grinding her into the ground. She had no money, but she ensured my birthdays were special, made memorable by the modest but wonderful gifts she managed to procure for me. She never got to see me make it in the world. And it pains me deeply to think that I never got the opportunity to repay her."

"Touching story. What's your point?"

"I know how much you want to help your mother. And I know you will not be able to do so properly unless you win this trial. So, we have a goal of mutual benefit."

"I can look after her. All I'm committed to is making sure that you foot the bill."

"Bradley, who do you think you're talking to? Do you think I don't know about your financial troubles? About your landlord trying to extract more and more rent that you cannot afford to pay? That in your desperation to secure your income you went groveling back to CDK? Don't try to pull the wool over my eyes. I know more about you than you can imagine."

Rafferty and Krieger. Of course, they must have enjoyed talking about me with Ashby.

"I don't care what you know, Ashby, but, win or lose, you will repay the money you took from my mother."

"No. I won't. Let me relieve you of that fantasy right now. I'm not what you'd call a gracious loser, you see," he said, digging his fork back into his dish. "If you lose, I will not just take a small pleasure in seeing your mother go uncompensated, but I will ruin you. That landlord of yours, David Thorpe? One word from me and he will double your rent. And if you try to lease an office elsewhere in the city, I will make sure whoever it is you rent from does the same. In no time you will be professionally homeless. Yes, buying office space might be an option but you won't be able to afford it. All you will be able to do is work from home. What a fine way to impress prospective clients." Ashby paused to fix his gaze on me with a rueful smile. "End up on the wrong side of that jury and, make no mistake, you won't be practicing law in this town ever again."

"You conceited bastard."

"And how would that be, to have to leave your daughter behind? And for her to see you scuttle off into the sunset with your skinny little tail between your legs?"

I stood up.

"You know what? After this trial I told myself I was going to let you walk away and let fate deliver you justice. But no, not anymore. I am going to bury you."

"Get Walter free and it's all moot, Bradley."

"No, it's not. I don't trust that you will pay me a cent if I win. And I'm not going to spend months in court trying to sue it out of you."

Ashby and I had a rock-solid cost agreement that meant I was getting paid on a rolling basis while working on Powell's case and in the court, but the final sum, the money that I'd use to clear my mother's debt, was a gentleman's agreement, if you could call a deal with the devil that.

"So, here's what we're going to do," I continued. "Tonight, you're going to transfer two million dollars to an escrow provider along with a boilerplate agreement that I get the money immediately following a not-guilty verdict for Powell."

"That's not necessary."

"If you want me to turn up to court tomorrow, it's necessary."

Ashby pondered the proposition briefly then nodded.

"Fair enough. I'll arrange it tomorrow."

"No. You'll do it tonight. Do it now and send the details through ASAP or I will withdraw myself as Powell's defense attorney first thing in the morning."

"You wouldn't dare."

"You'd be surprised what I'd dare to do. It might pay you to dwell on that a little."

Ashby did pause to think.

"Okay, Bradley. Have it your way. I'm about to see someone who I'm sure is perfectly qualified to make that arrangement."

"See to it that he does so by midnight," I said and walked away.

As I made my way to the elevator, I passed the bar, where I felt eyes upon me. I looked over to see Otto Benson and Harold Krieger. They were both getting off their stools, buttoning their jackets and looking at me with smug grins. It was Krieger who lifted his hand and waved.

"Not staying for dinner I take it, Madison?" he called out.

I punched the elevator button and turned to see the pair walk toward Ashby. He stood as they approached. They shook hands and exchanged jovial greetings. Then, as one, they turned and regarded me with amusement. Krieger muttered something and they all laughed. They were still laughing as I walked into the elevator.

CHAPTER 39

The trial resumed a little after nine the next morning. I got confirmation that the escrow deal had been set up just after eleven the night before. I was now assured that there was no way Ashby could either withhold or stall paying me the money he'd owe me. My head was clear to focus entirely on the trial.

As I made my way to court, my phone buzzed with a message from Jack.

"Got some solid stuff. Proceed with plan."

I was stoked. But before I'd get to see what Jack had found I had to call my first witness: Samantha Boylan.

As we ran through a few introductory questions, Boylan's intelligence and integrity shone. The jury heard how she and Nicola had met at work and had become firm friends. She said that despite Nicola being bright and bubbly on the outside she lacked self-confidence. Boylan said she had introduced Nicola to Walter Powell and that she'd socialized with him often.

"Ms. Boylan, were Nicola and Walter a good couple?"

"I thought so. But not everybody did. Walter, when you first meet him, can come across as a bit stiff, a bit cold even. But I got to know him and he turned out to be quite sweet with Nicola. I thought they would get married."

"But they had their problems, didn't they?"

"Yes, it wasn't all sunshine and rainbows. Nicola did have an issue with depression and Walter was very supportive of her."

"She was getting professional help?"

"Yes, she saw a therapist for a while. But after Walter broke it off with her, she went downhill."

"So much so that she threatened to kill herself?"

"Yes, one time she actually seemed determined to go through with it, and if it wasn't for Walter, she may well have done it."

"Did Walter save her?"

"Yes, he called her while she was at the cliff. He knew something wasn't right and demanded to know where she was. He kept her on the line, talking to her and listening while he got in a car and drove out to meet her. They didn't hang up until he was with her. He took her home and stayed with her until she was able to speak with her therapist."

"Was their break-up the reason she tried to kill herself?"

"Yes, for the most part. She was devastated that they were not together."

"Did she think the break would be temporary?"

"Yes, she held on to the hope that they would get married and settle down."

"And how well did you know Dean Swindall?"

"Not very well. I met him a few times."

"How did Nicola feel about Mr. Swindall?"

"She just didn't want him around. She didn't want him in LA, but she didn't have the heart to say that to his face. So she just treated him nice while trying to keep her distance."

"Was Dean Swindall what you might call a pest?"

"Objection!" called Haviland. "The question calls for a conclusion, and we are not here to listen to Ms. Boylan's opinion."

"Sustained," said Judge Austin.

"I'll rephrase. Did you ever see Nicola become upset by Dean Swindall's behavior?"

"Yes."

"Could you please elaborate for the court?"

"I was at Nicola's place one time and Dean just turned up unexpectedly. He knocked on the door and said something like he was in the neighborhood. It was clearly false but Nicola—she was so sweet—asked him in and offered him a drink."

"And what happened?"

"Dean had one drink and was fine, but then he threw down a few more and became drunk really quickly. And that's when his mood began to turn. Nicola and Walter were still together at the time and Dean started asking questions about Walter. This made Nicola very uncomfortable. But Dean kept on prying. Then he started to criticize Walter and told Nicola that he was a crook and that his boss was a crook and that she should not be associated with either of them in any capacity. He said he was worried about her. But all the while he was being slightly aggressive and I had to ask him to leave. We argued. He did leave but not before venting on her and saying some very mean things about her."

"And how did Nicola feel after that encounter?"

"She was really shaken up. And we both agreed that it wasn't Walter she should be scared of, it was Dean."

"Ms. Boylan, when you heard that Nicola had died, that she was found at the bottom of a cliff, what was your reaction?"

"My first thought was that she had killed herself. But then I thought she had been better and stronger in the weeks before her death. She had started to get her teeth into a serious project, an investigative story about police corruption. And that's when I thought there may be other reasons why she might die."

"Other reasons?"

"Yes. One minute she makes a call to the LAPD about some allegations about corruption and the next minute she's dead."

"Given what you know now, do you think Nicola was murdered?"

"Yes."

"Do you think Walter Powell could have murdered her?"

"No. Never. Walter wasn't perfect but he loved Nicola even after they split up. There's no way he had anything to do with Nicola's death."

"Thank you, Ms. Boylan."

I sat down and watched Haviland rise for his cross-examination. He buttoned his coat and stood at the lectern with his hands behind his back. He seemed oddly light of heart, as though he might be at risk of enjoying himself. I didn't think it would be anything other than a small-minded man's delusion.

"Ms. Boylan, you said Nicola Beauchamp might have had reason to fear Dean Swindall and no reason to fear Walter Powell."

"That's right."

"Well, could you please tell me again the nature of this investigative story Nicola had embarked upon?"

"I wasn't aware of all the details, but she had been given a tip-off about LAPD corruption. She mentioned the Rampart scandal to me and so it was clear that the thrust of her story would be unlawful activity by LAPD officers."

"How can you be so sure if she told you so little?"

"It wasn't just the words she said, it was the way she talked about the Rampart scandal. It was clear to me that she hoped to break a story of that scale; that and the fact that she had written the name and number of Detective Daylesford in her journal."

"Would it surprise you to know that Dean Swindall had given Ms. Beauchamp Detective Daylesford's number?"

"Objection!" I called. "Counsel is testifying. The court has neither seen nor heard any evidence to support Mr. Haviland's assertion."

"Sustained," said Judge Austin.

"Ms. Boylan—" Haviland was set to rephrase his question but Boylan jumped in.

"I'd like to answer that. You bet it would surprise me because I would have thought the last thing Dean Swindall would want would be a public investigation into—how should I put it?—questionable police behavior."

"But we have on record that in the days before Nicola Beauchamp died, the district attorney's office took a call from a woman who said she needed advice on a story she was working on. These calls are recorded and the transcription is here." Haviland held up the document. "Exhibit one-three-nine. The caller mentioned there was a potential police corruption angle to the story."

"Is there a question for the witness, Your Honor?" I asked.

"I'm getting to that, thank you, Mr. Madison. Now, what the court heard from Detective Daylesford was that the woman who called him claiming to be a reporter told him she was looking into a corruption story about how property developers secured land use approvals illegally. Yes, she claimed police were involved, but the evidence suggests the story was primarily about underhanded and unscrupulous businessmen. So, my question to you, Ms. Boylan, is, to your knowledge, was there potential for prominent figures in the property development business to be harmed by Ms. Beauchamp's story?"

"Objection," I called out. "Calls for speculation."

"Sustained," said Judge Austin. "The witness does not have to answer that question."

"Certainly, Your Honor," said Haviland. "Ms. Boylan, did Ms. Beauchamp ever talk to you about the relationship between Walter Powell and his boss Rubin Ashby?"

"Yes, she did."

"Was there anything she disapproved of about their relationship?"

Samantha paused to think before replying. I knew she wanted to be a team player and not give the prosecution anything, but she also wanted to offer what she knew with all honesty. "Yes, she felt that Mr. Ashby drove Walter too hard. She didn't like the way Walter was pretty much on call for Mr. Ashby 24/7. She said it was like Mr. Ashby owned him."

"But, as far as you knew, was the defendant happy or unhappy about this arrangement?"

"He didn't mind at all. He spoke about Mr. Ashby like he was some kind of guru and it was obvious he was willing to do just about anything Mr. Ashby asked of him."

Boylan winced at her words, knowing she had just given Haviland what he wanted.

"Willing to do just about anything asked of him," he said in a ruminating tone. "Interesting."

Haviland stepped to the side of the lectern, moving closer to the jury.

"Ms. Boylan, did Nicola Beauchamp believe Mr. Powell and Mr. Ashby were romantically involved?"

"No."

"Did she ever say she suspected that Walter Powell might be homosexual?"

Powell and I both jumped to our feet in unison.

"Objection!" I said. "It's inflammatory and calls for speculation."

"What is this? That is nothing more than slander!" shouted Powell.

"Mr. Powell!" barked Judge Austin. "Please, sit back down and remain silent. Mr. Madison, please control your client."

I pulled Powell down and talked in his ear.

"Zip it, Walter. We've spoken about this and how there was a chance the prosecutor would try to rile you. Any outburst or act of aggression will resonate with the jury. Take a few breaths. It's going to be okay. We just have to ride this out."

Judge Ashby waited for me to finish my hushed counsel.

"Now, Mr. Haviland—"

"Your Honor, my line of questioning pertains to—"

"Don't interrupt me, counselor. And do not test my patience."

"Yes, Your Honor. I am not seeking to impugn the defendant. I am trying to establish how the victim perceived the relationship between the defendant and his boss."

"Well get to it, post haste."

"Yes, Your Honor. Ms. Boylan, did Nicola Beauchamp believe there was something inappropriate about the relationship between Mr. Ashby and Mr. Powell?"

"Yes."

"Did she feel Mr. Ashby was sexually attracted to the defendant?"

"Yes, she did. But she never thought it was mutual."

"I see. But did she consider Mr. Ashby to be a rival not only for her time but for her affections?"

"Yes."

"Did she blame Mr. Ashby to some extent for her and the defendant splitting up?"

Samantha nodded. "That would be a fair thing to say. Yes."

"Could it be that Mr. Ashby, rather than police officers, was the target of her story?"

"She never said anything like that."

"Did she hate Mr. Ashby?"

"Yes."

"Is it not possible, then, that the danger in her pursuing her story did not lie with the LAPD but somewhere far closer to home?"

"I don't know what you mean."

"I think you do. You said the defendant would do anything for Mr. Ashby. Is it not possible Ms. Beauchamp was silenced before she could do Mr. Ashby damage?"

"Objection! Mr. Haviland, again, is testifying."

"Strike that for the record. Do that again, Mr. Haviland, and there will be serious consequences."

"No more questions, Your Honor."

Haviland returned to his desk looking as satisfied as a well-fed cat in the sun.

It was time to throw a grenade in his lap.

"Your Honor, may we approach the bench?"

Judge Austin nodded and beckoned us forward with a wave of his hand.

"Your Honor, I would like to call a witness who was not initially listed."

"Yes?" Judge Austin raised an eyebrow.

"Actually, I'd like to recall a prosecution witness."

Haviland's face balled up into a scrunch of bafflement.

"A prosecution witness? Your Honor—"

"Who?" Judge Austin cut in.

"Officer Dean Swindall."

Haviland at first looked relieved before suspicion and concern took over.

"And, Your Honor," I continued, "I request permission to treat the witness as hostile."

Judge Austin was emotionless. He waited for an objection from Haviland, but the prosecutor could not summon one.

"Granted," said Judge Austin. "Until tomorrow, gentlemen."

CHAPTER 40

Dean Swindall sat watching me like a rancher eyeing off a pesky coyote. Only this was not a problem he could solve with a bullet. Not here, at any rate. But you get that with subpoenaed witnesses; they're not on the stand of their own free will. And unlike his session with Haviland, Swindall could not see what was coming. And he didn't like it one bit.

"Officer Swindall, I don't want to waste anyone's time, so I'll get straight into it. We have heard already that you have known the defendant for a few years now. You weren't friends, though, were you?"

Swindall sighed, shifted in his seat and tilted his head. "No, we weren't friends."

"In fact, you have a deep dislike for the defendant, don't you?"

"I cared about Nicola and I didn't think he was good for her. And as it turns out, I think I was right."

I'd wanted to give Swindall some leg room to try to bury Powell and I was glad to see him use it. But it was always going to be a fine line as to whether my exchange with Swindall would sway the jury in favor or not. Obviously, I figured it was a risk worth taking. My aim, though, was to achieve a clear advantage. I'd called Swindall in to eliminate whatever indecision there was in the jury's mind about there being reasonable doubt. I wanted to leave them feeling certain that there was reasonable doubt. And with that certainty established, there'd be no way they could consent to a guilty verdict.

"Officer Swindall, you hated Walter Powell because Nicola chose him over you, is that right?"

"We've been over this. Yes, I hated him because I think he's phony and because he hurt Nicola."

"Officer Swindall, did that hatred of the defendant drive you to abuse your position as a police officer?"

"What? What are you talking about?"

"You went and saw Jaden Ross the day after Nicola was found dead, didn't you?"

"Yes, I did."

"Were you assigned to the case?"

"No, but I wanted to help where I could."

"But detectives had already spoken with Mr. Ross and he told them he had seen nothing."

"So?"

"Then you visited Mr. Ross and next thing we know Mr. Ross appears at the station declaring that he had seen two men drag Ms. Beauchamp to the cliff and that one of those men bore more than a strong resemblance to Walter Powell."

"I can't speak for Mr. Ross."

"Really? I beg to differ…"

"Objection! Abusing the witness."

"Sustained. Watch yourself, Mr. Madison."

"Of course, Your Honor. Officer Swindall, you told Jaden Ross to come forward, didn't you?"

"Yes. He said he had not been entirely open with Detectives Daylesford and Cousins."

"Yet he was open with you, is that right?"

"I had a discussion with him and I was able to convince him to tell the police what he saw."

"Officer Swindall, did you do a deal with Mr. Ross to get him to make a statement about Ms. Beauchamp's death?"

"No."

"Did you coerce him to?"

"No."

"You didn't say to him, 'Look, you go tell the police it was Walter Powell you saw that night or I'll make life hell for you'?"

"No."

"Because that's not the kind of cop you are, is that right?"

"Damn straight."

"You would never do anything like that. Because it would be illegal, wouldn't it?"

"Yes."

He didn't like where I was headed.

"You would never abuse your power as a police officer, is that what you're telling us?"

"Yes."

I picked up a document.

"I would like to enter this document into evidence, exhibit two-one-eight," I said, holding three copies up high and giving one to Judge Austin and one to Haviland.

"Your Honor," Haviland whined, "I have not seen this. It can't be admitted now."

"Your Honor, this is new evidence just arrived and I am submitting it at the earliest opportunity."

"Counsel, please approach," said Judge Austin.

After a two-minute pow-wow in which I explained the importance of this new evidence, Judge Austin allowed it to be entered. I then handed a copy to Swindall.

When Swindall saw what was in his hand, his face went white.

"Officer Swindall, could you please tell the court what you are holding?"

"It's a university paper," he said quietly, looking rather agitated.

"That's right. To be more precise it is the PhD thesis written by an anthropology student at the University of Tennessee in Knoxville. The paper addresses the subject of corruption in the Memphis Police Department, of which you were a member before you followed Ms. Beauchamp to Los Angeles. That's right, isn't it?"

"Yes."

"Now, could you turn to page seventeen and read the highlighted text, please?"

"Planting drugs was easy," Swindall began in a low voice.

"Louder please, Officer Swindall," I said. "The jury may not be able to hear you."

Swindall continued reading. "There was an endless supply in the evidence room—cocaine and grass mostly. So, you never had to buy your supply, know what I'm saying? And to get one of these nigger gang members off the streets, all you had to do was pull 'em over and, you know—'Ooh, look here. What's this?'"

Swindall finished reading and sat there expressionless.

"Officer Swindall, could you now turn to page twenty-seven and read the highlighted text, please?"

Swindall began again. "These tough-assed niggers are such pussies when you get them away from their gang. I'd beat the shit out of them until they were as timid as lambs. Do anything you want. Say anything you want. And who they gonna tell? We're the fucking law!"

Again, after he'd finished, Swindall sat there, motionless and ashen-faced.

"Officer Swindall, do you know who made those comments you just read out?"

"No."

"Really? They are completely foreign to you?"

"Yes."

"Now, the research paper does not attribute the quotes to anybody because that interview was conducted under the assurance that the interviewee's name would be withheld in order to encourage complete candor on their part. But when we approached the author of the paper, she gave us the recordings of those interviews."

I had the recordings on my phone and I plugged it into the input of the lectern and hit play. The unmistakable sound of Swindall's voice came over the court speakers, saying the exact words he'd just been asked to read.

"Officer Swindall, that's your voice, is it not?"

He was now irate. "That was given in confidence! It's illegal for you to identify me."

"I'm afraid it's not, Officer Swindall. Judge Austin has ruled that these recordings are admissible. They relate to how you conduct yourself as a police officer."

Swindall's mouth contorted into a bitter twist.

"Officer Swindall, you must appreciate that I am confused. You have told this court you are a good cop, that you play by the rules, that you would never coerce someone like Jaden Ross, but you have confessed in the past to bending the law to suit your needs. Isn't that right?"

"That was years ago, in Tennessee."

"This is not a question of time, Officer Swindall. It is a question of character as laid bare by the facts. I'll ask you again: did you lean on Jaden Ross to get him to fabricate a story that implicated my client in the death of Nicola Beauchamp?"

"That's an outright lie. No, I did not."

"Which part, Officer Swindall? What would you have us believe? Which version of you should the jury believe? The one who speaks about duty here in Los Angeles or the one who boasts about dishonor back in Memphis?"

"Objection!" Haviland cried. "Badgering!"

"Sustained."

"No further questions, Your Honor."

"Do you wish to call any more witnesses, counselor?"

"No, Your Honor. The defense rests."

CHAPTER 41

Judge Austin called a ninety-minute recess before closing arguments began. I returned to the office to run through my presentation with Megan. Throughout the course of the trial, I'd made notes on all the elements I wanted to use in my closing argument and Megan had compiled it into a presentation, complete with photos, graphics and images used in evidence. I'd set myself a target of twenty minutes. That was on the short side, but boredom was my enemy. I had to keep the jury riveted.

"Megan, could you come through?" I said as I arrived at her desk. "We need to get this nailed down."

From the look on her face, I could see something was not right.

"What's up?"

"Jack's in there," she said soberly, tilting her head toward my office. "You'd better go see."

"What's going on?"

"I'm not sure. But he's not happy about something."

Intrigued, I stepped into my office to find Jack standing at the window.

"Great job on the Swindall material, buddy," I said. "That really screwed that dirty son of a bitch. You should have seen—"

"I'm sure you skewered him with it," Jack said with a flat tone to his voice and his gaze still directed out at the view.

"What's eating you, Jack?"

"This case. That's what's eating me."

"What's happened? I thought everything was cool again. I mean I'm still working for those assholes but it's going to be done and dusted soon."

Jack turned around to face me.

"And that's what bugs me about you, Brad. It's just about the case."

"That's because it *is* all about the case."

I didn't want to convey what I aimed to do to Ashby if I lost the case and he didn't pay or carried through on his threats. I'd seen no need to bring Jack into that at all. But I could see him looking at me like he'd just noticed something off about me.

"No, it's about a young woman who was murdered, Brad. And it's about another woman who was probably murdered by the same person. That's two young women, dead. Their families utterly blindsided by a nightmare that is unrelenting and real. Suddenly, through no fault of their own, every second of their lives is a living hell. They can't sleep for imagining what their beautiful girl went through, the utter terror of her final moments, the cold brutality of her life being snuffed out, the thought that some worthless fucking piece of shit wanted her to die and took it upon himself to make sure she did. The people who loved them want to know what the fuck happened to these girls, and they want whoever killed them to be brought to justice. That truth is their only solace and what a fucking meager solace it is. But it's vital to their lives, to their sanity, to their ability to go on living. And it's the one small compensation the justice system can deliver to them. But it won't."

I'd never seen Jack like this before. He looked as if he was the one living the nightmare he'd just described.

"Jack, you know where I stand on all this. And you've been very clear about your position. So, if you want out, fine. If you want to stay, fine. We're pretty much wrapped up here anyway."

"This is what bothers me. You talk about it like you're installing a dishwasher. 'Yep, it'll be done by two.'"

"You're right. Sometimes, I have to think like that. I have to be objective because getting sucked into an emotional wormhole doesn't help me do my job one bit. In fact, it would make my job impossible. I would be useless. I can't win a case on belief or desire. Jesus, do I really have to tell *you* that? But there is a depth of purpose in what I do, Jack. The very least of which is every person's right to a fair trial. I'm a defense attorney. That's what I do."

"And who's Nicola Beauchamp's champion?"

"That would be Ted Haviland."

"What if that was your sister?"

"I wouldn't want Ted Haviland anywhere near the case. Thankfully, I don't have a sister."

Jack was back at the window, his bearing deflated, his gaze fixed on some meaningless point in the distance and his mind somewhere even farther afield.

"Well, I do. At least I did."

He spun away from the window and went to walk past me. I grabbed his arm.

"Jack, hang on, buddy. What's going on? I didn't know you had a sister. I've never heard you talk about her."

Jack shrugged his arm loose of my hand, stepped over to my desk and sat on its edge with his arms planted straight on either side.

"Her name was Nora. She was ten years older than me. My parents thought they couldn't have any more kids after years of trying, so Nora was their only child until my miraculous conception. She was the light of their lives, and mine. Beautiful, fun, smart and bold."

This was new territory for me. I'd known Jack for years. Not only was he my best friend, he'd saved my bacon on several cases, and not only saved my life but the life of my daughter. Personally and professionally, I didn't know where I'd be without Jack. That's why I'd asked Jack to be Bella's godfather. I wanted her to learn from this man, who was everything he said his sister was. Beautiful? Okay, make that handsome.

"Where is she?" I asked.

"We still don't know," said Jack. "When I was ten and she was twenty, she set off to travel the world. She went from Mexico to Central and South America, all the way down the Tierra del Fuego, traveling solo mostly. Got a boat to Africa, up to Europe, and then through Southeast Asia and into Australia. She ended up in Cairns, working in bars and teaching tourists how to scuba dive. When she wasn't diving, she was sailing around tropical islands or swimming on beaches where the jungle came right down to the sand. Then, one day, she just disappeared."

"What? What happened?"

"She had a routine where she'd call home every two weeks. One Sunday, my parents got a call from her. Four days later, the phone rings and it's an Australian cop saying Nora had been reported missing. And that's when our nightmare began. Dad flew out there; Mom had to stay with me. I heard phone call after phone call with Mom crying hysterically. But Nora was gone and gone for good. They found the guy who did it. He'd killed other girls—raped them and then stabbed them, slit their throats. They found the bodies of five of his victims out in the rainforest. He'd take them there to do what he wanted, out where no one could hear them scream, no one there to help, and then he'd go back home until he got the urge and the opportunity to do it again. They tried everything to get him to say where Nora was, but he took pleasure in prolonging Mom and Dad's agony. A year later, he died in his cell. Someone shivved him."

"My God, Jack. I can't imagine…"

"It's almost thirty years ago now, but there's never a day that goes by when Nora doesn't come to mind."

"Is that why you got into this game?" I'd always known that Jack wasn't investigating for the money. Cash he had plenty of and his life was exciting and full; he was a boy's own adventure in full bloom. I never suspected there was even the barest mark of tragedy on his soul.

Jack nodded. "It became the thing that I could do. Something to make sure Nora's killer never got away with it again, if you know what I mean. And then it became doing something just because I believed it was right, which brought me to you. Helping to keep the innocent out of jail or helping to put the guilty in there—I came to see it as two sides of the same coin."

"That's the truth, Jack. And you know you've helped me do that. There are at least six innocent men out there walking free right now who'd be behind bars if not for you."

Jack shook his head. "I know. But this one's different."

"How do you know? How can you possibly know that?"

"Erin Coolidge."

"Erin Coolidge. What about her?"

"Everyone seems to have given up on her, but I've been trying like hell to figure out what happened. In the process, I've spent a lot of time talking with Luke."

"Her boyfriend?"

"Right. Thing is he knows shit about what happened. He arrived home one day, was parking his car when he saw her pull out. Texted her. Got a message back saying she was off to comfort a friend. No sign of her since. He had no idea where she was going or what she was wearing."

"Have you got any leads at all?"

"I started where her car was found and worked outward. It's taken me weeks, but I've spoken to staff at every shop, bar, and restaurant in the vicinity. But you know how it is—those places churn through staff. No one saw her. No one remembered her. Then finally I got something."

"What?"

"A cafe three hundred yards from her car. The manager called me. When I first visited, he said his CCTV vision had been scrubbed. Then one of his staff, who got back from spending the winter waiting tables in Aspen, checked her diary and noted friends of hers had shot a student film at the burger joint next door on November sixteenth. They'd asked her to be an extra and so she went there for a couple of hours before her shift started."

"Did she see Erin?"

"No, but she got a hold of the crew members and got me access to the footage. And that's where I found this."

Jack had his phone out and was flipping through it as he spoke. He stood up from the desk to show me and hit play. The video showed two actors talking over Cokes and fries.

"I don't see…"

"There," said Jack and he hit pause, holding still the image of a woman walking by in the background who'd turned to check out the actors. "That's Erin Coolidge."

"Are you sure?"

He tapped through to her photo then switched between the frame and the photo.

"I showed this to Luke this morning. And he's positive it's her. But wait."

Jack closed the clip and searched for another.

"This is from the B-roll they shot. You know, the footage they splice into the main drama."

Jack found what he wanted and hit play. The vision was an elevated shot of the street outside the cafe.

"There's Erin," said Jack, pointing at a figure in the distance.

"You sure?" It was hard to make her out exactly.

"Same outfit. Time code fits. Definitely her. No question."

Jack hit play again; Erin Coolidge turned around and then embraced a tall man, kissing him on the neck.

"Who's the guy?"

"That's the sixty-four-thousand-dollar question. But to me it looks an awful lot like Walter Powell."

"How can you tell? You can't see his face. He's wearing a cap. You can't even see his hair color. All you've got is his build—tall and broad-shouldered."

"That's right."

"What are we looking at here?" I wondered aloud. "Erin Coolidge in the arms of her lover, her friend, or her killer?"

Jack frowned. "Maybe it's all three. Maybe Walter Powell was all three."

I sucked in some air. "Look, right now there's no way to ascertain who that guy is. I doubt it's Powell, but I can't say it's not possible." I looked at my watch. I was running out of time to prepare. "Jack, I'm about to deliver a closing argument that I hope will persuade the jury to exonerate Walter Powell."

"I know that."

"And I couldn't have done that without you."

"That's my point. If he walks, it's in no small part thanks to me. I'd be proud of that if I believed he was innocent."

"But you don't think he is?"

"No."

"Do you have evidence that he's guilty?"

"Nothing rock solid. But it stands to reason that whoever killed Nicola Beauchamp killed Erin Coolidge."

"Yes. And who had the motivation to do that? To kill both of them? The cops. You know what kind of cop Swindall is. You know Daylesford's reputation. If Nicola Beauchamp went ahead with her story, who knows, maybe both these guys would be exposed in yet another LAPD corruption scandal. We only have Daylesford saying the thrust of the story was criminal property developers, but he would say that, wouldn't he? Jack, you've been around long enough to know that the boot fits."

"You think they did it?"

"I'm not certain but I think it's highly likely. They had the motive and they had the means to make it look like a suicide. And then maybe Swindall adds an extra layer by leaning on

Jaden Ross to point the finger at Powell. This is LA, man. This sort of shit's been going on forever. When I was in Afghanistan, everyone saw the cops as being criminals in uniform. And plenty were: they ran drugs, kidnapped people, terrorized ordinary Afghans. And I tell you we're kidding ourselves if we think we are far removed from that here.

"Jesus, how many videos have we seen where a cop pulls out a gun and shoots an unarmed man dead? Shoots him in the back like a fucking animal. And they get away with this shit. And Dean Swindall, I guarantee you, is that kind of cop. He's confessed to planting evidence in Memphis. So that all stops now that he's in LA?

"And what about the bracelet? Are you okay with such sloppy handling of evidence or do you believe they stole that bracelet from Powell's bedroom and planted it at the scene? It's either sloppy or it's a setup."

"Doesn't mean that Swindall killed Nicola Beauchamp."

"Well, the prosecution has had its chance to prove Walter Powell did."

"Do you believe he is innocent?"

I paused before speaking. "What I believe doesn't matter, Jack. You know that."

"But I want to know what you believe."

"The truth is I don't believe one hundred percent that he's innocent. I don't like him. But my job has been to test the case against him to the best of my ability. Because you know what? I may not like him, but the bottom line is I'm not going to stand by and let an innocent man go to prison."

"Well, I swore on Nora's grave that I'd never help a guilty man walk."

"Jack, you can't always know. Sometimes we just never get the whole truth."

"Well, I'm not stopping."

"What do you mean?"

"I'm going to find out the truth, even if you have no need for it."

"Come on, Jack. Don't be like that. You know my job. I can't afford to let conscience be my guide on every client. I'm duty bound to ensure my client gets a fair trial."

"Yeah, of course. And that's how you get yourself to sleep."

"That's not fair, man."

"Well, I want to be able to sleep with a clear conscience when my head hits the pillow. I don't believe in God or anyone else for that matter making a judgment on my soul. I'm the judge."

"You won't accept the decision of a fair jury?"

"That's not enough for me." He put out his hand. I shook it on reflex, not knowing what he was going to say. "This is where you and I go our separate ways."

I dropped my hand. "Jack, come on."

"No, man. I don't need this shit. I don't need the money. I need to believe. We're done."

He marched out the door.

I contemplated us never working together again and the thought saddened me. But I had a closing argument to prepare, and I'd just about run out of time.

CHAPTER 42

The foyer outside the courtroom was crammed with people and press waiting to get in. I pushed through the crowd, still rehearsing my closing argument in my mind. Even the flashes that went off in my face could not derail my concentration. Since Jack had stormed out of my office, I'd surveyed the presentation Megan had prepared and proceeded to use every minute to get my thoughts in order.

"Counselors, are you ready to proceed with closing arguments?" asked Judge Austin.

After we both answered in the affirmative, Judge Austin addressed Haviland.

"Mr. Haviland, please begin."

Haviland got to his feet with some papers still in his hand. He bent over the table to place them there and tapped the pages into neat alignment before stepping up to the lectern. You didn't have to be a psychic to tell he was nervous.

"Ladies and gentlemen of the jury," he said, "sitting through this trial, you have been asked to consider whether Nicola Beauchamp was killed by the defendant sitting there—Walter Powell. And when you look at the evidence, when you look at the undeniable facts of this case, there is only one conclusion you can draw: Walter Powell, driven by blind loyalty to his boss, murdered Nicola Beauchamp.

"Evidence speaks very plainly. Very directly. And that's what it tells us: that Walter Powell murdered Nicola Beauchamp.

"On the night of November fifteenth, a man by the name of Jaden Ross is out getting some fresh air when he hears raised voices. It sounds like an argument. He then sees two men roughly leading a woman toward the cliffs off Point Fermin Park. The spectacle terrifies him. He is in no doubt that the poor woman's life is in danger. He is in no doubt that those two men intend to do her harm. Scared that the men might do *him* harm if they see him watching, he saves himself by retreating into his van. But I must remind you of this: you are not here to judge the moral fiber of Mr. Ross. You are here to decide whether the evidence convinces you that Walter Powell killed Nicola Beauchamp.

"Before Mr. Ross withdrew, he got a good look at one of those men. And he swears one of them was the defendant Walter Powell. And while Mr. Ross was safely back inside his van, Walter Powell threw Nicola Beauchamp off a cliff.

"We have sightings of the very distinctive car that Walter Powell drives his boss around in—a two-tone Maybach—at the scene of the crime.

"Then we have Walter Powell's bracelet. Ripped from his wrist and found at the bottom of the cliff near the body of Nicola Beauchamp. While the defense has invented a conspiracy theory to water down the strength of this bracelet as evidence, they failed. Yes, the bracelet was not turned in immediately. That's what's called oversight, made by a dedicated officer of the law who had hundreds of details to attend to as he carried out a thorough investigation into the callous murder of a beautiful young woman.

"You cannot diminish the significance of that bracelet, members of the jury. Please do not allow yourselves to be distracted by conspiracy theories. Before she died, Nicola Beauchamp clutched at something, at someone, to save her from her terrible fate, and all she could get hold of was the bracelet of her killer. Let me state it plainly: Walter Powell's bracelet was found at the bottom of that cliff.

"Members of the jury, you cannot save Nicola Beauchamp, but you can see to it that there is justice for her murder. You can take what she has given you—what she is telling you—as fact: it was Walter Powell who threw her off that cliff.

"There has been some debate as to why Walter Powell would murder his ex-girlfriend and do it in such a heartless, horrific way.

"You have heard that nothing came second to Walter Powell's devotion to his boss Rubin Ashby. You have heard that Nicola felt that Rubin Ashby was to blame for breaking up her relationship with Walter Powell.

"You have heard that she was given a tip by Walter Powell, a tip that would direct her to target the LAPD. But Nicola did not do that. She took that tip and sought to target Powell's beloved boss.

"You have heard that Walter Powell would do anything for Mr. Ashby. You have heard that Walter Powell regarded Mr. Ashby as a mentor who was showing him the pathway to riches.

"Nicola Beauchamp had the courage to pursue the truth, and it made an enemy of her former boyfriend. As far as Walter Powell was concerned, she had crossed the line. She was threatening to disgrace his Svengali, Rubin Ashby. She was intent on exposing the underhanded, criminal practices of property tycoons in Los Angeles. And Walter Powell simply could not allow that. He lured her under the guise of friendship, drugged her into a defenseless state and, with the help of an accomplice, threw her over a cliff.

"He took her to the place where she'd tried to kill herself before. And he hoped her death would be treated as a suicide.

"We cannot imagine the horror of Nicola Beauchamp's last moments. What must she have been thinking, betrayed by this man she had once loved, someone she considered to be her soul mate, someone she wanted to have as her husband? And how does he repay that adulation, that love that Nicola could not help but profess or display? How does he deal with the affection he no longer wanted? His actions could not be any more heartless or cruel.

"He eradicated her. He obliterated her as a threat to his esteemed boss. He expunged her from his life once and for all. Tossed her over a cliff like trash. He took everything from Nicola, everything that people adored about her—her love, her respect, her dignity and her very life."

The sounds of women in distress rose from behind me. Haviland had succeeded in transporting the courtroom into a vivid scenario. He'd made the terror real. There was not a soul there who did not have an imaginary outstretched hand in the vain hope of saving her. It was torture for Nicola Beauchamp's loved ones, but I could tell that the jury members were all jolted by the power of Haviland's words. It was going to be extremely hard for them to refuse his appeal.

"Now," he continued, "you must see to it that Walter Powell pays for this vile crime and that he pays dearly."

Haviland returned to his seat.

I hadn't underestimated Ted Haviland but I sure as hell never expected him to deliver a closing argument of such power and potency.

There was no doubt about it: to have any chance of winning, I had to swing for the fences. If I missed, I was done, in more ways than one.

CHAPTER 43

It took a few seconds for me to bring my presentation up on the monitor using the lectern's controls. Once in place, I turned to the jury. For the first time, I sensed a remoteness in them. Haviland had pulled them his way.

"Members of the jury, no doubt you have heard the expression that someone is being selective with the facts. That's when you cherry-pick elements of what you know to be true and present them in such a compelling way—and here's the important part—that they appear to convey the whole truth. What you heard from the prosecution was exactly that: a story that used only the parts he wanted to use.

"And I am not better than he is. That's not what I'm saying. What I will say is this: Mr. Haviland left out all the truths that conflicted or detracted or diluted the picture of truth he presented.

"What I would like to do is cover the facts that, if left to the prosecution, would never enter into your deliberations. They would never illuminate your reasoning. They would never give you pause to think twice. They could never compel you to entertain an element of doubt.

"If there's one thing the prosecution and I can agree on, it's that the death of Nicola Beauchamp was tragic.

"But did Walter Powell kill her? No, and I'll tell you why.

"First, let's look at the facts of the relationship between Walter and Nicola. She thought he was the one. He wasn't ready to commit. Or he just wasn't sure. But is there any evidence that he treated her cruelly? No, to the contrary. Everything that we have heard from firsthand witnesses tells us that Walter never cast her aside, even though they had broken up. He remained her friend. He treated her kindly and with respect.

"Who did Nicola call when she wanted to end it all after the break-up? Walter Powell. Who raced to her side, took her home and took care of her? Walter Powell.

"And consider this fact: considerable effort has gone into making Walter Powell out to be a killer. You have seen a witness here in court admit he had a change of heart prompted by a police officer whose character can be described as questionable and who bears Walter Powell the deepest of grudges. One day Jaden Ross says he saw nothing; the next, he says he saw two men leading Nicola Beauchamp to the cliff and one of them was Walter Powell. He couldn't tell you a thing about what the other man looked like.

"Do not allow yourselves to be fooled by this sloppy charade. This was a ruse contrived by Officer Dean Swindall, who believes that a badge allows him to be a law unto himself. He has admitted to planting evidence and other crimes. But his jealousy of Walter Powell drove him to seize the opportunity to pin the blame on his rival—the man who stole the love of his life away from him.

"The prosecution labored on about Walter Powell's bracelet. And as you heard, this bracelet was not submitted with all the other evidence found at the crime scene. Did Detective Daylesford forget to submit any other piece of evidence the day they found Nicola's body? No. Every single piece of evidence found at the crime scene was gathered, itemized, labeled and bagged in a very methodical way. You heard Detective Daylesford; if they are not absolutely diligent in following this process, they could wreck the case. But then we hear that Detective Daylesford found a bracelet that he'd bagged and labeled but had neglected to submit.

"Was there any other piece of evidence that he forgot to submit? No. Just the bracelet.

"And what happened between that initial investigation of the crime scene and Detective Daylesford handing in the bracelet? He and Detective Cousins visited Walter Powell. And while Detective Cousins interviewed Walter Powell, Detective Daylesford excused himself and didn't return for fifteen minutes. Then Detective Daylesford sent the bracelet to forensics.

"Those are the facts the prosecution would have you overlook, members of the jury.

"But there are some serious questions you must consider:

"How can you be sure Jaden Ross was telling the truth when he himself admits he lied to the detectives?

"How can you be sure Officer Dean Swindall was telling the truth when he has been exposed as a flagrant abuser of the privilege and power his police badge affords?

"How can you be sure Detective Daylesford made an innocent mistake when neglecting to hand in at the earliest opportunity the bracelet he told us he found at the crime scene?

"And when you think about Walter Powell, please ask yourself what reason did he have to kill Nicola Beauchamp? The prosecution did not give you a factual motive. The prosecution strung bits and pieces together to come up with something that sounded like a motive. They have no proof whatsoever that, for one, Nicola Beauchamp was about to expose Walter Powell's boss Rubin Ashby. There is no proof for this, only conjecture.

"Please think hard about these questions when you deliberate on your verdict.

"But you cannot convict Walter Powell on the questionable evidence that has been submitted to you. The story that the prosecution has constructed to try to explain what happened simply does not hold water.

"When you sift through the prosecution's case, you will see that it is not strong, even though they declare it to be strong. You will see that it is not right, even though they demand that you accept it as being right. You will see that they have got it dead wrong.

"You must find Walter Powell innocent. You must send a message to the LAPD and to the DA's office: they need to do better, much better. We don't throw innocent people in jail just because they tell us to. We don't ruin a young man's life because a police officer hates him. We don't stand by and allow a member of the public to be made into a murderer.

"No, let's apply our powers of reason, our strength of logic and our sense of justice here. Let Walter Powell get on with his life. He is not guilty and you should not send him back to a jail cell. If there is to be justice, then he should be as free to walk out of this courtroom as me and you are. Only you can do that.

That is the right decision. And I know that you will find it to be the right decision as well."

CHAPTER 44

Three hours after deliberations began, I was informed that the jury had reached a verdict. I made my way hastily to court, thinking the decision had come much sooner than I'd expected. It was impossible to think that the speed of the decision augured well for a not guilty verdict without considering the counterargument: that it was a promising sign for Haviland.

I've learned from past experience that it's unwise to try to convince yourself and others that you can read the jury's mind. Hope for the best, prepare for the worst; that's essentially what I'd told Powell, along with the contingencies that might follow a guilty verdict, such as an appeal.

As I walked down to the county courthouse, Jessica called.

"Which way is it going to go?" I asked. If there was anyone who had the early word on the verdict it was Jessica.

"How should I know?"

"Come on. You've got every security guard on jury detail wrapped around your little finger."

"Well, I'm hearing nothing. But it wouldn't surprise me if it went Ted's way. He closed beautifully."

"Thanks for the vote of confidence."

"You don't need me to blow your trumpet, Brad Madison."

"Says who?"

Jessica laughed.

"I see what you did there," she said. "I'm heading away for a few days. How about we catch up when I get back?"

"You're on. Where are you off to?"

"Washington, with a layover in New York to catch up with some friends."

"Washington? Business or pleasure?"

"Bit of both. But there might be a job going."

"Really?" The thought of Jessica leaving LA didn't thrill me. "What's the job?"

"Can't say. And nor can you."

"I don't know anything."

"You know too much already. No one knows I'm considering making a change."

"Who am I going to tell? Ted Haviland? He'll be thrilled—if he wins this case he'll be after your job anyway."

"Shut up. That's not even funny. Ted would be about tenth in line."

"Well, good luck." There was a slight pause where I thought about saying something like, "But I hope you don't get it." But I didn't, and the pause was long enough for me to think she'd have liked me to.

"Same to you. See you when I get back, handsome."

I was surprised Haviland wasn't in court and seated before I got there. After a few minutes, Powell was brought in. As usual he was impassive and impossible to read. Anyone in his position who wasn't sick with nerves was simply not normal, so I had to assume that beneath the stony exterior he was a wreck. When he sat down next to me, I noticed his brow was beaded with sweat.

"How are you holding up?" I asked.

My query was met with something that resembled curiosity.

"I can't wait to get out of these clothes. And then go to a nice Italian restaurant. Carpaccio and some vino rosso, that's what I want."

I winced and he smiled awkwardly, as though he wasn't surprised that his oddly timed stab at humor had struck a bum note.

"You know, I'm glad to see you hoping for the best, Walter, but the worst is not off the table. I'd advise you not to get too far ahead of yourself."

"Wowser."

I had to wonder if this behavior was how Powell was dealing with peak anxiety. Knowing that you're about to hear whether or not you'll spend the rest of your life in prison messes with your head heavily. There's no telling how the associated mindgames affect a defendant's behavior.

A moment later, Judge Austin appeared. He tended to a few matters before calling for the jury to be brought in.

He greeted the jury and then addressed the foreperson, Mr. Paul Nedimyer.

"Mr. Nedimyer, has the jury reached a verdict?"

"We have, Your Honor."

"Okay then. Mr. Powell, could you please stand and face the jury?"

Powell and I got to our feet and turned right.

In the seconds it took for these formalities to take place, I noticed with regret that I had misgivings about everything. Yes, as a defense attorney who takes pride in my work, I wanted to win. Yes, as a professional adversary whose goal it is to beat the opposition, I wanted to win. Yes, as a lawyer who believed the state had not proved its case beyond reasonable doubt, I wanted to win. And yes, as a son hoping to get his mother out of a deep financial hole, I wanted to win.

But did I feel a deep-rooted need to see Walter Powell walk free? No.

I just noticed, with a degree of sadness, that I was the least invested that I had ever been in the outcome of a trial. In some sense, I'd disowned it. When I thought of Walter Powell and Rubin Ashby—the type of people they were—I was reminded of that lunch I had with Jim Rafferty a few months back and how it was clear then that, despite the noble ambitions of youth, being a defense attorney didn't give me the moral high ground over a corporate lawyer like Rafferty. Earlier in my career, I was convinced I was better. Standing beside Walter Powell, I knew I wasn't.

Is it time to get out of this LA law game?

Look at Jessica. She may soon be working in Washington. Doing what, I wonder. Does it matter? It would have to beat this.

I envied Jessica for her initiative and the opportunity it might deliver.

"Let's hear it, Mr. Nedimyer," said Judge Austin.

"The Superior Court of California, County of Los Angeles, in the matter of the people of the state of California versus Walter Lindsey Powell, case number zero-seven-zero-three-one-six, we the jury find the defendant Walter Lindsay Powell not guilty."

There were no cheers from the gallery in response, just a restless hum. Powell's supporters had shown mannered restraint. I turned and gave him a quick smile. He lifted his chin up and I couldn't tell you what he was feeling. There was a trace of a smile but I couldn't be sure. He just looked smug.

I could hear a young woman sobbing behind me.

Mr. Nedimyer completed reading the verdict and then double-checked with each juror that that's what they'd agreed to.

After that, I turned to face Powell. He didn't look like he needed to hug it out and that suited me fine. I put my hand on his shoulder.

"Well, Walter, I guess you can make that reservation. You'll be eating Italian tonight."

Powell nodded.

"Do I just walk out of here?"

"No, you have to be processed first. I'll be meeting you again downstairs."

"I'm a free man. Not guilty. Why do they need me to do their paperwork?"

"It won't take long, Walter."

Powell just stood there looking at me.

"Normally, at this point, I'd get a thank you," I said.

Powell continued to regard me with this cold, constrained, asexual weirdness and said nothing. It was like he was surprised to be picked up on a basic courtesy and a bit annoyed that I'd done so. He went to say something then changed his mind to settle on, "Thanks, Brad."

He said this with a deliberateness that almost rendered it sarcastic.

"I mean it," he said. "I'm just glad it's over."

I felt a body press past me from behind. It was Otto Benson moving toward Powell for a hug. I bent over the table and began packing my briefcase.

I felt a hand grip my right shoulder. I turned around to find Rubin Ashby standing beside me.

"Bradley, congratulations. You did a marvelous job. I can't thank you enough."

Despite my fundamental detachment from the case, I was pleased to feel an indistinct relief about winning. It just felt good to win. Looking at Ashby's beaming, shiny face, the anger and loathing I held for him subsided somewhat. I gave him a polite smile and shook his hand.

"Thank you, Rubin. If you don't mind me saying, I'm looking forward to seeing the back of you."

"I understand. But I have one more request to make of you. I want you to join us tonight for a celebration."

"I'm sorry. I can't."

"Bradley. Please. Just for tonight, can we put aside our differences and celebrate that our team has won? And it's all thanks to you. We can't have our Super Bowl victory celebration without our quarterback, can we?"

I was shaking my head.

"Bradley. Please. Listen. There is something I want to give you. Something extra to show you I am not all stick and no carrot. But I want to give it to you personally."

"I'll think about it."

"Good. I'll get the details to you."

With that Ashby turned and hugged Powell, holding him close.

After Ashby moved past me, I looked over the gallery. I was surprised to see Jack making his way out, looking rather glum.

I got my things and went the same way.

Outside the courtroom, Detective Cousins was waiting for me.

"I don't like being proved wrong, Madison. But I guess I just have to accept that we had the wrong guy."

"Well, I hope you find the right guy. Shouldn't you be going after Swindall? Or Ross? That's who I'd be looking at. But who am I to tell you your job?"

"That *is* your job, isn't it?"

I laughed. "Yes, I suppose it is. To be honest, Detective Cousins, and for what it's worth, I believe you're both a good man and a good cop. The real McCoy."

He smiled and shook my hand.

"So long, Madison."

CHAPTER 45

The celebration party was held at the back of the Parlour Room, a vintage-styled cocktail bar in Hollywood. There were about thirty people milling around. I wanted to be in and out, deal with Ashby then get the hell away from these people once and for all.

The escrow money had been transferred and I'd called my mom to tell her the debt was as good as gone. It was nice to hear the relief in her voice.

As I made my way into the party, Otto Benson stepped in front of me. I hardly recognized him for the fact he was smiling.

"Brad, come on in. So glad you made it." He was drunk. "We are all very grateful to you for helping Walter. *I'm* truly grateful. You don't know how much it means to me to see Walter free."

Scanning the room, I could see most of the guests were drunk.

"You need a drink," said Benson. "We came straight here from the courthouse."

He reached over to a nearby table, pulled a bottle of Moet from an ice bucket and poured me a glass. He beamed as he raised a toast. "To our hero."

"Where's Ashby?" I asked after a sip.

"He wanted me to bring you straight over. This way."

I followed Benson through the crowd.

Ashby was seated on a large lush green velour lounge.

"Here he is. The man of the hour," he declared as I approached. He remained seated and waved out the people sitting next to him. "Please, let him in. And give us some space."

The lounge was emptied and I took a seat as Ashby moved around so we sat next to each other facing out toward the bar. As I looked out, I caught sight of Mitch. We didn't make eye contact and I looked away.

"What is it you wanted to do in person?" I asked. "As much as it's been fun in some ways, you and your crew aren't really my crowd."

"I understand. And I know I have upset you, and I don't assume you care to hear why I behave as I do. But you know that I rose from poverty. But risen is too passive a word. I've had to wage war to get where I am. I know that as a distinguished veteran, you might shudder at me using the war analogy. Let's just say that I've had to fight like hell to get where I am. I learned quickly, I learned young, that being liked by other people was never an asset. Wanting to be liked is a weakness that will be exploited as sure as night follows day. So, I decided I would never expose a single weak link to my rivals and opponents. I became hard, ruthless, heartless even. And I decided I would not attempt to hide it.

"You seem to be liked by your entourage," I said.

"Look up to me? Yes. Want to emulate me? Yes. Want to feed off me? Yes. But I wouldn't say they like me. Maybe some do but like I said, I'm immune to sentimentality."

"I get it. You're an asshole and make no apologies for it."

Ashby laughed. It was the first time I heard him laugh. "You've got that right," he said. "Now, Bradley, I'm guessing you think you've done okay out of this case, although I know we've had our moments."

"You mean your threats to harm me and my family?"

Ashby's face seemed to soften, though it was hard to be sure.

"I'll never apologize for my behavior, Bradley. I do everything I can to get what I want. And after your performance with that Ross character, I wasn't sure you were going to pull this off."

"There are no guarantees in a trial, and I never promise what I can't deliver."

"But you did deliver. Now, I told you that I have something for you. And I want to tell you that this is a gift to show that there are no hard feelings on my side. I know that you will gladly sever ties with me and Walter, but I wanted to give you a tip."

"What? That if given a choice between equity and cash, take the cash?"

Ashby laughed. "No, I got you one of these."

He pulled out his phone and showed me an image. It was of a smart modern kitchen with a balcony and a view.

"You bought me a kettle?"

"No." He flicked to another image. It was a floor plan. "This is a three-bedroom apartment in the heart of Santa Monica. *Your* three-bedroom apartment."

"What are you talking about?"

Ashby pulled some paperwork out of his coat pocket.

"This is the purchase agreement for number six one zero, one of the best condos in my Silicon Beach Plaza complex. It's not built yet, but in a year's time you could be calling this home. Move in, rent it out, sell it, save it for your daughter ... it's entirely up to you. You can do with it whatever you please. Whatever, this contract makes you Silicon Beach Plaza's first off-plan owner."

I was lost for words. It didn't seem right. I thought of how we'd heard about dirty cops getting apartments in return for their dirty deeds—leaning on council members to get land-use restrictions lifted.

"To be honest, I'd rather just get paid in money."

"This is better than money. This apartment cost one-point-three million. By the time you get the keys, it will have increased by fifteen percent minimum. This is my business, Brad. I don't just deal in cash, I deal in assets and as far as I'm concerned you have earned this as a reward—if not that, just take it as a symbol of both my deep gratitude and esteem. Walter means a great deal to me."

"I get that." I reached for the paperwork and flipped through it. "This is a hell of a tip."

Another bottle was brought to the table and after downing more champagne, I excused myself to visit the bathroom.

On my way back, I saw Powell sitting alone by the fire. He beckoned me over. He didn't look overjoyed but I guess that shouldn't have surprised me. Not for the first time, I wondered what on earth Nicola Beauchamp saw in him.

I figured that this could well be my last conversation with Powell, and I was curious to see if he'd reveal another side to me that I hadn't been privy to.

"Where's everyone gone?" I asked.

"We're all heading back to Rubin's house. He's organized a lavish dinner. His chef has prepared an Italian banquet."

"You don't seem as excited as you should be."

"Don't judge a book by its cover."

"You never seem to let your emotions show, Walter. You are without a doubt the most reserved person I have ever met. And you should count yourself very lucky because that verdict could have gone either way."

"But it didn't."

"No, it didn't but it could have. And you never seemed prepared to accept that."

"That's because I believed in myself."

"Well, good for you."

"And I believed in you, Mr. Madison."

"Thankfully it turned out well."

"Did you believe me?" he asked suddenly, again holding me with that cold-eyed stare.

"Believing you isn't my job."

"Do you think I did it?" he asked, spacing out the words. His mouth rose at the corner, an attempt at charm that just looked like a smirk. I didn't answer immediately and he didn't move an inch; he just waited passively for a reply.

"I don't know."

He took a sip of champagne.

"Would you feel used if I said I was guilty?"

Although the words jolted me, they were issued from Powell's mouth with the same dry, passionless tone with which he almost always spoke. But then I realized this was no awkward attempt at humor; he was serious.

And now I saw that his half-grin was not a hint of charm. It was the grin of a cold-blooded murderer.

"So, you killed her?"

Powell took in a deep breath and let it out sharply through his nose.

"With all the typing up and paperwork that's left, our contract has not officially expired, so attorney-client privilege still stands. Right?"

"Right."

"Then there's that old double-jeopardy thing. A murder I've just been acquitted of. So, what the hell... Yes, I did it."

He studied my reaction.

My mind was racing through the elements that I'd argued against in court. *Was Jaden Ross actually telling the truth? Was it true that he kept his mouth shut initially for fear of being blamed?* Given Swindall's involvement, it had always struck me as being such a contrived story.

"The bracelet?"

"No one stole it if that's what you're asking. It was the only piece of me Nicola managed to take with her."

"Why?"

"The prosecutor was right. I didn't want Mr. Ashby's name to be dragged through the mud. If I'd allowed that, I'd be killing my career."

"So, Nicola's story was going to target Ashby after all?"

"And others. But mainly Rubin."

"And so you killed her?"

He shrugged. "Well, no one would have been surprised if it was deemed to be a suicide. It's only when Swindall stepped in that they dragged me into the frame. And now I have you to thank for getting me out."

He was enjoying seeing the knowledge seep into my brain that I was now complicit in his crime. I'd helped him get away with murder.

"I'm going to leave before I knock you the fuck out, you psychopathic piece of shit."

I got to my feet.

"Okay. So long, Brad. Thanks for your help."

I marched for the door, hearing nothing, my vision a blur. What I'd just been told turned my blood cold and boiling at once.

I thought of Nicola Beauchamp's parents and what Jack said. They'd been condemned twice now, first by the grief of losing their daughter and then by seeing her killer acquitted.

And I'd helped the man who threw their daughter off a cliff get away with it scot-free.

CHAPTER 46

I was just like everyone else in the downtown dive bar: hiding in plain sight, hoping internal oblivion could somehow erase my presence from society. I drank steadily to hasten the onset of numbness. After four beer and bourbon shot rounds, I eased off and stuck with the whisky.

I kept my eyes on a boxing match being screened on the corner TV and strived to pick up the commentary. I was trying not to think, as though if I listened out for the TV hard enough, I could stifle the commentary running through my head. Of course, it was no use. What I was watching was a good light-heavyweight bout between a Pole and an Aussie, but what I heard was, "You fucking piece of shit," over and over again.

Every now and then I called out at the screen. I didn't know the fighters but they were made for each other. The Pole was taller, had longer reach, and was a tidy boxer with great ring smarts. The Aussie was shorter but broad-shouldered with obvious lead in his fists. The latter was landing the most telling blows, but the Pole kept his score ticking over with regular stiff jabs and crisp one-twos. It was a classic boxer versus puncher fight. The Aussie, his face already bloodied by the fifth, was clearly the underdog, and he lifted the crowd whenever he landed, so it was him I was rooting for.

But no matter how absorbed I was in the fight, it couldn't drown out my thoughts.

Here you are, you fucking loser: divorced, alone and morally bankrupt. Not long ago, you felt grubby for virtually begging Jim Rafferty for a job. You thought you were better than him, and then you go and take a case that was all about the money. Yeah, there was your mom's plight. Yeah, you wanted to be the hero for her and prove what a dipshit your brother was. Now look at you. You've taken a pile of cash and an off-plan apartment from a man you despise.

You knew Powell was guilty. Deep down, you knew. You knew Jack was right. You worked your butt off; you applied all your intelligence and lawyerly smarts to get a guilty man off. How could you do that to her parents? Can you imagine how they must feel? Seeing you in your expensive suit, waxing lyrical about the indisputable existence of doubt, persuading the jury to set her murderer free?

You made a mere game of justice. You made a mockery of it.

And her parents watched you in agony, perhaps wondering what kind of person could defend so eloquently, so artfully, so expertly, so vaingloriously the man who threw their child off a fucking cliff.

Me, that's who.

It's my job.

I can set aside my emotions.

It's the law.

It's the Sixth Amendment.

It's my job.

It's my job.

It's my fucking job.

"Smash him!" I shouted at the screen.

The Aussie had landed a heavy right cross that stunned the Pole, who for a split second remained almost motionless, his knees buckled and shaking, his gloves lowered.

"Take him out!" I shouted. But the Aussie seemed able to do nothing but admire his handiwork. "What are you doing? Go for the kill, man!"

But the moment was lost. Ever the pro, the Pole backed away and recovered.

"Your guy's a moron. What a fucking dope," sneered a drunken stranger to my right.

"He's no moron. He could get another opportunity if he keeps hitting like that."

"He won't. He's a dumb fuckin' chump."

I kept my eyes on the screen, but I could tell by the man's tone that he didn't want to discuss boxing. He wanted to start something. And, you know what, I might have just been into that.

I turned to get a look at him. Three yards away. He was a hefty Samoan who looked like he was taking time out from running with the Hell's Angels. Leather jacket, dirty blue Norton T-shirt, and a heavy chain hanging down his chest. Tatts covered his skin wherever it showed; his hands inked in letters I couldn't read.

"So, the guy who's in the ring fighting for the WBC light-heavyweight title is a chump? As opposed to some deadbeat drunk in a downtown bar?"

He stared at me, stunned that the suit had given him lip.

"What did you say?" he said, sliding off his stool.

I did the same and stepped toward him.

"You heard me, asshole."

With my heart suddenly pumping fast, my senses swung from dullness to aggression. I was glad this was happening, almost grateful to this son of a bitch for giving me the opportunity to properly thrash out my demons. We stopped a foot apart.

Before either of us went beyond the point of no return the barman stepped in between us.

"Fellas, we're going to have none of that kind of shit in here. You hear me? Tiny, go finish your drink and then hit the road. You've been baiting people all night and I'm putting a stop to it."

Tiny didn't move.

"Go get your drink then head on home, Tiny. It's been a long day."

"You better hope you don't see me outside, cocksucker," Tiny said and walked back, swaying, to the bar. He picked up his whisky glass, threw it down, gave me a stare and then made for the door.

The barman stood straight in front of me.

"You on a death wish, stranger? That dude just got out of prison. He's lost out here in the real world, and he's looking for any excuse to go back home. He will fucking kill you, and I'm not even joking."

My tense bearing eased off. I dropped my head and rubbed my eyes.

"I could have—"

"Bullshit. You could *not* have. Not unless you're carrying a knife or a gun. Tiny would fucking stomp your brains into jelly. You look like you use your brain for a living. So, my advice for you is to sit back down, pull your head in and give it thirty before heading home to bed."

I got another drink into me before that time elapsed. It was long enough to see the end of the fight. The Pole won in a unanimous decision. The Aussie had blown it. He'd joined my Team Loser. Tiny was right. What a chump.

The boxer and me both.

The barman called me a cab and went out front to see if Tiny was waiting for me.

"He's gone. When your cab gets here, you just make like David fucking Copperfield and disappear quick, you hear me?"

I nodded.

I left him a hundred. A small price to pay for some timely wisdom.

CHAPTER 47

I woke up in my clothes, rolled over and felt something stiff in my suit jacket. I felt for it and took it out. It was the purchase agreement Ashby had given me.

I unfolded it and looked it over. On the last page, I saw the words "Cooper, Densmore and Krieger" above the signature of Harold Krieger.

Of course, it should have come as no surprise to me that Jim's firm was handling the Silicon Beach Plaza project. It made me feel that Jim and I were actually bedfellows, just two of the many minions who kept the world spinning just the way Rubin Ashby wanted it to.

I wondered whether Ashby knew all along that Powell was guilty. He must have.

I checked my watch; it was just after five thirty. There was no way I was going to get back to sleep. That seedy hangover feeling throughout my body and brain made staying in bed almost unbearable. I got up and jumped in the shower.

My mind began to turn on the person I least wanted to think about: Walter Powell.

If he killed Nicola, I thought, *he probably killed Erin Coolidge too.*

I thought of the B-roll footage Jack showed me.

Was that Powell greeting Erin Coolidge with a big, warm hug?

If so, was he, at that moment, thinking about how and when he was going to kill her?

No, he'd have already hatched a plan.

At that moment, Erin Coolidge didn't know she was about to die, but he did.

It no longer made sense to hang on to the doubt I'd expressed to Jack when he showed me the footage. The only thing that made perfect sense was that Powell killed Erin Coolidge.

These thoughts spun around my head for a few moments. Then suddenly an idea struck me.

In an instant, I became charged, eager to get back on the job. It was too early for the office, so I hit the gym for a good hour before heading into work with some fire in my belly.

I'd realized something.

A damning piece of evidence against Powell might have been sitting under my nose all along.

He may have gotten away with one murder. But he wasn't going to get away with two. Not on my watch.

CHAPTER 48

I was in the office by seven thirty. As I walked from the elevator, my phone pinged and I saw an alert on the home screen. This was nothing unusual because I'd subscribed to every media outlet in LA since taking on the Powell case, wanting to be notified of any story featuring my client or Rubin Ashby. This alert was different though. It was nothing about the case; it was all about Ashby.

The night Roger Russell dropped into my office, he told me to forget about seeking revenge on Ashby. He said Ashby was headed for a fall. Do your job for the man and then walk away, Roger advised. And I promised him I would. Except that I didn't want to just let fate deal with Rubin Ashby. I wanted to make sure that his Costa Rican bribery scandal would be the event that brought down his house of cards.

So I'd picked up the phone that night and called Samantha Boylan and asked whether her paper might be interested in some information on Ashby. Of course, they jumped at it.

I'd given Boylan the tip on one condition: that she couldn't publish her story until Powell's trial had finished. And now, a day after Powell was acquitted, Boylan's story was out.

"Property mogul Rubin Ashby's crooked Costa Rican cash cow," the headline read.

I tapped through to the story.

It was all there and more: the bribery story Roger had told me fleshed out in detail plus a land-sale Ponzi scheme that Boylan had managed to unearth. Hundreds of land-home packages had been sold to US citizens as future retirement homes set in comfortable estates in a tropical paradise, but not one had been built or was ever likely to be.

Boylan located several properties and verified they were lying idle with no sign of building, no development applications filed. They were fraudulent dreams sold with no intention of converting them into brick and mortar reality. She'd also located other land that had been sold despite it being part of a national park.

There were scores of victims—retirees, mostly—who'd handed an Ashby company a hundred-grand deposit and had never heard from its staff again.

These facts alone made this a damning story, but it got worse; Boylan quoted an inside source stating Ashby was out of control.

This source said the property mogul had a "Midas complex" and a "pathological lack of sympathy for the people he hurt." He said, despite taking their money and having no concrete plan to deliver them anything in return, Ashby actually thought he was doing those poor people a favor, "as though just having a relationship with him somehow improved their lives." He said, "The delusion of the man knows no bounds."

Boylan didn't stop there. She uncovered the fact that Ashby siphoned his loot through two shelf companies registered in the Bahamas: Arrogate Enterprises and Zenyatta Securities.

I grabbed a coffee and sat at my desk feeling quietly exhilarated. The truth-telling about this dangerous rogue had begun and I took some pride in giving Boylan the tip-off. In truth, though, I never thought it would be this explosive.

I imagined Ashby's reaction upon seeing the story. He would be apoplectic. I had seen a nicer side to him the previous night at the celebration drinks, but fuck him.

This was my revenge, at last, and it felt good.

This was a man who had not only ripped off hundreds of people, my mother included, he had also lied to protect a murderer. Not for the first time I wondered what Ashby knew about the murder.

Who's to say it wasn't him who declared that Nicola Beauchamp had to die?

Who's to say he didn't order Walter Powell to kill her?

Who's to say Ashby wasn't the one who helped Powell throw the poor girl to her death?

And what of the property he had given me the night before? I felt nothing about it. Yes, it was tainted goods, but I hadn't decided what I was going to do with it yet.

I had to find out who Boylan's source was. Maybe they might be willing to help me expose Erin Coolidge's murderer. I know she was technically still a missing person, but right then I was in no doubt she'd met the same fate as her friend.

Boylan picked up after one ring.

"Hey, Brad."

"Wow. What a powerful story. I would love to be a fly on the wall in Ashby's office right now."

"Well, I would have liked to have gotten it out sooner but a deal's a deal."

"Thanks for holding. But back when I called you, I couldn't even imagine what a spectacular job you'd do. Congratulations."

"Thanks, Brad."

"Is your editor happy?"

"Are you kidding? She's thrilled. She wants follow-ups, of course, but right now I don't have anything."

"Samantha, look, I know this is delicate, but I really need to get in touch with the mole you quoted. I want to help find Erin Coolidge's killer and I think they might be able to help."

There was a noticeable pause that immediately validated the apprehension I had about asking the question.

"Hell, Brad, I can't reveal my sources. To *anybody*. Period. You know that."

"Come on, Samantha. It's not like you're outing them. They may want to help find justice for Erin."

"I can't. Sorry."

"Samantha, who was it who—"

"Don't you dare hold over me the fact that you fed me the story." She was scolding me but in a nice way.

"Okay. Okay. But can you at least give me Erin's number?"

"What for?"

"Never you mind."

"Hang on a minute."

As Boylan searched for the number, I noticed Megan had arrived for work. I watched her through the glass as she set her things down before coming to the door to say hi. I waved and she saw I was on the phone. She hand-signed to ask if I wanted coffee. This would be one from the cafe nearby, not the pot in the office. Hell yes, I said, by way of a vigorous thumbs up. She scooted off.

"Here it is," said Boylan. "You ready?"

"Fire away."

After I got the number, I hung up and went to search the files in the Powell case. I pulled a bunch of thick folders from the cabinet and took them back to my desk.

Before long I had what I wanted.

Earlier that morning, it had occurred to me that if Walter Powell was involved in the murder of Erin Coolidge, a key piece of evidence may have been sitting here in my office. And now I had it in my hands: Walter Powell's phone records.

It took all of ten seconds to confirm what I suspected: the day Erin Coolidge disappeared she received two calls from Powell. One call lasted twelve minutes. The second was just a few seconds.

I compared the time of the second call with the time stamp I'd noted earlier from the B-roll Jack had sourced—the moment Erin Coolidge answered her phone. The times matched perfectly.

I sat for a minute trying to compose a text message I needed to send urgently. I needed Jack's help and so I had to persuade him to rejoin my team. Problem was, I couldn't tell him that he was right. I couldn't tell anybody that Walter Powell had confessed to murdering Nicola Beauchamp. Like Boylan, there was a professional code to which I was bound. I could never violate the confidence of my client. The fact that I hated my client and what he did didn't change the fact that attorney-client privilege was sacrosanct.

I wrote the text: "Jack. I want to find Erin Coolidge's killer. Your instincts were spot on. We need to team up and nail these fuckers."

A few minutes later, I got a message back: "You didn't say please."

"Please. With cherries and shit."

"Starting when?"

"Now. I want you to get on Powell's tail."

"On it."

And while Jack was doing that I was going to see if there was another way I could find out who that mole was.

If Boylan wouldn't tell me, maybe someone else could.

CHAPTER 49

I watched Mitch emerge from the Ashby Realty Corporation building and stride toward my car with haste and slightly hunched shoulders.

"Are you scared to be seen with me?" I asked as soon as he'd gotten in and closed the door.

"Just drive, would you? Ashby's on the fucking warpath and if he sees me with you, he'll start grilling me. That article's got him hyper-paranoid about who's betrayed him. And Otto Benson's running around like a pack hound, sniffing for the slightest hint of disloyalty to feed back to Ashby."

I pulled the car out into light traffic.

"I don't get it. Why would it be a problem to be seen with me?"

"It doesn't have to make sense. The guy's loco and he is out for blood. Any employee who gives him reason to suspect they are informing on him he's going to fire. But not before having Vinnie and the boys break every bone in their body. And that reporter was your witness, wasn't she?"

"Um, yeah."

"Well, there you go. Me, you, reporter; to Ashby, that'd be a no-brainer line of dots to join up."

After a minute or so, when we were well clear of Ashby's office, Mitch eased up. He rubbed his hands on his thighs and looked out the window as he prepared what he wanted to say.

"I hear you sorted Mom out," he said. "Thanks for that."

It wasn't like all my anger toward Mitch had evaporated after Mom had recouped her money. I still thought he was an asshole for getting her involved and doubly so for asking her to cover his own doomed investment. But I had to let it go. I needed Mitch now and I had to keep this exchange on good terms. But it wasn't brotherly love that had gotten us back together. I'd texted him saying I needed his help and that if he came through, I'd make it worth his while.

"I'm just glad it worked out," I said. "But there's something I need from you."

Mitch stretched his legs. "Yeah, you said in your text message. You also said you'd make it worth my while. What does that mean?"

"I'll get to that. What I need to know is who the informer is. Someone in Ashby's inner circle clearly wants to see him taken down. I need to find out who that person is."

"What makes you think I know?"

"You set up Ashby's shelf companies in the Bahamas."

I had my eyes on the road, but I could feel Mitch looking at me.

"What are you talking about? I had nothing—"

"Jesus, Mitch. Don't lie to me! I'm over it! I'm trying to solve a murder here, and I really need your help. What I really need is for you to be totally straight with me. Can you do that?"

"Yeah. Okay. I set them up but that was all. It was a job Benson gave me to do because he knew I'd done something similar when I was involved in a couple of start-ups. You know, to boost credit opps and borrowing power."

"No, I don't know. I have no idea what you're talking about."

"How did you know it was me then?"

"Are you kidding? Arrogate? Zenyatta? Come on, who else but you would name companies after Breeders' Cup Classic winners?"

"Yeah, well. I did pretty well backing those two."

"I don't care. It's not the horses I'm interested in. What I want to know is any thoughts you may have on who in that company would want to see Ashby taken down."

"Well, no one likes him. Apart from Otto, it seems. And Walter."

"Mitch, you read Samantha's story. Who came to mind when you read the comments from the source she found?"

Mitch hesitated.

"Hell, it's a frickin vipers' nest in there. Ashby has gathered round him a bunch of guys who like nothing better than to make a lot of money fast."

"No shit, Sherlock. But this person has to stand to gain from Ashby being taken down. Who would that be?"

Mitch shook his head.

"I really don't know. As far as I know, as long as Ashby wins, everyone wins. I don't see who profits from him losing. I mean it looks to me like this source or mole or whatever just wants to hurt Ashby on a personal level because if he goes down, we all go down."

"Are you sure about that?"

"Bro, there are so many branches of Ashby's business that I know nothing about. I'm sorry, I can't really help you there."

I pulled out an envelope and a pen from my inside coat pocket. "Do me a favor, will you?"

"Yeah?" he said uncertainly as he took the pen and paper.

"Write down all the names of everyone you know who had anything to do with Ashby's Costa Rica projects. Playa Dorada and that other Ponzi land-deal shit he had going. Anyone. Anyone you can think of."

"Why?"

"Mitch, I need you to do this, please. No one will know you gave me the names."

Mitch began to write. After he'd jotted down some names he stopped and held up the envelope.

"Okay, that's it. That's everyone."

"Thank you," I said and went to take the list off him. But he snatched it away.

"You said if I helped you, you would make it worth my while."

Now why didn't this surprise me? I wasn't about to be dicked around by Mitch now. I shot my hand out and took the paper out of his hand and put it back in my pocket.

"You'll get your list back," I said. "And you'll know that you helped bring the person who killed Erin Coolidge to justice."

Mitch was silent for half a minute. I thought he might have been sulking.

"Well, I hope it helps then."

"Have you heard anything at all about her? Has anyone in that company ever mentioned her name or anything that might have had something to do with her disappearance?"

Mitch shook his head.

"Believe me, I've thought about that, but I seriously have heard nothing that I could even vaguely relate to her or what might have happened to her."

I'd driven in a big loop and pulled over on Westwood Boulevard a couple of hundred yards short of Ashby's building.

"I'll let you out here. Thanks, Mitch."

We shook hands. Mitch held on firmly.

"Watch yourself, Bro."

After he got out, I took a photo of the list and sent it to Samantha Boylan. I gave it a few seconds and then I called. She answered straight away.

"Is it anyone on that list?"

"Brad, I can't tell you."

"I'll just read them out and you say yes or no."

"How would that be okay? I can't tell you yes or no. It would be no different to me giving you their name."

"Okay. How about this? Can you just tell me if the name is on the list?"

Boylan paused.

"Is the name not on the list?" I asked.

Silence.

"Are they American or Costa Rican? Come on."

"Why do you need to know?"

"They might help me expose Erin Coolidge's killer."

Boylan breathed in deeply and exhaled audibly.

"Brad, for the last time, I can't tell you. That's all I can say. I'm on a deadline. I've got to go."

"Deadline? A follow-up story on Ashby?"

"Bye Brad."

Damn it. I was back to square one.

I hit the road and headed back to the office. As I pulled up at some lights my phone pinged with a message.

Maybe Boylan has had a change of heart. Maybe she's going to confirm the name.

But it was better than that. Something unexpected and—I don't use the word lightly—astonishing.

It was a message from Jack that contained a photo and a single word: "Bingo."

I stared at the image, processing what it contained and everything it suggested.

"Un-fucking-believable," I muttered. "Son of a bitch."

Quick as I could, I spun the car around and headed back into Westwood.

I had to see Rubin Ashby. Immediately.

CHAPTER 50

I called Ashby after I'd parked and told him I had something urgent to discuss and needed to speak to him alone.

"Now's not a good time, Bradley," he said with a tone that suggested he wasn't sure if I wasn't to blame for the article.

"Now is the best time for you to see me. I promise."

Intrigued, Ashby consented and assured me that we would have complete privacy for our meeting.

When I approached the reception desk, the woman who I'd rudely ignored in the past stepped out from behind the counter.

"Mr. Madison," she said softly, "Mr. Ashby has asked me to show you to his private rooms."

She led me to a single elevator door that stood opposite the ones that accessed Ashby's office. She produced a card that allowed the call button to function and pressed it. When the door opened, she ushered me in. Once I was inside, she used the card again to press the floor button. That done she stepped out.

"Thank you, Mr. Madison."

When the elevator door opened, Ashby was standing there waiting with his feet spread, his arms folded, phone clutched in his left hand and pinching his chin with his right.

"Hello, Bradley," he said and shook my hand and beckoned for me to follow.

He led me to a room fitted with a bar and two leather sofas facing each other over a low glass table. It was a floor higher than his office but had the same view.

"Please, have a seat," he said. We both sat on the edge of our respective lounges, which, it dawned on me, were totally inappropriate to discuss a matter of such importance. Ashby seemed to read my mind. He too was too on edge for such comfort.

"My apologies," he said. "I had to bring you here, otherwise the whole office would be alerted to your presence. So, what did you want to discuss?"

"This," I said as I pulled out my phone and handed it to him.

Rubin Ashby's eyes fell onto a photo that showed Walter Powell and Otto Benson greeting each other with an embrace … and an open-mouthed kiss.

The color drained from his face.

"There are more," I said, and he began to flick through them one by one. I could see all the implications rise in Ashby's mind amid the searing questions and the obvious, treacherous answers. Within a few moments, his face had morphed into a furious scowl.

"Fucking Benson," he seethed through gritted teeth and shot to his feet. "I'm going to kill him."

I stood up and approached Ashby. "No, Rubin. You can't. Hear me out."

In the half-hour or so before this moment, I'd had to make a serious reassessment of Ashby. Until I'd seen the photos Jack sent, I had thought Ashby was not just Powell's master but his accomplice in the deaths of those two unfortunate women. I'd assumed he'd lied for Powell because he desperately wanted the young man he had affections for to be spared prison. I'd assumed he'd forgive Powell anything, even murder, and would willingly lie to help him get away with it. Now it seemed evident that Powell had strung him along about why he needed an alibi.

I stood in front of Ashby who was wrestling with a storm of emotions.

"Benson's the one who sold me out to the *LA Times*," he seethed. "That ambitious, ungrateful snake. I knew he was ambitious but I never suspected he would do it this way. He's trying to ensure that any problem within my business lies at my feet and mine only.

"But I'm telling you the truth when I say I had nothing to do with those dodgy land deals. That was something Benson set up and handled on the side."

"I know, my brother told me Benson ordered him to set them up," I said.

"The fucking weasel wants to see me not only disgraced but behind bars, leaving him to reassure everyone that there has been a changing of the guard and that he can take over. It is a coup by stealth."

The first name Mitch had written on the list was Otto Benson. Although Boylan had confirmed nothing, it seemed most likely that Benson was the mole.

"That certainly makes sense. But where do you see Walter in this?" I asked.

"Well, obviously Benson has him fooled too. Walter would never knowingly betray me." Ashby's face softened. He obviously didn't want to entertain the hurtful possibility that

Powell had turned against him too. "This is the work of one man, I assure you. Just as I assure you he has spent his last day on Earth."

Ashby went to storm out of the room. I grabbed his arm.

"Rubin, listen to me. For you, this is business. And it's also personal, given your fondness of Walter Powell. But that's not what I'm looking at. I didn't just come here to show you these photos. I came to ask for your help."

"My help? What do you mean?"

I had to be very careful about concealing the knowledge of Powell's confession and that he was my primary target.

"I think Otto Benson killed Nicola Beauchamp, and whoever killed her killed Erin Coolidge too. I'm sure of it."

Ashby was thrown into deep thought. "I covered for Walter on the night that Beauchamp girl was murdered. And Benson had asked me to cover for him too if asked. I never thought they were involved. I can't imagine Walter even contemplating such a thing. If Benson was involved Walter must not have been part of it. He was found not guilty by a jury."

I didn't want to argue the toss, saying that the jury did not find him innocent, they just were not sufficiently convinced of his guilt. "In any case, there were two men involved and one of them may well have been Benson," I said. "Let's just take a moment to really think this through." I beckoned for Ashby to sit. We resumed our places on the lounge chairs.

"Now, both Powell and Benson came to you seeking an alibi for the night of Beauchamp's murder. Let's set Powell aside for the time being and assume Benson killed the girl. Why would he do it?"

Ashby shook his head, the logic of such an explanation defying his reasoning. Then something Samantha Boylan had told me came to mind.

"Rubin, all along it has been assumed that Nicola Beauchamp was killed to silence her. Depending on who you talk to, she was seeking to expose police corruption so the cops killed her. Or she was seeking to expose you for corrupt property deals because she thought you stood between her and Walter."

"Yes. Those were the theories put to the court during Walter's trial."

"Exactly, but what if both were wrong?"

"What if they were? Why would it matter?"

"Because Samantha Boylan told me that Nicola was nervous about raising something with Walter. Swindall said so too. No one knew exactly why and we all had to guess."

"So?"

"Well, Samantha told me Nicola was urged to broach this subject—whatever it was—by Erin Coolidge. She said it was something Erin had noticed or something to that effect. Which means that maybe it was just an observation made by Erin of something to do with Walter. And it prompted a question that Nicola didn't want to ask but felt she had to ask. Maybe that's why she was apprehensive about seeing Walter. Not just because she feared his response but because she also feared the truth."

I tapped the photo on my phone.

"What if she was steeling herself to ask Walter and Otto if they were lovers. She didn't want to ask because she didn't want to know the answer. If Walter was gay, then there was no hope of her getting back together with him. Erin had caught on to the fact that Powell and Benson were more than just good friends, and she urged Nicola to confront them."

"I see," said Ashby, his face screwed up into a painful grimace. "And Benson would know that I would cut him off completely if I ever found out."

I had to say these words. "Yes, because he knew that you were in love with Walter."

Ashby sat in silence for a few moments while it all sunk in. "Yes," he said, as though he was finally admitting to himself what so many others knew. "I was in love with Walter. Not that I expect you to understand." He leaned forward and wiped the corners of his eyes with a knuckle and with a sniff regained his composure. "So Nicola Beauchamp was killed in order to keep their secret from me?"

"It's only just occurred to me, but it makes sense every way you look at it. But, as I said, I've long believed that whoever killed Nicola killed Erin too. So, I assume that in putting her suspicions to Powell and Benson, Nicola may have said that it was Erin who suspected that they were lovers."

Ashby got up and went to the bar. "Benson is already dead. He just doesn't know it yet." He poured two glasses of whisky.

"Rubin, you can't do anything to Benson. If he killed Erin Coolidge, I need to see that he faces the full brunt of the justice system. Justice for these young women trumps your thirst for revenge, as much as I get that you want to see that traitor hung, drawn and quartered."

Ashby drained his glass in one gulp. "Okay. What do you want from me?"

"Look, this is out there but it's all I've got: Walter Powell used to brag to Nicola and Samantha about 'knowing where the bodies are buried.'"

"Where the bodies are buried?" Ashby looked confused.

"You know, he was saying property development was a high-stakes game and some people had been killed and buried underneath the foundations of construction sites, never to be seen again."

"The boy has a vivid imagination," said Ashby, looking at me coldly.

"Actually, he gave both Nicola and Samantha warnings as reporters never to go digging too deep because that's where they would end up. You can't say it's all just an urban myth, Rubin."

"Where are you going with this?"

"Okay, let's assume Erin Coolidge has been murdered by Benson. Let's say Powell helped him. The body has never been found. Erin Coolidge was seen by her boyfriend driving off to meet someone. I now know that that someone was Walter Powell. I have footage of him meeting her on Nebraska Avenue. Then she disappears off the face of the earth. Your Silicon Beach Plaza construction site is not too far away. I'm thinking there's a chance Erin Coolidge's body is buried there."

Ashby didn't blink.

"No, not Silicon Beach. Nebraska Avenue."

"Nebraska Avenue?"

"Yes. I've got another site there. It's not that big—just a block of twenty apartments. But..." Ashby's voice trailed off with his thoughts.

"But what?"

"They're due to pour the foundations tomorrow."

My mind was racing. I had no evidence that Powell and Benson murdered Erin Coolidge. I needed to flush them out. Pretty soon I had an idea.

"Rubin, listen. Can you do something for me? If it works out like I hope it will, Benson will get what is coming to him real soon. It will be pretty to watch, I assure you. And after he's gone down, you can clear your name of any wrongdoing in that Costa Rican mess. You'll have the likes of my brother to vouch for the fact that Benson was the brains behind that scam."

Ashby placed his phone on the table, leaned back in his seat and sighed.

"Okay. What do you have in mind?"

Before I could speak, Ashby's phone buzzed and its screen lit up with a message. He lurched forward and grabbed it. Upon reading the message, he bared his teeth, seething.

"It's that reporter," he said. "She wants me to respond to a claim that there's a link between me and Erin Coolidge."

That must be the follow-up piece Boylan is working on. She must be going harder at Ashby. I had to try to get her to hold off.

"I'll call her," I said and hit Boylan's number.

"Brad, I—"

"Samantha, I know you're working on an Ashby follow-up piece."

"How do you know?"

"Because I'm with him right now. And I'm not shitting you when I say this, but you are being used by your source."

"There's no way I'm killing this story, Brad."

"I'm not asking you to kill it. Just hold off on it for twenty-four hours. One day."

"Why?"

"Because I'm hoping that by tomorrow we'll know exactly what happened to Erin Coolidge."

"I'm going to need more than that, Brad."

"Samantha, I can't give you anything right now. Can you please just hold? You don't know the whole story."

"Which is why I contacted Rubin Ashby. But he's not going to talk to me, is he?"

"One day, and he'll give you all the time in the world," I said, nodding assertively at Ashby, who was shaking his head and mouthing the word "No."

"Brad, I can't. My editor is screaming for the story as is. I should have filed twenty minutes ago. There's no way she'll agree to hold. I'm going to have to run a line that Ashby was contacted but declined to comment."

"When will it go live?"

"Six in the morning."

"Samantha, what's one day?"

"In the news game? Plenty," she said and hung up.

I spent the next five minutes trying to pacify Ashby. He'd resumed his threats to exterminate Benson immediately, but after a while I got him to calm down. And I got him to listen to me. More specifically, I got him to listen to the plan I had for making Otto Benson pay for everything he'd done.

And by the time I'd finished, he was on board.

CHAPTER 51

Later that afternoon, Ashby called to say he'd set the plan in motion. As agreed, he'd called a meeting to inform his staff that works on all his construction sites had to cease indefinitely. After the day's shift there wasn't to be a single worker on site, no deliveries, no removals—nothing. He said the delay would be indefinite.

He said Benson had piped up immediately. After saying the company would be facing huge financial losses—hundreds of thousands of dollars every day—he asked why it was necessary.

After insisting that what he was about to tell them mustn't leave the room, Ashby revealed that he'd gotten a tip from a contact in the DA's office. The *LA Times* article had prompted the LAPD to take a closer look at the supposed link between the Silicon Beach Plaza site and the missing girl Erin Coolidge. They had just filed for a search warrant and would be on site in the morning.

The questions came at Ashby from all corners but mostly from Benson and Powell.

"What do you mean 'search'?"

"I mean they'll do whatever they want; they'll have a look around, probably bring dogs, and if they want to excavate, they'll excavate."

Why would they excavate?

"Why do you think? They're looking for a body."

"So why shut down all the sites if they're just interested in Silicon Beach Plaza?"

"Because I need to be seen to be cooperating fully. If they don't find anything at Silicon Beach Plaza, they'll go on to the next site. So, I'm getting proactive. I'm going to invite them to investigate whatever they want. The sites will be clear and waiting for them."

"But we're pouring the foundations at Nebraska Avenue tomorrow."

"Not anymore we're not. I'm not going to pour those foundations only to have to dig them up again."

"What will we tell the workers?"

"Tell them they've got a couple of paid days off. I've got nothing to hide. The cops aren't going to find a thing. And in a couple of days we'll forge ahead as before, except that there should be some good press about this company for a change—that we cooperated fully and the LAPD is directing its attention elsewhere."

Ashby reported that once the meeting was over, Benson stuck by his side like a loyal hound. He was sure his offsider's brain was working overtime in a perturbed state and that he'd wanted to stick to Ashby like glue to pick up any extra scraps of intel on this strange turn of events.

Come nightfall, Jack and I were stationed at the Nebraska Avenue site, ready to detect and record any movement.

Occupying one corner on the Corinth Avenue intersection, the development was boarded up with scaffolding rising sixty feet above the street. As the clock ticked past midnight, the street remained empty save for a stray dog. An hour later, though, a black van pulled up outside the entrance to the site.

Jack was watching through the viewfinder of his zoomed-in camera, taking both video and stills. No one got out of the van and within a minute it drove off again.

Minutes went by without seeing so much as a piece of litter blow past.

"Maybe there's another entrance," said Jack. "I'm going to check the back lane."

"I'll come with you," I said.

"No. Someone needs to stay watching this side. I'll keep my phone on silent—you do the same—and text me if you see anything."

"Okay," I said. "Have you got a gun?"

"What do you think?" Jack produced his Smith & Wesson semi-automatic. And once he'd checked his weapon, he was out the door.

About five minutes later, he texted me a couple of video clips. They showed Benson, Powell and Vinnie entering the site from the lane. At the very start, a fourth man was seen going in first but only his back was visible.

The second video was of a large blue plastic barrel.

I only got to watch each clip once before a text message landed: "Get in here now!"

I sprang out of the car and entered the lane off Corinth Avenue.

There was a small security gate that led into the site. Parked next the entrance was the van.

My heart was racing. Was Jack's message a trap? The tone was urgent. But how was I to find him? It seemed self-evident that he'd contact me once I'd gotten inside. I assumed I was okay to enter so long as I did so quickly. But then again, maybe I was reading a whole lot of nonsense into his stark directive if it was him who sent it.

As quietly as I could, I opened the gate and slipped through. It was pitch dark, but I could see I was enveloped by a maze of scaffolding bars. The walkway I found myself in opened onto the interior of the site, which was lit by ambient light. As I stood there waiting for my eyes to adjust, a waft of foul air reached my nostrils. It was a dead animal smell.

I walked toward the light and bumped something large and heavy. I felt at it and tapped it. It was a large plastic container.

Was this what Jack had filmed?

I got to the interior edge of the scaffolding and looked around. I saw nothing but a network of channels dug into the earth with steel bars in place, either lying parallel with the ground for the footings, or rising up vertically for the columns.

I could hear nothing but my own breathing. I ventured to text Jack.

"Where are you?"

As soon as I sent the message, I saw a patch of ground amid the network of footings light up. I realized with dread that it must be Jack's phone.

"Go ahead," a voice said from behind. "Go pick it up. Your friend's not gonna need it anymore."

I turned around and could make out two figures in the dark.

"Where's Jack?"

"You'll find out. Now move!"

I walked slowly out into the open area of the site. I stepped over two rows of footings and picked up the phone. I turned to see Otto Benson and Vinnie, the latter holding a gun on me.

"Let's go," said Benson. "This way."

Benson walked ahead and with a wave of his gun Vinnie told me to follow. Benson flicked on his phone flashlight and walked back into the well we'd emerged from. As he neared the entrance gate, he turned right and lit up a large blue plastic barrel as he passed it.

"What is that?" I asked.

"Shut your mouth," hissed Vinnie and jabbed the gun into the small of my back.

I followed Benson up six flights of stairs. The top opened onto a landing, a kind of platform for the builders to load and unload materials by crane. Three figures were there waiting: Jack, who was seated on the ground, Walter Powell, who had a gun to Jack's head, and a third who remained obscured by shadow.

It was the third man who spoke.

"Well, if it isn't Brad Madison," he said in a voice that I was stunned to recognize immediately.

The speaker then stepped out to stand right in front of me.

It was none other than Harold Krieger.

He read the flinch of puzzlement on my face. "I know. I wasn't expecting to see you tonight either. But you just keep making poor decisions, don't you? And now, I'm afraid, you've made a fatal one."

"I must admit, Krieger, it's a hell of a surprise. I never thought you were involved in the sordid deeds of these three. I always thought you were a prick, but I thought you were Ashby's prick."

"Ashby is an erratic narcissist who, by way of repeated lapses in judgment, has made himself a severe liability to the prosperity of his own company. When Otto came to me with a plan by which I could keep Ashby's highly lucrative business but not have to deal with Ashby, I was all ears."

"So you approved of the murder of two innocent women?"

"That was not part of the plan. But Otto assured me it was necessary or else his takeover plan would be ruined."

"Even if you kill me, your plan has failed. Why do you think Ashby halted the construction works? The LAPD has made no move to search any of his sites. It was all just to flush you out. And out you came, all three of you, emerging from your evil filthy burrows to do your odious work."

"Ah, work. Well, I never had the pleasure of hiring you, Brad. But I will enjoy firing you."

"Enjoy your freedom while it lasts. We've got video of you idiots coming in here. It's been sent to both Ashby and an *LA Times* reporter already. Even without my dead body to account for, you'll have a lot of explaining to do."

Krieger smiled. "I take it you're referring to Samantha Boylan."

"That's right."

"Vinnie. Otto. Over here for a moment, if you wouldn't mind," said Krieger as he stepped away from me toward the edge. When the two men had joined him, he took a document out of his pocket. "Do you know what this is?" he said to me.

"Your 'I'm-a-slimy-cocksucker' signed confession? Courageous of you to put it in writing."

"It's an advance copy of an *LA Times* story that's being published at six in the morning."

As much as I was intrigued, I didn't want to let Krieger know and stoke his evident conceit. "Fascinating."

"Yes, it is. And why would I have an advance copy? Because it's a proof copy. Ms. Boylan sent it to me to check that she had quoted me accurately."

Krieger smiled as he saw the revelation dawn on me.

"You're the mole?"

Krieger laughed. "Ah, yes. Not that Ms. Boylan knows. While, thanks to Otto, I have provided sufficient proof to her that I am a reliable source, she has never met me nor spoken to me. I have communicated with her only by way of encrypted messages. She has absolutely no idea who she is dealing with."

I remembered Boylan telling me over and over again she couldn't give me the name of her source. And she wasn't even prepared to tell me that she didn't actually know. She'd stuck to her source-protection guns like a trooper.

"When this story is published, it won't be me who'll face some tough questions," Krieger said. He then took the folded article and opened Vinnie's leather jacket. "Vinnie, could I please entrust this to your safe hands?"

The big man looked a little surprised and flattered by the gesture. He relaxed his arms to allow Krieger to tuck the article away. Krieger patted Vinnie's chest lightly. Then he delivered a sharply lifted knee into Vinnie's groin. The henchman doubled over in so much pain he lost the grip on his gun. Quickly picking up the weapon, Krieger nodded at Benson, who responded instantly. He kicked Vinnie in the face with full force, straightening my old rival up so quickly that he staggered and struggled for balance. Benson then moved in front of Vinnie and delivered a straight kick into his chest, sending him over the edge. Vinnie barely had the chance to scream before he hit the ground.

Krieger and Benson leaned over to see the result. Krieger came forward to address me once again.

"Now. So when the police come tomorrow and find poor Vinnie skewered on those steel bars, they will wonder who killed him. And they will wonder why he is in possession of that article, and that reporter will tell them that he is the person who has helped her lift the lid on Rubin Ashby's nefarious wheeling and dealing. They will know Ashby's connections to the Philly mafia and they will know what a corrupting influence he has been since he moved to Los Angeles. And before long they will be suspecting Rubin Ashby of murder."

Krieger resumed his position in front of me, smiling as though he could see the future and very much liked what he saw. "And of course, when they find Vinnie, they will find two more bodies—yours and your friend's here. Both killed with Vinnie's gun. So, it won't be too hard to see that Ashby was cleaning house. Especially when Otto and Walter testify that they heard Rubin order Vinnie to kill you, just as he'd ordered him to get rid of Nicola Beauchamp and Erin Coolidge."

"And when that's done," this was Benson talking now, stepping toward me and eager, I guess, to take some credit for the grand plan, "Ashby will be off to prison while we steady the ship and get the full benefit of Silicon Valley Plaza and other projects in the pipeline."

"I assume that's the body of Erin Coolidge in that barrel?"

"Yes," said Benson. "And they'll find it in the back of Vinnie's van."

Jack and I had worked together a long time and, some time back, we considered what we'd do if we found ourselves at the mercy of people who had guns pointed at our heads. Nothing too sophisticated. It was just a signal to let the other guy know you're about to make a move.

It wasn't something to say aggressively because that would only put your gun holder on notice, and when they are scared you're going to try something, your chances of coming out of it without being shot are practically zero. It had to be something submissive, flattering and disarming. So, we figured the plan would be to clear your throat then use the words, "Okay, looks like you got me." But there'd be a big pause after the "okay" because "me" was the trigger word. At the sound of "me," it was time to strike like lightning.

I'd been watching Krieger all this time with Vinnie's gun, trying to act like he knew what he was doing, but it was clear that he was a novice shooter at best. His hand shifted restlessly on the grip. He didn't seem conscious of where he was pointing it at all times. I mean he had it pointing at me but as he waxed lyrical about his brilliant plan the aim of the gun wavered, the tension in his wrist slackened.

It's not a science and it would be a mistake to think that, at the first sign of trouble, he wouldn't pull the trigger fast and accurately enough to put a hole in my head. But this nine-iron-swinging, argyle-vest-wearing, pot-bellied asshole was about to learn he should never wave a gun in the face of an ex-Marine like you own him.

"Harold, can I just say something?" I said, holding up my hands.

Krieger smiled. "What? Your last words? Be my guest." As he stood there, he extended the gun out closer to me and shifted his legs to strengthen his stance. Shit. I was having the opposite effect on him, like he was expecting me to be coming at him with more than words. To hell with it. As I said, there were no guarantees about any of this, but I was not going to let this bastard take me out without a fight.

"Okay," I said, taking a moment to breathe and drop my hands to a non-threatening height. I even relaxed my body, shifting my weight back from Krieger and then looking to the side as I prepared my words, disengaging my eye contact with him. I had no idea whether I'd gotten him to ease off a little, but a little was all that I'd need to acquire the most vital thing I needed—the element of surprise. "Looks like you got me."

As I spoke the last word, my actions were fast, sure and violent. My left arm shot forward and grabbed his gun arm just below the wrist. In the same motion, I pushed my left arm out, pushing the gun away from me, and pivoted to my left, taking my head and body out of the gun's aim. The next instant, I shot my right hand straight out and snatched the gun from Krieger's grip. In the same movement, I leaned in toward him and as my arm crossed his body, I launched my head under his chin. Almost knocked out by the head butt, he began to fall. To help him down and keep him there, I put a bullet in his leg before training the gun on Powell.

In the space of a second, Krieger had gone from holding all the cards to writhing on the ground in agony. And by the time

I had the weapon on Powell, Jack had disarmed him and had wrestled him to the ground.

I kept the gun on Benson while Jack sought to tame Powell, who stupidly didn't know when to stop struggling. Jack had to wrench his arm back and dislocate his shoulder before Powell conceded.

"You want to try something stupid, asshole?" I said to Benson, who was struggling slack-jawed to process the shocking turn of events. He held his hands up and shook his head. "Okay then, get on your knees."

Instead of obeying my order, Benson stood there. And I saw it happen: I saw the exact moment that he fully realized it was all over. A few seconds earlier, he was sure his plan had worked; that he'd be walking away with a multi-million-dollar company, that he'd gotten away with two murders and that the blame for killing Jack and me would never fall at his feet. Now he knew with sudden and horrendous certainty that his life as he knew it was over; instead of his choice of condos with water views, all that he had ahead of him was a five-by-ten cell in San Quentin.

I saw his feet swivel, then he went to sprint for the ledge.

"Oh, no you don't," I said as I dropped the gun and lurched after him. I tackled him from behind, wrapping my arms around his thighs. We hit the ground and the momentum took Benson half over the edge. He tried kicking me, but I wouldn't loosen my grip. I lifted my head to see how I could restrain him better. That's when I saw Jack's legs appear in front of me.

Two gunshots sounded and Benson screamed. He ceased trying to wrest his legs free. I got to my knees and dragged him back onto the landing, well away from the edge.

I couldn't see any blood on him.

"Where'd you shoot him?" I asked Jack.

Looking down at Benson, Jack flicked a couple of fingers past his right ear. "Just a couple of warning shots. Took all the will out of him."

We relieved Benson and Krieger of their belts and tied their hands behind their backs. Jack stood over Powell as I made a call.

About five rings in, the phone was answered.

"What is it?" said the voice of a just-woken man.

"Detective Cousins?"

"Yes. What time is it?"

"It's just past two. It's Brad Madison. I'm at a construction site on Nebraska Avenue, Santa Monica. You're going to want to get over here right away."

"Why's that, Brad?"

"The body of Erin Coolidge is here. I'm holding the men responsible for killing her and I'm worried that I might just lose all self-restraint and shoot them right between the eyes."

"I see. Well, you stay cool, Brad. I'll send some squad cars over and get there pronto."

CHAPTER 52

I was so wired from the night's events it took me a long time to get to sleep. Not wanting to be woken early, I slept past nine o'clock. When I did awake, I checked my phone and found messages from Megan and Ashby. Megan I could understand—she'd naturally be wondering where I was. Ashby? Well, maybe he was eager to dine on our success.

I got up and called Megan first and filled her in on everything that had happened. I said I'd come into the office at about lunchtime, and asked her to hold the fort for me. I then called Ashby.

I'd spoken to him hours earlier after I'd called Detective Cousins. It shocked him to learn that Krieger was one of Benson's co-conspirators. He sounded relieved and grateful. He was going to be completely exonerated of any involvement in the deaths of Nicola Beauchamp and Erin Coolidge, and the Costa Rican land scam would be shown to be all Benson's work.

Not that his future was going to be a bed of roses. His reputation as a ruthless visionary had taken a big hit. Some of his more unsavory activities had been exposed and the media, with the help of his rivals, might move in to finish the job. And they still had the Playa Dorada scandal to hang him with.

Then there were questions about him possibly having corrupted or intimidated various Los Angeles council members in order to get what he wanted. No, looking ahead there were plenty of reasons for him to sweat.

Hoping for a brief conversation, I called him back.

"Bradley. Thanks for getting back to me. You've seen the article, I gather?"

Ashby was outdoors somewhere. I heard the beep of a horn and cars setting off from traffic lights.

I had no idea what he was talking about.

"What article?" I asked as I set about making coffee.

"The *LA Times*. You haven't seen it?"

"No," I said, putting Ashby on speakerphone and bringing the site up on my cell.

"It's another hatchet job. This source of theirs says those two young women were working on a story that was going to damage me. They say I'd go to any lengths to keep my corrupt deals secret. So, the inference is that I had Nicola Beauchamp and Erin Coolidge killed to stop that story going ahead."

"You're not denying making corrupt deals to get your way then?"

"Don't be naive, Bradley. To win in this game you have to be creative, ruthless and sometimes brutal. But it wasn't me who killed those girls."

"I'm not saying you did. But they got caught up in your game."

"Not my game. Benson's."

"You play a pretty brutal game too, you know. Hell, you threatened my family."

"I apologize for that. I was doing everything I could to win."

"To win *your* way."

"Yes. That's the only way I know."

"Be honest with me. How would you feel if someone started investigating whether or not any council members were intimidated into voting to approve your Silicon Beach Plaza project?"

Ashby didn't miss a beat.

"Who's fed you that nonsense?"

"Don't deflect."

"I'd be delighted. They can come at me any way they want, Bradley, but there's no way they're going to pin anything on me. Nothing's going to stick. Like I told you, I fought a war to get where I am, so I won't start trembling if some reporter tries to make a name for themselves by cutting me down. Many others have tried the same thing and they've all failed. They have no idea what it takes to dominate in the construction game. It's a cut-throat world, that's for sure, but I don't have a scratch on me. You get me?"

"Are you saying you wouldn't be worried if they found out you paid some dirty cops to lean on some vulnerable public officials?"

"Nice try, Bradley. Let's see who talks. My bet is no one will. No one that matters, anyhow."

"So, you're not going to speak to this *Times* reporter and set the record straight? With the arrest of Benson, Powell and Krieger, the opportunity's there for you to polish up your image."

"Maybe. But the authorities are in the process of rectifying matters now. They've got Erin Coolidge's body and they have her killers. Justice will be done and I will be exonerated."

"And what about Walter Powell?"

Ashby paused a while. I heard him release a deep sigh.

"I gave Walter everything and he threw it back in my face. I helped save him once, thanks to you, but I'm not lifting a finger to help him now. The stupid boy; he's gone and thrown his life away. As for me, I'm going to sit down, have my breakfast, read the news, drink some coffee and then get on with my day. Walter is on his own."

I heard Ashby walk indoors and then take a seat.

"You've still got a lot of enemies, Rubin."

I heard a waitress greet him. "Shakshuka and Americana coffee," Ashby said without cupping the phone. "Bradley, you don't get to where I am without making enemies. Which brings me to you."

"What do you mean?"

"What I mean is that I thought Harold Krieger was a friend but he turned out to be an enemy. And with this Playa Dorada case coming up, I need a lawyer I can trust."

"Oh, no you don't. The only reason I worked for you was to get my mother out of a financial hole that you dug for her. I'm not going near that case. Not my bag anyway and you'll be in good hands with Jim Rafferty on the team."

"If you think I'm sticking with Cooper, Densmore and Krieger, you're crazy. First thing I'm doing after breakfast is firing them." There was a brief pause. "Just a second, Bradley, there's a young man here who's after something. Can I help you?"

"You're Rubin Ashby, right?" I heard a voice ask.

"Yes, that's right, but I'm kind of in the middle of something. No! Wait! No!"

"This is for Erin!"

I heard a gunshot. Then another. And, as people began screaming, another two.

"Rubin!" I shouted. "Rubin!"

Finally, there was one last shot.

CHAPTER 53

"Want one?" asked Mitch, who'd appeared in the doorway of our parents' garage holding two cans of Sierra Nevada pale ale. It was mid-afternoon and I'd spent the day moving a whole bunch of stuff out of the house for the garage sale.

"Thanks," I said. I took a can, lifted myself up onto Dad's old wooden workbench, and ripped off the ring pull. I'd taken my time going through all my old belongings to see if there was anything I wanted to set aside. I'd decided that, along with some jewelry that Mom said Bella should have now, I was taking my Glen Plake poster back with me to LA. Other things, like a couple of Dad's rods and some ski gear for Bella, would have to wait until I got them sent back before Mom and Dad's movers came. "You just get in?"

"Yep," said Mitch. He came over, put his beer on the bench and ran his eyes over the wall of tools Dad had arranged in perfect order.

"Dad's sure got some beautiful tools here," I said. "You better claim what you want because that stuff will sell in a heartbeat."

Mitch picked out a beautiful old mortise gauge and inspected it. "Whatever happened to those sailboats he carved for us?"

"Don't know." They were long gone but never forgotten, such was the allure of their dark-stained and varnished wood and their bright sails. They were beautiful things to behold. And their absence never diminished what they had placed in our hearts and minds. The memory of those boats summoned a strong sense of my father's being—his warm presence, his gentle nature, his loving spirit, his old-school know-how. They were eternal gifts.

"I just wouldn't use any of this stuff," he said.

"You used to. Dad was always stoked to see what you'd come up with. Remember that wooden snowboard you made?"

Mitch laughed. "Yep. I was ahead of my time. Could have been Madison snowboards instead of Burton."

"Yeah, well. You never know. You might get back into carpentry some day. You were very good at it."

I knew that Mitch had been somewhat cast adrift in the wake of Ashby's death. And to be honest, it had shaken me up a little too because once I'd found out who'd shot him, I realized it could have been avoided.

The killer was none other than Luke Wells, Erin's boyfriend. He'd read Boylan's article, in which her source practically said Ashby had the young photographer killed in an act of self-preservation, and had gone to Ashby's offices and followed him to the cafe. Once Wells was certain Ashby was dead, he'd turned the gun on himself.

Boylan hadn't seen the video I'd sent until well after her story was posted. They did pull it down, but Ashby's body was stone cold by then.

Wells must have been trailing Ashby the whole time I was on the phone to him. I never called Boylan to talk about the murder, no matter how much I wanted to point out that she and her paper were complicit in Ashby's murder. I had no desire to rub it in. In time, she'd find out that her source was Harold Krieger, that she'd been used and that the consequences were devastating.

With Benson and Powell in prison awaiting various charges, Ashby Realty Corporation had folded. In the ensuing weeks, Paul Spears, head of Calbright Properties, had moved in to take over various Ashby projects, including Silicon Beach Plaza and Nebraska Avenue. It wasn't yet clear if he'd retain any of Ashby's staff, including Mitch.

After I found out about Spears, I texted Jim Rafferty, asking if he was the brains behind the move. He said yes before adding that he'd be replacing Harold Krieger as managing partner. So, another big Tetris block had just fallen into place for Jim Rafferty.

Krieger was out on bail but faced a string of felony charges he had no chance of beating. He was going to go to prison for at least ten years, no question, but in the meantime he'd been stood down from CDK, which would soon be CDR, Jim assured me.

I'd taken a call from Walter Powell, who said he had nothing to do with Erin Coolidge's murder and that he'd been seduced by Otto Benson, who'd then blackmailed him to help kill Nicola Beauchamp. When I told Powell I wouldn't touch his case with a ten-foot pole and referred him to someone else, he seemed genuinely puzzled and taken aback. It was like he'd assumed that I was professionally obliged to help him.

As for Mitch, he'd be testifying against both Benson and Powell, that much was certain, but as for work, I gathered he was in limbo.

"Mom says you're not staying for the sale," he said.

"That's right. I'm taking off in the morning. I've got an afternoon flight out of LAX."

"Where you going?"

"Scotland. Roger Russell and I are going to spend a week on the single malt trail. And then I'm flying out of London to Bangkok."

"You're going to Thailand? For how long?"

"Three weeks. Going to get up into the mountains for some trekking then kick back on a tropical island beach."

"Sounds tough. You going alone or do you plan to pick up a ladyboy in Bangkok?"

After I almost spat my beer laughing, I wiped my mouth with my forearm.

"I'll be in very good hands; don't you worry about that. But she's blonde, beautiful, one hundred percent American and all woman."

For a second, I imagined Jessica greeting me at Bangkok airport wearing a Singha tank top and sarong. I smiled at the thought and couldn't wait to get there.

"Mitch, there was something I wanted to give you before I go," I said, reaching into the back pocket of my jeans. I retrieved an envelope and handed it to him.

Mitch held it in his hands and gave me a quizzical look.

"This is the list of names I gave you," he said.

"Exactly. I said if you helped me, I'd make it worth your while. So, there it is. I'm giving you your list back."

"Gee, thanks, Bro," Mitch said sarcastically.

"You're welcome," I said.

Mitch looked set to screw the list up and throw it in the trash. "I told Mom I'd get some steaks for dinner, so I'm going to head into town."

"You want to open that envelope first?"

"What?"

"Open it."

Mitch ripped open the envelope like he was going along with a joke that he knew he'd be the butt of. He pulled the folded document out of the sleeve and opened it. Being in the real estate game, and working for Ashby, Mitch knew exactly what it was immediately.

"A purchase agreement for a Silicon Beach Plaza condo. This is one of the best. And it's yours? Hell, Brad, when did you buy this?"

"I didn't."

"Ashby gave it to you?"

"That's right. And now I'm giving it to you."

Mitch's jaw dropped slightly.

"What? Brad, this condo will be worth one and a half mill the day you get your keys and from there it'll shoot up close to two before you know it. Ashby may be all kinds of weird but Silicon Beach Plaza is going to be one of the most sought-after addresses in LA. This isn't as good as gold; it's better."

"And now it's yours. I'll arrange for it to be transferred into your name. If that's okay with you?"

Mitch was dumbfounded.

"Bro, I can't accept this."

"Yeah, you can. Make a new start, Mitch. Get yourself another job, don't waste all your money on the ponies and before you know it you'll have this to call home."

Mitch's eyes were beginning to water.

"I've got a job," he said. "I heard back from Spears today. He says he could use someone like me on the sales team. It's a little drop in salary but the commission's pretty good."

"That's great news," I said. "But isn't Paul Spears just another dodgy property developer."

"Dodgy. Savvy. It's all the same in this business. But thanks, Bro," he said, tapping the contract. "I don't know what else to say."

"How about we go get those steaks?" I said and jumped off the workbench. I downed the beer then scrunched up the empty can. "Then after dinner you and I head into town and have a few more of these."

"Don't think I'm going to go easy on you at pool."

"I wouldn't have it any other way, Mitch."

At that moment, it was nice to think that while my parents were having to let go of our family's past, they could at least believe their sons would be there for each other in the future.

THE END

GAME OF JUSTICE

NOTE FROM J.J.

Thanks so much for reading *Game of Justice*. I really hope you enjoyed the ride.

Please make sure to leave a positive review on Amazon. It means an awful lot to an independant writer like me.

Just as helpful is if you recommend my book to your friends.

All the best

J.J.

BLOOD AND JUSTICE

PREVIEW

CHAPTER 1

"Brad Madison!" the voice barked into my ear, making the greeting sound more like a command.

I'd answered an unknown number, but I recognized the caller immediately. Even after twenty-plus years, the gravelly tone was unmistakable. A deeply ingrained Pavlovian response had me in two minds: should I drop and give him twenty, or snap to attention?

"It's Henry Tuck here," he said, but the reminder wasn't needed. For thirteen long weeks, I ate, slept, breathed, and crossed five realms of hell to the tune of that voice. As my drill instructor, or DI, at Marine Corps boot camp, Sergeant Henry "TNT" Tuck was my ceaseless tormentor. In the perverse way of the military, that made him my mentor.

What does he want with me now?

And how did he get this number?

Tuck had not been put through by my secretary, Megan Schaffer. He hadn't looked me up online. Someone had given him my private number.

In the brief conversation that followed, Tuck offered no reason for the call. He just said he wanted to come and talk to me face to face. Then, once the arrangements were made, the call was over. Whatever it was that Tuck wanted, I felt I owed him. Big time. I was indebted to that man for life.

Tuck had taken a shine to me at boot camp. At least, he'd taken a shine to seeing me with my face buried in the ground, shouting, "Yes, sir!" "No, sir!" "Aye, aye, sir!" through a mouthful of Parris Island dirt. No recruit wants special attention from their DI, but that's what Tuck gave me. In the process, he instilled in me the life-and-death virtue of obeying orders. To civilians, this may sound like little more than power and pedantry. But in the heat of battle, when you have the lives of a dozen or more men riding on your decision, you need to get shit right. Not by doing it your way. Not by weighing up pros and cons while precious half-seconds slide by. Not by wondering whether you want to or not. *A Few Good Men*'s Colonel Jessop may have lost the plot like Colonel Kurtz, but no one said it clearer or saner: "We follow orders or people die. It's that simple."

When the civilian version of Henry Tuck walked into my office three days after he called, it took a little adjusting to see him without his wide-brimmed smokey. That hat had a rancor all its own. When his eyes drilled into you, it stared you down too, as though you'd also roused its wrath. His hair was thinner and silver all over but still cropped short. He was in his mid-sixties now with all the facial lines to show for it, but he looked fit and sharp. As he stepped toward me and offered his hand, he showed me something I'd rarely witnessed all those year ago: his smile.

Addressing him as Henry, as he insisted, took some adjusting too.

He ran his alert blue eyes over my office and the shelves of books I'd surrounded myself with, and nodded his head with satisfaction.

"Glad to see you're doing well for yourself, Madison."

"You look fighting fit, Henry," I said as I invited him to sit. "I bet you could still put recruits to shame in the gym."

I wasn't humoring him. He was a lean two-hundred pounds, about my height—six, two—and he moved as lightly as a man half his age.

"What can I say?" he said as he took his seat. "I watch what I eat, I stretch, and I can still bench two-sixty. How about you?"

"Two-eighty-five. But I'd be more than happy with two-sixty at your age."

"Listen," Tuck said as he tapped a hand on his chair, "I didn't mean to be all top secret on our call the other day. I just hate talking on the phone—never liked it—and so I always keep it super brief. But the reason I'm here is that I have two problems I'd like your help with. Kevin Allman recommended you. Said you were a good operator."

Allman was a former DI of Tuck's generation who now worked for a non-profit called Second Life that helped vets with PTSD. He'd sought my input on a fundraiser five years ago and I've helped out occasionally ever since. That Allman saw fit to give Tuck my private number was okay with me.

"What kind of problems are we talking about, Henry?"

"Two divorces, you might say."

Henry then paused, disinclined by nature to be expansive. I didn't want to have to prod him to go into more detail, so I waited for him to fill the silence.

Henry breathed in deeply then exhaled.

"I've been married to Laura for twenty-seven years," he said. "And, for longer than I can remember, if it hasn't been me threatening to leave, it's been her. But we stuck at it. Recently, though, I decided I couldn't do it any more. So I moved out, and now I want to proceed with a divorce."

I felt deflated all of a sudden. That's what family law does to me. I hate it. Give me criminal law any day with its cast of lowlifes and liars and its smattering of innocent souls. It's not every day that I fight to save a client from a travesty of justice, but when I do there's no better job in the world. Family law is a downright ugly, sordid mess that I was happy to steer well clear of.

Problem was I'd just recently defied my own conventional wisdom and take on a divorce case. A bitter one—surprise, surprise. But I only did so as a favor for a friend of a friend. Well, a friend of my ex-wife Claire, who practically begged me to help.

Henry must have guessed I was considering looking for an out.

"I know divorce is not your bag, Madison. If you want me to go somewhere else, I will."

I waved my hand. That was never going to happen. Like I said, I owed Henry.

"Don't be silly, Henry. Of course, I'll help you. But tell me this: who is she?"

"What are you talking about?"

"You know exactly what I'm talking about."

The skin on Henry's face was still taut and, as I guess he had done every day since his late teens, he'd shaved that morning, so there was no hiding the fact that he was clenching his jaw.

"Her name's Fernanda. Fern for short."

His manner was ever so slightly defiant.

"And she's how old?" I persisted.

"Thirty-four," he said. He tilted his head to adjust the aim that his eyes kept on me, alert for the slightest hint of ridicule, I suspect. "And don't try that all-your-Christmases-coming-at-once line on me. We had the DI reunion last weekend in San Diego and the boys never let up. But they're nothing but jealous. They even admitted it. And as it happens, it was talking about Fernanda that led me to you. Kevin practically insisted I come to you."

I could just imagine those DIs standing around, ribbing Henry for all it was worth before getting back to hanging crap on their former recruits.

"So, your relationship with Fernanda is out in the open?"

Henry shrugged. "There's nothing to hide. We're in love."

I was leaning back in my chair now, relaxed and impartial.

"How'd Laura take it?" I asked.

Henry's lips pressed into a flat frown. "As well as can be expected. She thinks I'm a fool."

I paused for a moment to consider what I was going to tell Henry. Yes, my instinct was to think that Laura was right but he didn't come to me to be judged. "You want my best advice, Henry? Get your settlement with Laura agreed on with little or no input from lawyers."

"Too late for that," he said, shaking his head. "When I told her that I was coming to see you she said the next call she was making was to her own lawyer."

"Any idea who that might be?"

"Don't know for sure but I could take a pretty good guess. A couple of years ago, her sister Martha took her husband to the cleaners after he cheated on her. And I'll never forget the name of those lawyers after Laura told me. Paxton and Punch. Man, did they give that fella the old one-two."

I had heard of Paxton and Punch. My reservations about dealing in family law only deepened.

"Henry, that firm may as well be called Paxton, Punch and Pitbull, because that's what they are. They're ferocious. And if Laura has engaged them, you're in for the fight of your life."

"Come on, Madison. There's plenty of money to go round. I'm not looking to screw Laura over. I just want to get on with my life."

"You say there's plenty of money, Henry. But sometimes plenty ain't enough. Just how financially sound are you?"

"Well, that's the other thing I wanted your help on."

"The second problem?"

"Yeah, the second problem. You could say it's another divorce."

"God Almighty, Henry. You better not be telling me you've got two wives you want to leave."

"No. It's a business. Something that I poured a lot of money into."

"And?"

"Well, when I told my business partner that I want to get my money out, he wasn't real happy. He said it wasn't a good time. He wants me to wait a year, at least."

"How much money are we talking?"

"About two million. It's a security company that's gone from strength to strength. It's been growing fast for five years."

I raised my eyebrows. Some business smarts must be nestled in that love-addled brain of his.

"And you don't want to wait, obviously?"

"Madison, I don't want anyone telling me to put my life on hold. I want to cash in my chips, and I want to cash them in now."

"Okay," I said, tapping away at my computer keyboard to bring up my calendar. "We're going to have to make another appointment. Thursday or Friday next week looks free if that suits you. Meantime, I'd like you to send me the partnership agreement."

"Okay."

"Is there a dissolution strategy in the contract?"

"A what?"

"A dissolution strategy. It's kind of a prenup for partnership agreements."

"I have no idea."

"Okay, I'll check that out. Have you got all the financial statements?"

"Yes."

"Send me those too, will you?"

"Will do," said Henry. He was looking relaxed now. Having someone to help was clearly a weight off his mind. "I think I came to the right place. Thank you, Madison."

I stood up and put my hand out. "I want that paperwork ASAP, okay? I wouldn't mind betting Paxton and Punch have already gotten a head start on us."

I walked Henry to the door. As I returned to my desk, I heard Megan book him in for the following Thursday at three o'clock.

A couple of days later, I got an email with a rudimentary list of Henry's assets. The email was sent from his girlfriend's account.

But he never showed for his three o'clock.

A few days after leaving my office, Henry Tuck took hold of his Beretta M9 service pistol and fired a bullet into his right temple.

CHAPTER 2

I fell in with a line of men entering the small chapel and took a seat in a pew midway up the aisle. The place was three-quarters full and more mourners were still coming in. Men, mostly. Some wore suits while others looked like they'd had to rummage deep through their drawers to find a suitable tie—heck, any tie. And then there were the bikers. They may never have met Henry, but when word gets around that a soldier has fallen, a lot of vets make a point of attending the funeral. They'll be damned if they'll let someone who'd had the balls to serve leave this world alone.

Like me, they'd always carry survivor's guilt. Funerals bring death near again, to coldly graze the soul. They give rise to sobriety—there by the grace of God go I, and all that—and gratitude for having the fortune to be alive.

"Always go to the funeral." I don't know who came up with that as a guiding principle to death, but I agree with it wholeheartedly. Do it if not for yourself but the deceased's family. They'll take heart from those who show at the service, the strangers in particular. It's something I will instill in my daughter, Bella.

But I wasn't here for the family, I was here for the dead. For the life of me, I could not work out why Henry would choose to kill himself so soon after our meeting. He'd displayed the verve of a man who relished the future. I did want to pay my respects, but I also wanted answers.

Henry and I had unfinished business. He walked out of my office with a spring in his step and a glint in his eye. He did not look like a man fixing to kill himself.

Not long after I'd taken my seat, a man crossed in front of two people to claim the place beside me.

"Madison," he said, still on his feet. He held his smile and an outstretched hand while I took a couple of seconds to recognize him.

"Pete Chang," I said, standing up and taking his hand enthusiastically. "Good to see you. My God, you haven't aged a day."

"What can I say? It's the Asian genes. My grandfather could pass as my older brother."

"What are you doing here, anyway?"

"Same as you, I guess. When I heard old TNT had kicked it, I got down and gave him fifty."

When I got the news of Henry's death, the first thing I did was call Doug Ward, an LAPD detective whose nephew I'd helped beat a first-time DUI. Ward told me Henry's death was a boilerplate suicide. Besides the fact that there was no note, Henry had done a meticulous job of it. He had gotten dressed in his good clothes, laid himself down on his bed, and fired. Ward said no one reported hearing a shot. What they did report was a godawful smell coming from his apartment. Forensics estimated Henry was dead for three days before they found him.

It may have made sense to the cops, but to me it just didn't add up. I came to the service hoping either Henry's wife or his girlfriend could help me make sense of it all.

Sitting across the aisle from me in the front pew was a woman I assumed to be Laura Tuck. In a yellow floral dress, she sat staring ahead, waiting for the minister to begin speaking. Now and then she dabbed her eyes with her handkerchief.

I then scanned the crowd and, to my surprise, there was no one who could be Fernanda.

"You know she left him," Peter said in a hushed tone, leaning sideways into me.

"He told me he left her. After twenty-seven years of not quite marital bliss."

"No, not his wife. The girl he ran off with."

"Fernanda?"

"You know her?"

"No. He told me a little bit about her. Well, a little bit about his situation. He came to see me about handling his divorce."

"Well, it looks like he jumped the gun." Pete shook his head. "Shit, I didn't mean that pun."

"Who told you she dumped him?"

"One of Henry's DI buddies. You remember Sergeant Longley? I was speaking to him before I came in."

As the service got under way, we fell silent, but I ruminated on what Pete had told me all the way through. I may not have known Henry too well, but from our brief contact I knew that if Fern had dumped him it would have been a crushing blow.

After the service, the crowd began to shuffle out from the pews and into the aisle. Pete and I were standing together when he grabbed my shoulder firmly.

"Listen, Madison. I've got to go now, but what are you up to tonight?"

I had absolutely no plans other than a few hours at home watching SportsCenter.

"Not much," I said.

"Why don't we grab a meal together, have few beers and do a proper catch up?"

I'd been keeping to myself in recent months. So much so, turning down social invitations had become a reflex. But not this time. Pete was a good man, and the thought of us hanging out and shooting the breeze appealed to me. Besides, I wanted to know what else he knew about Henry's situation.

"That'd be great, Pete," I said. "Let's do it."

"My family's got a restaurant. China Doll. It's on Sunset. How's seven?"

"Seven's fine."

"Don't you dare pull out on me, Madison."

"I won't."

We shook hands quickly and Pete shifted into the aisle and made for the door. After a moment, I followed him then waited outside to see if I could get an opportunity to speak with Laura Tuck.

A string of mourners consoled her before she began making her way to the parking lot.

"Mrs. Tuck," I said as I approached, and she turned to face me.

"Yes?" she said and waited for me to introduce myself.

"I'm so sorry for your loss, ma'am. Please accept my sympathies."

"Thank you," she said flatly. Her tone surprised me. It was like I'd earned her disapproval without ever meeting her.

"Mrs. Tuck. My name's Brad Madison. I'm a friend of Henry's. Well, I was one of his recruits."

As I spoke, her expression hardened into a glare.

"So you're Brad Madison."

"Yes, ma'am."

"Well, you have some nerve approaching me."

"I'm sorry. I don't understand."

"Don't play me for a fool, son. You were helping Henry to divorce me."

I guess he must have told her.

"Well, Mrs. Tuck, the truth is we never got that far. And to be honest—"

"Don't play the nice guy with me. And don't introduce yourself as a friend when you're just his lawyer. You were going to leave me destitute."

"We had one conversation during which Henry made it clear he wanted to do right by you."

"If you were any kind of friend, you would have advised him to come to his senses and save his marriage."

"I didn't get the chance to advise him on anything, ma'am."

"Sure, you didn't. If you had done the right thing instead of trying to make a buck out of that fool, he'd still be alive today."

"I'm sorry you feel that way. I won't bother you anymore." I bowed my head quickly and turned to walk away.

"I bet you feel proud of yourself," she called out to me as I walked. "I suspect you'll be chasing some kind of payment to come out of his estate. You leech."

I kept silent. I kept walking.

Family law. Like I said, it's the pits.

END OF PREVIEW

Books by J.J. Miller

THE BRAD MADISON SERIES

Force of Justice

Divine Justice

Game of Justice

Blood and Justice

Veil of Justice

THE CADENCE ELLIOTT SERIES

I Swear To Tell

The Lawyer's Truth

Stay in touch with J.J.

Sign up for J.J.'s newsletter

Email: jj@jjmillerbooks.com

Facebook: @jjmillerbooks

Website: jjmillerbooks.com

Printed in Great Britain
by Amazon